A FIERY WHISPER
#1 TILDAS ISLAND SERIES

TAMSEN SCHULTZ

ALSO BY TAMSEN SCHULTZ

THE WINDSOR SERIES

WINDSOR SHORT STORIES

THE TILDAS ISLAND SERIES

For more information visit www.tamsenschultz.com

To the people of the Virgin Islands

ACKNOWLEDGEMENTS

I always wonder how many people actually read this, so if you do, I'd be curious to know what you like to see. As for what I want to write, the first thing is to thank everyone involved in the book...Woody and Rebecca (my editors), Stephanie (my PA and marketing guru), Valerie (my cover designer), and of course my friends and family.

The Tildas Island series is, obviously, a new series for me. Over the last few years, I've been lucky enough to spend a fair bit of time on St. Thomas and I became fascinated by the beauty of the islands as well as its history and the current complexities. It's a stunning place to vacation and switch your mind off, but if you're interested, I'd highly recommend looking a little deeper at the history and culture(s) of the area. There is a nod to that history both on the cover and in the name of the Tildas Island, itself – have a look here (https://www.virgin-islands-history.org/en/history/fates/the-three-rebel-queens) and then see if you can find them. Feel free to email me if you want confirm your finding or know more!

PROLOGUE

DR. SUNITA SHAH sat in a sunken leather chair across the desk from where FBI Special Agent in Charge, Ronald Lawler, looked down on her. She was quite certain he'd swapped out furniture before her arrival for just that purpose. Passive-aggressive tantrums were his specialty, and Ron Lawler was not a man to miss an opportunity to put her in her place. But the other thing Ron Lawler was not, was a man worth spending any time thinking about.

"So, Tildas Island?" he asked. He was drumming his fingers on the top of the five files she'd handed him. "Nice gig if you can get it." The scent of stale coffee and bad breath wafted toward her.

"It's a task force, not a holiday," she responded, nodding to the files. He regarded her for a moment, then picked up the first.

Tildas Island, a US Territory in the Caribbean, had recently been selected by the governing body of the Organization of World Leaders as the location for their first-ever World Summit. In eighteen months, presidents, prime ministers, shahs, kings, queens, and other world leaders would be gathering on the island approximately half the size of Omaha, Nebraska.

With the sudden spotlight on the region, just about every alphabet agency in DC had realized their intelligence on the area—and hence the government's ability to protect against any threats—was woefully lacking. So, two weeks ago, she'd been tapped to lead the task force that would spend the next eighteen months in the region gathering every bit of intel possible so that by the time of the conference, security would be locked down tighter than a nurse swaddling a newborn babe.

"You want Damian Rodriguez?" Ron asked, looking up from the file he held in his hands. "He just ran an unsanctioned investigation that included all but deputizing a journalist."

Sunita shifted her gaze from the window that she'd been staring out of to Ron. She smiled but remained silent. She didn't have to justify her decisions to him, or to anyone for that matter. A condition of her taking the role as the supervisory director of the task force had been complete control over the team and how it functioned. Lawler's sign-off was nothing but red-tape.

Of course, another reason behind her smile was because she knew, at this moment, that Agent Rodriguez was talking to the very same journalist Lawler referred to about the very same unsanctioned investigation. The young agent was no doubt sinking his career on a matter of principle—having promised the journalist the story in exchange for her help—and Sunita admired the hell out of him for it. That he'd also been an Army Ranger and a top field agent, before his recent activities, didn't hurt.

Lawler picked up another file and held it up as he fixed his gaze on her. "Dominic Burel has been on probation three times since he joined the Bureau two years ago." Ron was too seasoned of an agent to think she'd simply made a bad choice.

But he wasn't smart enough to figure out why she'd chosen whom she'd chosen. She'd give him a little leeway on Burel, though because his record *was* a little sketchy. But, she had access to files on the former pararescuer that only a handful of people even knew existed.

"And Alexis Wright? Seriously, Sunita? FBI Barbie?" he said, slapping Burel's file down and picking up the third.

Sunita cocked her head. "Making derogatory comments on people's looks, Ron? You know what they say, glasshouses and all."

His eyes narrowed on her.

She didn't mind letting him question an agent's ability, but she'd damn well draw the line when he crossed it. It was true, Alexis Wright was stunning. The daughter of a famous R&B singer and a Swedish supermodel, Alexis wasn't just gorgeous, she was loaded, too. A fact that seemed to get more attention than her stellar scores at the academy and her impeccable record in the field. The only legitimate complaint had come from her supervisor who'd said the agent had been distracted a bit lately. Sunita gave that observation little weight, though, as she knew that Wright had just defended her Ph.D. four days ago, having completed her course of study without ever mentioning it to any of her colleagues. To say Agent Wright had a penchant for extreme privacy would be an understatement.

"Jake McMullen is a cowboy, and you want to take him to the land of fun and sun?" Lawler asked, holding up the fourth file. Tildas Island was famous for being a getaway for the rich and famous with all the trappings of luxury that came with that.

"I'll sign off on him, but he's not allowed to drive any government vehicles," Lawler said, setting the file down. In her mind, Sunita rolled her eyes. It was a childish response, but then again, so was Ron's illusion that he had any control over whom she picked or how she ran her task force.

Jake McMullen *was* a cowboy, but he was a cowboy who had been a professional surfer before an injury had ended his career at age twenty-four. He brought that same daring streak that drove him to ride twenty-plus-foot waves to his job with the FBI. And no one in the Bureau knew the ocean like Agent McMullen—a handy trait to have when they'd be surrounded by water.

"And Benita Ricci? Really? That woman has a chip on her shoulder the size of Long Island," Lawler said, holding the fifth and last file.

At least he hadn't commented on her appearance. And again, to be fair, Ricci did have a bit of a chip on her shoulder. But unlike Ron's negative impression, Sunita believed Beni—as she was known to her colleagues—to be tough as nails and one of the best no-nonsense agents she'd seen in recent years. Ricci wasn't *nice,* but she was damn good at her job. In fact, while Sunita was planning to let the dynamics play themselves out, she fully anticipated Rodriguez and Ricci would become the de facto leaders of the team. All five members were strong agents, and each had a little extra *something* she knew would contribute to the success of the task force, but Ricci and Rodriguez also had that elusive, unnamable quality that made people want to follow them.

"I don't know where you pulled these names from, Sunita, but it's like you looked for every misfit in the Bureau. Are you sure you don't want to take Agent Webster or Agent Kapinski?" Ron asked.

Sarah Webster and Stanley Kapinski were two of Ron's pet agents. Loyalty in the Bureau was important if an agent was interested in playing the politics game, and no one was more loyal to Ron than Webster and Kapinski. Which was exactly why she hadn't even thought of considering the two.

Instead of answering, Sunita rose from her seat to her full

height of five feet, one and three-quarters inches, swiped a pen from Lawler's desk, and handed it to him.

"Sign the transfer papers, Ron. I have agents I need to round up and a task force to get off the ground."

CHAPTER ONE

DAMIAN RODRIGUEZ SET his bag down on the tile floor of his foyer and closed the front door. After two weeks away, he took a moment to absorb the peculiar musty scent he'd come to associate with his new home on Tildas Island in the Caribbean —humidity with a hint of decomposition and undertones of floral sweetness—he glanced around the room. Sunlight streamed in through the open shutters, casting slanted lines across the living room furniture to his right and long shadows across the dining room table to his left. Dust motes danced in the beams, and the temperature inside, though not as cool as he normally kept it, felt just a little crisper against his skin than the air outside.

Even in February, and even at ten in the morning, he was glad he'd had one of his teammates stop by the night before to set his AC to a lower temperature. He was used to summers in DC, but having moved to Tildas Island as part of an FBI special task force three months prior, he'd quickly realized that those few hot months in the DC swamp had nothing on the Island where temperatures rarely dropped below eighty—even at night.

After over thirty hours of travel from Rome, where he'd been for a friend's wedding, weariness weighed on Damian and coffee was the first order of business if he was going to make it through the day. Leaving his bag where he'd dropped it, he headed into the kitchen and set the kettle on the stove. After filling the French press with grounds, he leaned against the counter and stared at nothing in particular as the water heated.

Insignificant thoughts filtered through his mind as he waited —flashes of memories from the wedding, the amazing wine he'd had at dinner two nights before, and the seemingly interminable flights and layovers between Italy and his new home. Living the island life seemed like it should be a dream, but the reality was much more complicated than bumming around in the sun with a beer and listening to Jimmy Buffet.

The random thoughts slowly faded, and the bone-deep fatigue that came from travel and jet lag started to press down on his body. He was glad he'd taken a few extra days off. The time difference between Tildas Island and Italy wasn't much— only six hours—but between the festivities, late nights, and long travel, he was feeling every one of his thirty-seven years.

A knock came at his door just as the kettle whistled. Thinking it was one of his four teammates, he called out, "Come in, the door's unlocked."

Yet one more thing that was different down on Tildas Island, people actually left things unlocked—cars, doors, even shops sometimes. He wasn't usually one of those people, but he'd found that as each day passed, he had to remind himself more and more often to lock things up.

He poured the water into the press and set the lid on top, and still, none of his teammates came barging in. Inhaling the scent of fresh coffee like it was aromatherapy, he tamped down his irritation—as minor as it was—at whoever was going to make him leave his kitchen and answer the door. Maybe he could wait them out.

Another knock sounded, this one fainter, maybe even slightly tentative. With a tired sigh, Damian left his coffee to steep, and made his way to the front door. Gripping the handle, he yanked it open.

And every annoyed comment that hovered on his lips died.

He froze, his hand still on the handle, then blinked.

"Charlotte?" He managed to force the name out even though his mind was still struggling to comprehend that she was standing on his front porch. He was also vaguely aware that his mouth hung open in shock.

He snapped his jaw shut and blinked again. Yes, it appeared that Charlotte Lareaux was standing not three feet away from him. The very same Charlotte Lareaux who, at one time, he'd thought was *the one*.

Despite his attempts over the past year to forget her, to push her out of his mind, and most definitely out of his heart, that traitorous organ gave a lopsided thump, then started thudding against his ribs. To counteract the unwelcome, though, unfortunately not surprising, reaction to her, he narrowed his eyes and drew his shoulders back.

"What are you doing here?" he asked. She lived in DC and had no reason to be on Tildas Island, let alone a reason to seek him out.

She stared at him and didn't answer right away. In those few seconds, he took in her appearance and frowned. Dressed in capri-length running pants and a sleeveless exercise top, she was soaking wet. He could even see the footprints her drenched sneakers had made on the sun bleached wood of his porch.

Her face was pale, but most concerning was the look in her eyes; the deep brown pools looked at him in confusion. With her brow slightly furrowed and the corners of her eyes pulled tight, she stared at him.

"Charlotte?" he asked, this time he gentled his voice. He wasn't used to seeing Charlotte anything other than confident—

oh, he'd seen her in just about every mood possible from giddy to pissed-as-hell. But underlying all those had been a foundation of confidence that he'd always found both frustrating—because she'd often taken it to the extremes and used it as a shield to keep him out—and sexy as hell.

But this, this vacant, utterly lost expression on her face baffled him.

He didn't reach for her, but he relaxed his posture and took a step closer. "I didn't know you were on the Island. Is everything okay?" He hated to think that the only reason she'd come see him was if something *wasn't* okay, but then again, at least that meant she trusted him at least a little bit, didn't it? Not that he was looking for her trust.

Finally, she seemed to wake up a bit. Her gaze fixed on his, and though her eyes still looked a little wild, he could see her struggling to focus on him. Slowly, she shook her head.

"I don't know, something…the dock…it hurts."

Her words filtered into his mind just as he noticed a thin stream of blood making a track down her bare calf. His gaze jerked from her leg back to her face as alarm shot through his system.

A tear streaked down her cheek. "I'm so sorry," she rasped. Then she collapsed.

Damian moved swiftly and caught her against him. Instantly, her damp clothes soaked through his shirt, and despite the heat, goosebumps chased across his skin. Gathering her in his arms, he stepped back into his house and kicked the door shut behind him. Without breaking stride, he made his way into his bedroom and set her gently on his king-sized bed.

Panic lanced through him like lightning when he glanced down at his light blue t-shirt to see it stained with blood. Working quickly, he removed her shoes and socks as he pulled his phone from his pocket.

Pulling up a contact and hitting the dial button, he did a

cursory examination of Charlotte's body to see if he could glean where the blood was coming from. He didn't have to look too hard, and by the time he'd run a hand up one leg, blood had already started to pool on the blanket just below her ribs.

"Rodriguez, welcome back," Benita Ricci answered her phone.

"I need your help, stat, Ricci," Damian said, bending down to see if he could get a better look at what was causing Charlotte to bleed so much. Gently he pulled the bottom of her shirt up, revealing the wide waistband of her pants.

"Burying-a-body kind of help or some other kind of help? You know I'm there for you either way, but I'd like to be prepared."

Damian's lips almost twitched into a smile at that. In the three months since they'd started on the special task force, Beni had become a good friend. She could be abrasive and annoyingly tenacious at times, but her ability to read people and situations was almost otherworldly, and he could always count on her to tell it like it was.

"No bodies. Hopefully," he added. "But bring your kit," he said. Beni had been a medic in the Army before joining the FBI and now acted as the team's de facto doctor.

"I'm out the door already. Where are you?"

Damian sucked in a breath when his fingers caught on a tear in the fabric at Charlotte's waist. No, not a tear, a slice. His stomach pitched as he traced the two-inch line, and he was glad he hadn't had a chance to drink any of his coffee because he wasn't sure it would have stayed down.

"I'm at home. Come quickly and come alone. My friend's been stabbed."

CHAPTER TWO

DAMIAN WAS SEATED BESIDE CHARLOTTE, pressing a folded towel as hard as he dared against her side when Beni let herself into his house. He glanced up when she paused in the doorway to his bedroom.

He could see a thousand questions in her eyes, but thankfully she didn't pause to ask a single one. Instead, she entered the room, set her medic bag on the bedside table, and crouched down to get a better look.

"I didn't want to undress her until you got here," he said, letting Beni gently peel his hand from Charlotte's side. She took the towel from him and started to lower the top of Charlotte's pants.

"I'm not promising she won't need to go to the hospital, but I'll see what I can do," she said as she bent down to get a closer look. "The waistband has probably been keeping this pretty compressed, so as this comes down, you might see a lot more blood. You going to be okay with that?"

Damian swallowed. "I'll be fine."

Beni paused and glanced up. Her eyes, an unusual mix of gold and green, studied him.

"Why don't you go get some more towels," she said.

"I'll be fine," he repeated.

"Sure, fine, whatever," she said, turning her attention back to Charlotte. "It looks like she's been in the water, so once we get these pants off, I want to flush the wound with antiseptic and antibiotics before stitching her up. I assume you're fine with her resting on a soaking bed when we're done? If not, I'm going to need more towels."

Damian muttered a curse at the point she'd driven home, then rose to retrieve more towels. By the time he returned, carrying every one he could find in his bathroom and closet, Beni had Charlotte's pants pulled down to the tops of her thighs.

"Get her pants all the way off," Beni ordered as she examined the wound. Damian chanced a look at two-inch gash that marred Charlotte's waist then quickly looked away. He wasn't squeamish by any account, but seeing so much blood flowing from Charlotte's body made it a little hard to breathe.

He worked quickly, not bothering to ask Beni what she thought Charlotte's chances were—he wouldn't contemplate any option other than full recovery, and he knew Beni operated with the same objective.

"I'm going to roll her to her other side just a bit and I want you to slide two towels underneath her," Beni said as soon as he'd stripped Charlotte of her soaked jogging pants.

When they had the towels tucked enough under Charlotte so that they wouldn't move once Beni started to flush the wound, she gestured Damian closer. "Now, I need you to hold this in place while I listen to her lungs," Beni said, nodding to the towel she still held against Charlotte's side.

Smart woman that she was, she didn't give him any chance to hesitate. Grabbing his hand, she placed it over hers, then slid her hand out from underneath. Instinct kicked in and, despite the fear inside him clawing to get out, he held the compress tightly in place. With nothing but the sounds of Beni going through her kit filling the room, Damian forced himself to look at Charlotte, really look at her.

With Creole heritage on her mom's side, her skin was darker than his, but he knew her appearance often confused those who needed to put labels on people because she wasn't *quite* white or *quite* black or *quite* any one thing. She'd pulled her long, black hair into a low ponytail, and he spotted an errant piece of sargassum seaweed caught in the strands near her temple. He reached to remove it then snatched his hand back when Beni returned to the bed, a stethoscope in hand.

Slipping the ear tips in, Beni pressed the diaphragm against Charlotte's chest. He stilled, willing Beni to hear nothing but clear lungs. If the knife had nicked, or worse, punctured, Charlotte's lung, they'd have no choice but to take her to the hospital —something his gut told him they should avoid if possible.

He breathed a little easier, when Beni met his gaze and said one small, but important, word, "Clear."

Common sense had told him her lung probably hadn't been punctured—if it had, it was unlikely she would have been able to walk up the steep trail that led from the beach to his house— but even so, it was good to have Beni's more experienced opinion.

Dropping the stethoscope back in her bag, Beni began pulling out supplies. She talked him through the process as she prepared syringes; first, she'd flush it with saline, then with antiseptic, after that, she'd clean it with an antibiotic solution before stitching the skin together. She told him he'd have to watch Charlotte for any signs of internal bleeding—swollen belly, stomach pain not associated with the wound, and a few other things. It was useful information, but he was pretty sure the only reason Beni was talking was to give him an anchor to hold on to.

By the time the syringes, needle, and sutures were prepped and set out in a tidy row atop a towel that lay across Charlotte's flat stomach, Damian had taken Charlotte's hand in his and moved to stand beside her shoulder.

"She may be unconscious, but I think it's more from fatigue, and maybe loss of blood, than anything else," Beni said, picking up the first syringe. "Her heart rate is slightly elevated from the injury, but it's not erratic or high enough to be a concern in itself. That's all good, but it also means she's going to feel what we're about to do, and she may or may not wake up. You need to be ready to soothe her if she responds or, worse case, restrain her if she starts to fight."

Damian nodded and placed a hand on Charlotte's cool shoulder. When the content of the first syringe filled the wound, Charlotte jerked and moaned. Instantly, Damian dropped to his haunches and ran his fingers across her forehead and through her hair, murmuring words to comfort her.

"That had a little analgesic in it too, so the next few shouldn't hurt as much," Beni said, as she reached for the second syringe.

After that, Damian tuned Beni out and focused on Charlotte. He had no idea why she was on the island, let alone what had happened to her. Nor did he know if she'd gotten caught up in something and been specifically targeted or if what had happened to her was random.

Indiscriminate violent crime wasn't common on Tildas Island, though—at least not targeting the tourists. But whoever had done this to Charlotte had not only stabbed her but left her for dead by tossing her into the water to finish the job.

But, he found it hard to get his mind around the idea that she might have been specifically targeted. Charlotte was an economist and didn't typically run in the circles that included killers—although, to be fair, her work did give her access to classified information which might be of value to others.

"Damian?"

He turned to see Beni studying him.

"I'm done," she said. Damian's eyes went to the row of tidy stitches then back to Beni. "The wound was pretty clean and straightforward to stitch. Infection is what we'll need to worry about now. I'll put a bandage over it before I leave, but let's move the towels out from underneath her and get her top off. Do you have something more comfortable we can put on her?"

He rose and helped roll Charlotte a little to the side so they could slide the soaking towels off the bed. The bedspread was still a little damp from Charlotte's clothes, but Beni had been right, it would have been drenched without the towels.

With Charlotte still partly on her side, Beni grabbed a pair of surgical scissors and cut off her fitted jogging top. Once Charlotte was on her back again, Damian gently pulled the bedspread out from under her then tucked it back around her body. Grabbing a tube of what he assumed to be antibiotic ointment and a gauze pad, Beni knelt, shifted the blanket just enough to see the wound, and bandaged it up.

"She's still so pale," Damian said, as Beni rose and stood beside him at Charlotte's side.

"She lost a lot of blood," Beni said. "Not enough that I think she needs a transfusion, but enough to slow her body down. Those exercise pants of hers, and the wide waistband, probably saved her life by compressing the wound. But she's cold, Damian. At this point, that's what I'm most concerned about. I don't know how long she was in the water, but the fact that she was cold to the touch when I got here and that hasn't changed is worrisome."

"Do I need to warm up some blankets for her?"

Beni shook her head. "Who is she?"

Damian's gaze traveled to Charlotte's face and memories—ones he'd tried to keep buried—came flooding back. He cleared his throat.

"She's a friend."

"A little more than a friend?" Beni countered.

Damian hesitated then inclined his head. "At one time."

"She needs you now, Rodriguez. I don't know how she ended up with that," she said, gesturing toward the knife wound. "But my instincts are telling me it wasn't random."

He didn't want to think someone had intentionally tried to kill Charlotte, and he couldn't fathom why. But he also couldn't deny Beni's observation. "I agree."

For a moment, they stood, side-by-side, watching the steady rise and fall of Charlotte's breathing.

"You need to get her warm, Damian. The old fashion way."

Damian's eyes flitted to Beni then back to Charlotte. He knew exactly what Beni referred to. He didn't want to agree, but he was smart enough to know that sharing his body heat would be the best way to warm Charlotte.

"Help me get a shirt on her?" he asked.

Beni nodded and, working in tandem, they managed to get Charlotte into one of his softest cotton shirts. When she was back under the blanket, he stripped off his shirt, shucked his pants, and climbed in beside her wearing nothing but his boxers —his years in the military making him anything but modest. It felt awkward lying nearly naked next to an unconscious woman who had made it clear she had no room in her life for him, but he pushed aside the personal misgivings and focused on the clinical aspects—she needed body heat; he had body heat.

"I gave her a little something for the pain," Beni said as she packed up the last of her things. "She'll need more when she wakes, but don't let her take more than one of these, not until I can examine her again," she added, placing a pill bottle on the bedside table.

"Now get some rest, both of you. I'm going to re-stock my kit and run a few errands. She doesn't just need you, Damian, she needs all of us," she said, referring to their full team of five agents. "We'll get this figured out. But in the meantime, I think we can agree that as far as the rest of the world is concerned, our friend here needs to stay dead."

CHAPTER THREE

WARMTH SURROUNDED Charlotte as she slowly woke. The loveliness of being cocooned in comfort was her first thought, but that was quickly followed by the realization that her body felt like it had taken a beating and not come out on the winning side.

She drew a quick breath at the shock of pain that consumed her. Had she been kicked in the side by a strong man with a big-ass boot? Where was she and what the hell had happened?

As she cataloged the sensations that assailed her—a warm, but not too warm, blanket, soft sheets that caressed her bare legs, and the deep, throbbing pain in her side—she became dimly aware of voices. Two of them.

The quality of the sheets told her she wasn't in a hospital, and so, bracing herself for the unknown, she opened her eyes. Even as she took in the fact that she was lying on a large bed in someone's bedroom, her gaze instantly zeroed in on two figures she could see through the open bedroom door.

Damian Rodriguez was talking to some woman wearing a green t-shirt, jeans, and boots. Charlotte's gaze lingered on the boots, and for a moment, she wondered if the woman was the source of her pain. But she dismissed the thought—whatever else Damian thought of her, Charlotte knew that he would never stand by and let her get hurt. No, if Damian was talking with her, especially in such a personal setting as someone's home, chances were she was a friend. Or maybe even more, which was a thought Charlotte didn't want to contemplate.

Either way, neither Damian's presence nor the woman's went far in answering just what had happened to her, and in an effort to clear some of the lingering sleep-fog from her brain, she moved to sit up.

Pain, so nauseatingly intense, shot through her and she dropped her head back down onto the soft pillow. Closing her eyes, she took several deep breaths. When she no longer felt like she was going to vomit, which she thought might actually kill her with the strain it would put on her stomach, she opened her eyes.

"I'd ask you how you feel, but I think I can hazard a guess," Damian said from beside the bed as he looked down on her, his face so achingly familiar. The woman had entered the room as well and stood at the foot of the bed.

"How...I don't remember..." Charlotte's voice trailed off. Hating how confused she felt, she made to sit up again, though what that might accomplish she hadn't a clue—just an errant display of some control, perhaps?

"Here, let me hold your weight," Damian said, slipping an arm behind her and lifting her as he grabbed a pillow and shoved it between her back and the headboard. Her stomach still hurt like the devil, but at least the pain was slightly more manageable.

"Damian," the woman said, then nodded toward something.

Charlotte turned her head to see Damian shaking a pill out of a bottle. He handed it to her along with a glass of water. She supposed she should ask what it was but she couldn't muster the energy and she trusted Damian—her trust in him had never been their problem. Instead, she dutifully took the pill and chased it down with a sip of water. Then she downed the rest of the glass. When had she gotten so thirsty?

"Give it about ten minutes, and you'll start to feel it kick in," the woman said. "It's not an opioid, so it won't make you woo-woo, but it will take the edge off."

Charlotte almost smiled. The woman might be Damian's new girlfriend, but Charlotte had to like a person who could use the word "woo-woo" in complete seriousness.

"What happened?" Charlotte asked.

"You don't remember?" Damian countered.

Ignoring both the questions, the woman muscled Damian out of the way as she spoke. "Since Rodriguez hasn't bothered to introduce us, I'm Benita Ricci. You can call me Beni, though. He and I work together."

Beni reached for Charlotte's hand and, for a moment, Charlotte panicked. Raising her arm to shake Beni's hand would require the use of her stomach muscles and anticipation of the pain lanced through her. Thankfully, instead of the greeting, Beni wrapped her fingers around Charlotte's wrist and started taking her pulse. "I'm also the team medic and the one who stitched you up," Beni added, then dropped her gaze to her watch to count the seconds.

"Stitched me up?" Charlotte asked, her gaze going to Damian.

"Do you remember anything?" he asked.

She frowned and tried to conjure her memories. "I remember going for a run this morning. The sun wasn't up yet, but several paths around the resort are well lit, so I was running those." She paused and, like a sieve, bits and pieces of her morning came filtering back through her mind.

"I stopped at the dock to watch the sunrise." She hesitated. She remembered what she *felt* more than what happened, and she struggled to find the right words. "I was just about to turn and head back to my room. I remember thinking about a report I needed to send before my meetings started for the day. But then I was grabbed from behind. I never saw him, and it happened so fast, but I felt something in my side and then I was falling. I remember hitting the water, but not much more than that until I woke up with my arm stuck on one of the pilings. I was hanging there, bobbing up and down with the waves. That saved me, I suppose. I don't know how long I was there, but everything felt so foggy, like my mind couldn't work properly."

She paused again and raised her gaze to meet his. "I saw the pictures of Matty and Dash's vacation here last month," she said, mentioning her best friend and husband, the couple who had introduced her to Damian. "One of them was the picture of the three of you on your porch. Matty knew I was coming to the Island and where I was staying and showed me where you lived. I must have had that in my mind when I crawled out of the water because the next thing I know…" Rather than finish her statement, she gestured to the room. Neither Damian nor his colleague needed to know that on the first day she'd arrived, she'd gone for a walk on the beach and spotted his home. She also didn't fool herself into thinking it didn't mean something that even when delirious and nearly dead, she'd remembered not just that Damian was nearby, but exactly how to find his house.

"You said that you never saw *him*. Are you sure it was a man?" he asked.

Charlotte nodded. That small detail was clear as day in her mind. "He came from behind. I remember looking down and seeing his forearm across my chest. It was thick and covered with coarse, blond hair. And I could see his thumb. Of all the details I could have noticed, this seems like a weird thing, but in the moment, I remember thinking I'd never seen a man with a missing thumbnail before."

"No nail at all?" Damian asked.

Charlotte shook her head. "None."

Damian and Beni, who'd finished checking Charlotte's vitals, shared a look.

"You were stabbed," Beni said. "You have ten stitches in your side, and while I flushed it with antibiotics, I want to give you a couple more doses, intravenously, over the next few days. Now, do you know why anyone would want to do this to you?"

"Jesus, Beni, she just woke up ten minutes ago and just learned she was stabbed," Damian said. "Give a woman a chance to catch her breath."

Charlotte glanced over to where Damian stood. He'd moved to the end of the bed while Beni had been poking and prodding her, and hadn't returned to her side when his colleague had finished.

Out of the corner of her eye, she saw Beni flash a dismissive look at Damian. "She doesn't look like a woman who needs to catch her breath, Rodriguez. Based on the little bit of research I've done on Dr. Lareaux since she showed up on your doorstep six hours ago, I'd guess she wants answers even more than you do."

"I do," Charlotte said, cutting off anything else Damian might have said. "But without giving it much thought, no one comes to mind. If you looked into me, you know I consult with both public and private sector businesses. It's possible that I pissed someone off along the way, but no one comes to mind."

"Pissed someone off enough that they'd travel to Tildas Island to kill you?" Beni asked.

"Or it's someone who's here with her already," Damian said.

"We're looking into that," Beni responded to Damian, though her gaze never left Charlotte. There was very little that intimidated Charlotte, not with the life she'd had, but Beni's scrutiny was coming pretty close.

"You look like you have something to say," Charlotte said to Beni.

The agent's lips twitched, then she spoke. "I do. After I stitched you up, I took your room key from your pants—pants that saved your life, by the way. I will never complain about exercise clothing again—"

"Beni," Damian cut her off.

Beni shot Damian a quelling look then continued. "After having a little look at the security footage from this morning and seeing you leave for your run, I figured out your room number and made a little visit. The cleaning staff had already been through, and I wouldn't know if anyone had been in and taken anything anyway, but I can tell you, it looked pretty clean. Your laptop and phone were even sitting on the desk."

"You say that like the room being clean has more meaning than it just being clean because housekeeping had been there. I'm an economist and not *that* in touch with the criminal element, so you're going to have to spell it out for me."

"It means that if no one searched your room, or searched it and left your laptop, chances are, they aren't looking for something you *have*," Damian said. "They're worried about something you *know*."

Instantly, Charlotte's mind started spinning. In her field of expertise, which included monitoring and advising on the global flow of money, she *knew* a lot of things. She even knew a lot of things that were highly confidential and not for public disclosure. But did she know something worth *killing* for?

"Or something that they think you might learn," Beni added.

Charlotte looked at Beni and raised her brows in question.

"I already brushed your laptop and phone for fingerprints, but I'd like to take it to my tech guy to see if someone has been in it recently and either done a data dump of everything on your hard drive or left anything on it that could monitor your activities—although, admittedly, if you're supposed to be dead, that latter is unlikely."

Charlotte thought about all the data on her computer, most

of it was encrypted and protected more than the usual laptop, but having someone she didn't know go through it, gave her pause.

"How much will he see?" she asked.

"We have a tech guy?" Damian asked at the same time.

"*I* have a tech guy," Beni said, then turned to Charlotte. "Just logs, none of the data."

"Who's this tech guy?" Damian pressed.

"You know Jim, who does the security system at the resort?" Beni asked.

Damian nodded.

There was more than one resort on the island, but Charlotte knew that the one Damian and his team were most concerned with was the one where she'd been staying. It was just down the cliff and around the point from Damian's house and it was also the location of the summit scheduled to occur in just over a year that was being hosted by the Organization of World Leaders.

"His brother John is a whiz," Beni said. "I've been trying to get him onboarded as a real consultant for us, but passing the background check has been a little bit of a challenge. He had some trouble as a kid and young adult," she added as an aside to Charlotte. "Anyway, he prefers captaining his boat charters—he doesn't have a lot of patience for sitting still—but if you can give him something quick and discrete, I've never met anyone better."

She felt Damian's gaze, and she shifted her focus to find him watching her. "It's your call, Charlotte," he said.

"Would you?" she countered.

He nodded. "Beni trusts him, and I trust her." The words were barely out his mouth when he flinched. It was subtle, but she saw it. A shadow of the heartache she'd felt when they'd broken up flickered to life, but while the reminder of their relationship hurt, she tamped that feeling down. She wasn't going to compare the relationship she and Damian had to the one he had with his colleague and it wasn't fair to think he'd meant it that way.

"Go ahead," she said, turning to address Beni. "I'd like my phone back as soon as possible, though, so I can call a few people. Also, I'll need to let the team I'm meeting with here on the island know I'm okay. They'll have missed me today and will start to worry."

At her comment, Beni and Damian shared another look. "You got this, Rodriguez?" Beni asked.

Damian grimaced but nodded. "You can use my phone for the time being, but we need to talk about a few things before you make any calls," he said, addressing Charlotte. "Beni, why don't you give her the antibiotic injection then head out with the computer and phone. We can all convene here tomorrow morning to figure out a plan."

Beni nodded, but Charlotte's attention was on Damian. He was avoiding her gaze, which wasn't something he usually did. Or at least it hadn't been something he'd done when they'd been together. She thought about pressing the matter, but held off when Beni started swiping a spot on her arm with a cold, antiseptic wipe. Two minutes later, she was withdrawing the needle from Charlotte's vein and placing a bandage over the injection site.

"You can get up to use the bathroom, move to the couch, that sort of thing," Beni said as she packed up her medical bag. "But don't do too much more than that for now. Your body has been through a trauma, and the best thing to do is let it rest and heal."

"Can I shower?" Charlotte asked.

Beni nodded as she zipped her bag. "I've left waterproof bandages on Damian's table, as well as supplies to replace the bandage that's on there now. Just don't overdo it, or you will seriously piss me off." She said it with a smile, but Charlotte was pretty sure Beni wasn't joking.

"Make sure she eats and sleeps," Beni said to Damian as she

headed toward the door. "Pain killers are on the bedside table. Call me if you need anything more."

Both she and Damian watched Beni leave. Then, when the door shut behind her and they heard her jogging down the front steps, she turned to meet Damian's gaze. Her heart hitched, skipping a beat or two. This was the first time since they'd broken up just over a year ago that they were alone—well, alone and both conscious.

His dark eyes watched her, and she searched his face, looking for any sign that might give her a hint as to what he was feeling. She saw nothing there, no clue as to his thoughts. His posture was even annoyingly benign. But then she saw it, the tiny movement in his neck, his artery beating faster than normal. She still didn't know what he was thinking, but he was most definitely thinking something.

"Damian," she said. She sounded like a fighter acknowledging her opponent. She couldn't help it, though. With her injury and, more to the point, the fact that she'd sought him out, even in her delirium, she felt at a disadvantage when it came to the game of hiding their feelings.

Damian cocked his head ever so slightly to the side and crossed his arms. "Charlotte," he said. "I think we have a few things to talk about, don't you?"

CHAPTER FOUR

At his words, a wary look entered Charlotte's eyes, and Damian hated it. He didn't hate it enough to not feel some satisfaction at seeing it—after all, if she cared nothing for him, she wouldn't have that reaction—but he wasn't that much of a dick to enjoy it. He also wasn't that much of a masochist to want to rehash their relationship. Again.

"We need to talk about contacting people," he clarified. "About who you can reach out to and what you should say."

Charlotte hesitated then nodded. "Before we do that, may I use the restroom? At some point, I'd like to shower, too, but not sure I'm quite up to that yet."

In three strides, he was at her side, pulling the blanket back and helping her swing her long legs over the edge of the bed. There, she paused to catch her breath.

"This is going to hurt like hell, isn't it?" she said, already clutching his arm.

"Probably, but if you made it up the cliff from the beach to my house when you were in pain and bleeding, you can make it ten feet to the bathroom with aid from pain killers and me."

He smiled when she chuckled. "Well, when put that way, I feel a little pathetic worrying about this."

"You should, it's nothing," he said, drawing another quiet laugh from her.

"Now you're just trying to goad me, and yes, before you ask, it's working." And with that, she used his arm for leverage and rose. He heard her suck in a quick breath and let it out slowly, but then she took a step. And then another.

They made the journey in small increments, but never stopped moving. When they reached the door to the en suite bathroom, Charlotte braced a hand on the frame and took another few deep breaths.

"Okay, that was painful, but not as bad as I thought it would be," she said.

It was on the tip of his tongue to point out that it rarely was. Charlotte was cautious by nature and, given her childhood, she had every right to be, but somewhere along the way, she'd also forgotten that for every hard thing she'd ever done, for every risk she'd taken—including dating him—she'd come out the other side just fine. Maybe a little emotionally or intellectually bruised, but fine. Because Charlotte was nothing if not a survivor.

Instead of speaking his thoughts, Damian eased his hold on her and took a half-step away. "The bathroom is small and you should have enough things to lean on or hold onto between here and the toilet," he said. "Holler if you need help, but while you're doing your thing, I'll dig up a washcloth and toothbrush so you can at least rinse your face and brush your teeth before getting back in bed."

Ten minutes later, he was lifting her legs back onto the mattress and tucking the blanket around her.

"You hungry or thirsty?" he asked once she was safely back in bed. *His* bed to be precise, but he was probably better off with a little imprecision.

"A little of both," she admitted. "I don't think I can eat much, but I am a little hungry and wouldn't mind another glass of water."

"Dominic brought by some curry soup—I know you can handle spicy food, but this isn't the hot kind of curry and it will be easier to stomach right now," Damian said. "And Alexis brought you some clothes, which you can look at later, but she also brought some of this magic tropical fruit juice she gets from somewhere but won't tell any of us where. It's really good when mixed with sparkling water."

"Both of those sound great. I'll have to thank Dominic and Alexis, but I don't know who they are," she said.

There had been a time when she'd known all the people on his team, and her words were another stark reminder of just how far they'd drifted.

"Dominic Burel and Alexis Wright are on my team," he said, even as he made his way out of the bedroom and into the kitchen. His house was small enough that if he spoke loudly, she'd be able to hear him.

"The fifth member is Jake McMullen. Dominic is from Louisiana, and I don't know who taught that man to cook, but out of the five of us, he is definitely the best chef. Alexis is a little bit of an enigma, but she has some serious people skills—she's great when it comes to soothing people or making them comfortable enough to talk with us. I think she's studied psychology, though she hasn't confirmed or denied it. Regardless, even if she has, whatever she learned probably only complemented her innate skills." As he spoke, he reheated the soup that Dominic had left on his stove and poured two glasses halfway full with Alexis's juice.

"And Jake?" Charlotte asked, her voice sounding much stronger than even an hour earlier.

Damian chuckled. "You'll have to meet him yourself—which you will tomorrow when the team comes by—but he's a little crazy. Was a professional surfer in his younger years, but when an injury took him out of the pro-tour, he said, 'thanks, but no thanks,' to entering the family hotel business, and joined the FBI." As he spoke, he carried the full glasses into the bedroom and handed one to Charlotte while he set the other on the bedside table.

"Try that," he said, nodding to the drink. "I'll be right back with the soup."

He was ladling soup into two bowls when Charlotte called out and asked him to bring more juice, making him chuckle. Alexis had a lot of secrets, and as a former Ranger, he could appreciate that, but he *really* wished she'd share where she found her tropical concoction.

A few minutes later, he was settled into a chair beside the bed, holding his own bowl of soup, and two topped-off glasses of juice on the bedside table. He took a spoonful as he glanced at Charlotte and considered the best way to tell her that for all intents and purposes, she needed to stay "dead."

But the words died on his lips as he watched her take a dainty taste of soup. The sight didn't render him speechless because it was sexy or erotic, as seemed to happen in a lot of the romance books he'd read—and yes, he read a lot of them because who the fuck didn't like a happy-ever-after—but because for the first time since she'd shown up on his doorstep, he allowed himself to feel how truly bizarre this whole situation was. He hadn't seen Charlotte in just over a year, and their break-up had been a cluster-fuck of epic proportions—they'd both hurt each other, and they'd both said a lot of things they hadn't meant. At least he had.

And yet here they sat. Charlotte reclined in his bed—albeit with a stab wound—having dinner and a relatively nice, if not unusual, discussion. They'd both even laughed a time or two since she'd awakened. He didn't want to forget the gut-wrenching days that followed their split—they were too defining to let go of altogether—but that he found he could let those memories go just for a little while, felt good.

And he missed her.

Sitting here with her, even in the circumstances they were in, forced him to acknowledge that even through the pain and hurt, he missed her. What that said about him, he didn't know and, as he took another bite of soup, he decided that maybe he didn't *need* to know. For now, it could just be what it was, and they could focus on getting her healthy and keeping her safe.

"Tell me what's on your mind. You've got that little line right here," Charlotte said, pointing to a spot between his eyebrows. "And by the way, you were right about Dominic's cooking. Don't tell my mother, but this could rival hers." She gave him a mock salute with her spoon.

Damian smiled at that. Nanette Lareaux was a southern woman through and through and cooked like one too—she also ran the catering side of the business she'd started with Carmen Viega—the mother of Charlotte's best friend, Matty.

"I'm pretty sure he adds pixie dust and the blessings of angels to just about everything he makes," he said. He wasn't about to tell Charlotte what had really been on his mind, but they did have things they needed to discuss.

"There isn't a lot of random violence on Tildas Island," he started. "And while it's possible what happened to you was just that, I don't want to take that chance."

Charlotte regarded him for a moment. "I want to go back to the part of that statement about not taking any chances in just a little bit, but given that they didn't appear to break into my room or steal anything, doesn't that argue for it being random? I know you said they might be after something I *know*, but these days, how much do you *know* that you don't also have some-where on your electronic devices? If they were worried about that, it seems like they'd at least take my computer and phone."

Rather than answer, he shifted in his seat, dug into his

pocket, and pulled out a piece of paper Beni had given him. "Any chance this is one of your email accounts?" he asked, handing it to her.

Charlotte reached for the paper, read the address on it, then arched a brow at him. "Doclareaux69? If I were going to put a sexual innuendo into an email address, I'd be much cleverer than that," she said, handing the paper back.

Damian tossed it on the bedside table. "Yeah, it didn't sound like you, but I had to ask. The reception at the resort received an email purporting to be you from that address. It included your room number and a message saying that your aunt had fallen ill on a neighboring island and that you had to leave early that morning to see her. You also asked them to let your colleagues know."

"You're shitting me?" Charlotte's spoon clattered into her bowl. "And the resort staff believed that? Why on earth would they think I'd ask them to tell my colleagues anything? The meeting was—is—small and intimate. There are only ten of us here, and until today, we'd been locked in a room together for three days. Didn't it occur to the reception that it was weird that I didn't tell my colleagues myself?"

"We, on the task force, are looking at it as a good training exercise," Damian said with a rueful grin. Since he and the team had arrived on the island in November, they'd been working with the resort and its employees on privacy and security protocols. Apparently, they needed to go back to some of the basics.

"Given that someone impersonated me to excuse my absence so that no one would raise the alarm, I grant you that the fact that my computer and phone were left in my room isn't as relevant as I thought it might be," Charlotte said.

Damian nodded.

"Which is why you don't want to—can't—treat this as a random attack," she clarified.

He nodded again. "And because it's likely you were intentionally targeted, we want to limit the number of people you contact. Your mom and Matty are okay, but we don't want you to reach out to anyone else. It's better for whoever did this to you to go on thinking you're dead. At least until we know what's going on."

"Dead and washed out to sea," Charlotte said.

Damian grimaced at her blunt assessment. "We may not know much yet, but there is one thing we have going for us—in the absence of a storm, the currents and tides on the island aren't that strong, at least not close to shore, and it's unlikely anything heavier than a bottle would get washed out to sea. So, whoever did this probably isn't local. And if they aren't local, they should be easier to trace since the only way on to and off of the island is by boat or plane."

"Always the silver lining," Charlotte muttered as she set her empty soup bowl down on her lap. "I still can't fathom what I could know that would make someone want to kill me, though you can be sure I'll be thinking about it all night. But before I set my mind to it, may I borrow your phone to make those calls?"

Damian rose and collected their dishes as he spoke. "Of course, it's charging in the kitchen. Let me take these to the sink and I'll grab it and bring it back. While you're talking to them, do you mind if I take a shower?" he said, gesturing to his bathroom.

He could see the moment it dawned on her that not only was she in his house, but she was in his bedroom. Her eyes widened a touch as she looked around, then her gaze met his again.

"I'm only one person, Charlotte," he said. "It's a small house. One bedroom, one full bathroom, although there's a half bath off the pantry. There's a pullout couch I'll sleep on tonight, and if you even think about protesting and try to insist on sleeping on the couch, I'll eat the rest of Dominic's soup."

In the beat of silence that followed his statement, he left the room before she could say anything. Returning a few minutes later, he handed her his unlocked phone—no need for her to know that the day of their first date was still his code.

"I'll be done in ten minutes," he said. "I assume that's enough time for you to have a quick call with both your mom and Matty?" He waited for her to agree, and when she nodded, he continued. "Please remember to tell them to keep this to themselves. When I'm done with my shower, I can help you to the bathroom again, and then, if you don't mind, it's been a long day and I need to get some sleep."

Charlotte nodded again but didn't say anything. His gaze held hers for a moment—a moment when all the anger and hurt and love he felt threatened to roar to life and strangle him.

Clearing his throat, he took a step back. "I'll be done in ten minutes."

CHAPTER FIVE

CHARLOTTE SLOWLY DIALED Matty's number as Damian gathered clothes from his closet. As soon as the bathroom door closed behind him, she hit the call button. It wasn't that she intended to say anything she didn't want Damian to hear, but she didn't trust that Matty wouldn't lead them down a conversation trail she hadn't planned.

"Hey, it's me," she said, as soon as Matty answered. They'd known each other since they were both in diapers; there was no need to identify herself.

"Hey, you. Why are you on Damian's phone?" Matty asked.

"How did you know I'm using Damian's phone?" Charlotte countered, already glad she'd decided to wait until the man in question was in the shower before calling.

"Shocking as this may sound, in the two years you two dated, he and I actually became friends. I have his number in my phone."

It was hard to miss the sarcasm in Matty's voice, but even so, her comment took Charlotte aback for a moment. She and Damian had spent a lot of time in the Hudson Valley of New York, visiting with Matty, her husband Dash, and their twins,

Daphne and Charlie. It made sense that Matty considered Damian a friend too, but even so…

"I guess that never occurred to me," Charlotte said. She and Matty had no secrets; it wasn't worth trying to pretend she wasn't surprised that her best friend had stayed friends with her ex.

"Unlike some people, I didn't wipe him completely from my life. Now, are you going to tell me why you're using his phone? I know you're on Tildas Island. Are you back together?"

"I got stabbed," Charlotte said, cutting off any more of Matty's speculation.

Silence followed for a long moment before Matty spoke again. "Are you just saying that to get me to stop asking you about Damian? Or," Matty paused and took a deep breath before continuing. "Or, did you really get stabbed?"

At the concern in Matty's voice, tears sprang into Charlotte's eyes. She hadn't expected anything else—the two of them had been looking out for each other since the day they'd met—but even so, saying the words made the events of earlier that day, and the terror of it, all too real.

In a halting voice, she told Matty everything she knew, reassuring her friend over and over again that she was going to be okay and that Damian and his team, particularly Beni, were helping her. Mindful of Damian's warning to keep the attack quiet for now, she declined Matty's offer to come down to the island.

And when she found herself declining the same offer for the fourth time, she decided it was time to end the call, especially if she wanted to call her mom before Damian finished.

"I'm more than grateful that you're willing to fly down," she said. "But it's not a good idea right now. Besides, Daphne and Charlie's birthday is in two weeks, and I know you're in the middle of planning the party. How are they?" she asked, not able to help herself. Yes, she needed to call her mom, but Daphne and Charlie were the brightest light in her life, and being an honorary auntie was her favorite thing.

"I love them more than life itself, but they're three years old and being total assholes," Matty grumbled, but no one would miss the affection in her voice. Back when she and Matty had been three, the idea that they'd both be living the lives they were now was about as likely as them colonizing Mars. But with a bit of luck, the love of one very powerful woman, and a lot of hard work, both of them—and their mothers—had built lives for themselves that they all treasured.

"Yes, well, they are your assholes, so give them a kiss for me and tell them I'll see them at their party," Charlotte said with a smile.

"You think you'll make it?"

"Yes," she answered. If she had to charter a flight to stay under the radar, she wasn't going to miss that party.

"Call me. Every day," Matty said.

"Yes, mom," Charlotte said, grinning to herself. Usually, she was the one "mothering" Matty.

"Ha, funny. Go call your mom and tell her to call me if she needs to vent her worries on someone other than you."

Charlotte chuckled at the comment because there was a very high probability that her mother would do just that. "Will do. Love you."

"Love you, too. Oh, and before you hang up, I just have to say that while I know the reasons you ended things with Damian, and you know I agree with you, you may want to think about what it was in your heart, or your soul, that drove you up that cliff, in the state you were in, to his doorstep. You ran to him when you were hurt, maybe even dying, terrified, and in pain, Char. That has to mean something. I'm not saying what it might mean because that's not my place, but you and I trust so few people that sometimes it's easy to stop trusting ourselves too, and that's never a good thing."

Matty's words ran uncomfortably close to a few stray thoughts Charlotte had let herself have recently. Rather than try to lie to her friend, which Matty would see right through, she simply said, "I know."

On the other end of the line, Matty exhaled. "Take care of yourself, physically, mentally, and emotionally. I'm here if you need me."

"And I'm grateful for it every day."

She ended the call just as Damian stepped out of the bathroom dressed in nothing but boxers and a t-shirt, a wave of steam following him. Attraction had never been something they lacked, and though her gaze wanted to linger on the man before her, she forced her attention back to the phone.

"Not surprising, my call with Matty took a little longer than I planned. I just need to call my mom, and then you can have your phone back."

Damian studied her for a moment, then nodded. "Take your time. I'll go make up the bed."

Charlotte watched him leave then dialed her mom, this time taking a moment to notice that like Matty's number, his phone also recognized her mother's. It was disconcerting to think he might have been in touch with both her best friend and her mother in the year since they'd split, but she didn't have much time to consider the thought before her mom answered and she was swept into one of the more difficult conversations she'd ever had.

By the time she'd finished, exhaustion weighed heavily on her shoulders. Damian appeared in the doorway then moved into the room. Without a word, he took the phone from her and helped her into the bathroom again. She couldn't manage a shower—that would have to wait until tomorrow—but at least she managed to brush her teeth and wash her face again.

When she finished, Damian helped her back into bed and handed her another pain killer. "I know it hasn't been very long, but Beni said you could take one more before you go to sleep."

Gratefully, she took the tablet from him and swallowed it down.

"Call if you need anything," he said.

She nodded. "Thank you, Damian."

A muscle in his jaw ticked, and he gave a sharp nod. "Goodnight, Charlotte," he said, then walked away, closing the door behind him. She stared at the door for a long moment, then sleep slowly took its hold.

Hours later, when Charlotte woke, she was still on her back, in the same position in which she'd fallen asleep. The light streaming through the crack in the curtains was strong and pure. Another beautiful day in paradise. She supposed.

She turned to eye the distance between the bed and the bathroom and her muscles screamed as her body shifted. The pain killer had allowed her to sleep, but with such minimal movement the day before—and what was feeling like none during the night—her body was protesting any change in the current state.

The good news was that at least the pain from her stab wound seemed to have abated. It still throbbed, and she wasn't about to run a marathon or even go for a walk on the beach, but she did feel like she could make it the bathroom on her own.

Ignoring the stiffness of her body, she tossed the blanket aside and swung her legs over the edge. Once upright, her eyes caught on a small stack of carefully folded clothing at the end of the bed. Leaning over, she snagged the top piece—a button-up tank top—and as she pulled it toward her, a note fluttered to the bedspread.

"*Some of what Alexis brought. Thought you'd want it when you get up, but let me know if you want to try to shower first,*" it said.

Damian wasn't perfect. She wouldn't have been attracted to him if he hadn't had his own scars, like she did. But he was damn close. And she hated that she sometimes hated that about him. As she did now.

With a sigh, she gathered the clothes and rose from the bed. She was smart enough to know that most, if not all, of her frustration came from feeling so helpless. But that didn't make it any less real.

Ten minutes later, dressed in the tank top and a pair of low slung cut-offs—not something she'd normally wear but were damn comfortable—she opened the bedroom door.

Five heads turned in her direction, and five sets of eyes tracked her entrance.

Damian was standing next to Beni, leaning over a dining table, looking at something. At the end of the table sat a shockingly good looking man who had to be Dominic Burel. It was a guess, but she thought a pretty good one because standing to Dominic's side was another man with sun-kissed skin, brown hair highlighted with sun-bleached streaks, and a swimmer's body. There was no doubt in her mind *that* man was Jake, the former pro surfer. And beside Jake, stood a tall, gorgeous woman who had to be Alexis. Wearing a suit and heels, Alexis was the same height as Jake, and though her skin was darker than Charlotte's, Charlotte could see a smattering of freckles across her perfectly patrician nose. Her gaze noted the pastel blue color of Alexis's eyes, but what really caught her attention was the huge longhaired, black cat perched in Alexis's arms and draped over her shoulder. Even from where she stood, Charlotte could hear the animal purring.

"I didn't know you had a cat," she said. Inane words, to be sure. There was probably a lot about Damian she no longer knew.

"It's my neighbor's," he said, breaking away from his team and striding toward her. Taking her elbow, he led her to a seat at the table opposite Dominic then quickly introduced her to his team. She thanked Dominic for the soup and Alexis for the clothes and juice then let her eyes swing from member to member. She had no doubt they were all quite capable—she *knew* Damian was, and he seemed at ease with them in a way he wouldn't have been if he didn't have confidence in his teammates—but they also seemed to represent the diversity of the island. If they ever needed to go undercover, they'd have their bases covered for probably just about every scenario, at least from a superficial perspective.

"Why don't I make you some coffee and Beni and the team can walk you through what we're thinking so far. We have a few questions, too, if you're up for it?" Damian asked, hovering at her side. Funny, she never thought of Damian as the hovering sort. Attentive yes, hovering, not so much.

She nodded. "Coffee would be great, thank you. And maybe some more of that juice if you have any?" she added with a glance and smile at Alexis. Alexis didn't exactly look unfriendly, but she didn't smile back.

Damian disappeared into the kitchen, which lay to the right of where she sat, and she could hear him turning on the tap and moving around as he prepared the coffee.

"His name is Steve," Alexis said, dumping the cat in Charlotte's lap. "He's a good judge of character. I'm going to help Damian." With that, the woman disappeared. Charlotte spared a fleeting thought about whether or not Alexis and Damian were involved and then decided she was turning into a bit of fishwife —she'd initially thought Damian and Beni were together, and now Alexis? First of all, it wasn't any of her business, and second, she owed Damian more than that. He wasn't the kind of man who couldn't be friends with women or the kind of man who assumed friendship always meant something more.

With a little shake of her head, she started to stroke Steve and turned her attention to Beni. "I'm not sure how much more I can tell you other than what we talked about yesterday, but I *am* a little more clear-headed."

Beni nodded then turned toward Dominic, who spoke.

"We're tracking arrivals on the island in the past week of men traveling alone. We know your meetings started four days ago and so we're looking a few days before that too. But we also noticed that you landed on the island eleven days ago. You didn't check into your hotel until the night before your meetings started. Can you tell us where you were?"

Steve's purring rumbled against her thighs and under her hand as she answered. "I have a friend with a boat down here. He met me at the airport, and we spent a week traveling around the islands."

At the sound of breaking glass from the kitchen, everyone turned. "I just dropped the glass," Alexis said, her voice floating toward them in the silence that followed the shattering sound.

Charlotte glanced at Beni, who had switched her attention to a map spread out on the table. Finding no connection there, she turned back to Dominic. Jake took a seat just as a door in the kitchen slammed.

Ignoring whatever was going on in the kitchen, she continued. "He's a former professor of mine, and his daughter came down too. She works for the World Bank and is a bit of a mentee of mine. We really didn't do much of anything, just swam, snorkeled, a little diving, and maybe more drinking than we should have. They dropped me at the resort dock the night before the meetings started."

Alexis entered the room carrying a mug. "Damian said sugar, no cream," she said, setting the coffee down in front of her along with a tall glass of the juice.

"Thank you," Charlotte said, unsure what to think about Alexis. Beni, Jake, and Dominic seemed interested in hearing her story, in helping to figure out what might be going on. Alexis looked to be withholding judgment; although Damian had said she was a bit of an enigma, so maybe Charlotte shouldn't think about it too much.

She took a sip of her coffee to hide a rueful smile. *Of course* she'd think about it. The sad truth had hit her when she'd looked into Alexis's discerning eyes.

Charlotte wanted Damian's team to like her.

It had been a long time since she'd cared whether or not someone liked her—whether they respected her was something she cared about deeply, but *liked*? They either did or didn't. And she had plenty of friends so it wasn't anything she ever felt the need to force. But here she was, like an insecure teenager, hoping this group of four people *liked* her.

"Where's Damian?" she asked.

She saw Beni and Alexis share a look. "He had some errands to run in town. Mostly grocery shopping. He just returned from Italy yesterday," Alexis said. Charlotte was surprised to learn that. That he hadn't mentioned it once yesterday, spoke volumes. But even in her surprise, she could read between the lines of Alexis's answer. Damian needed space from her.

Hating that her presence in his life, in his home, made him feel that way, she refocused her attention back on Dominic. "I'm not sure what else I can tell you. I'm not sure I'll remember every beach or bay we stopped at, but I'll probably remember the restaurants where we ate and the dive shops we used."

"What about while you were out. Did you encounter anyone?" Beni asked.

Charlotte took a sip of her coffee and shrugged. "We met the usual boaters out and about. You know, the ones you strike up a conversation with because you happen to be eating at the same restaurant, boating in the same waters. No one any of the three of us knew."

"What about when you arrived on Tildas Island?" Dominic asked. "Anything unusual happen since then?"

Charlotte didn't hide the sardonic grin. "You mean other than getting stabbed and left for dead. No, nothing unusual."

Dominic grinned back, making Charlotte laugh. He was

almost uncomfortably good looking. Like Helen of Troy, his smile could launch a thousand ovaries, of that she was sure—not hers, but that didn't mean she was immune. Or blind.

"What is the topic of the meetings you were having?" Alexis asked.

Here Charlotte hesitated. The meetings weren't exactly top secret—they weren't even government-sanctioned—but they were sensitive.

"We're all cleared, Charlotte," Jake said, the first words he'd spoken since he'd greeted her. "Our clearance is as high as yours, and even though the topics of the meeting might not have anything to do with your attack—and so wouldn't be something that would meet the need-to-know criteria—we can't rule it out."

She looked down at Steve, sprawled across her lap, his fur like a soft black rug covering her thighs. She scratched behind his ears and he turned his head, urging her to a favorite spot. Jake was right; they couldn't rule it out.

"It's not that," she started. "The meetings aren't supported or funded by the government, so technically there's no security clearance needed." She paused, working through the best way to talk about something that was more a *feeling* than a reality. "There have been a few unexpected market reactions, globally, in the past six months. There's not much more I can tell you than that because we—the colleagues I was meeting with, and I —don't know what's causing them. They could be due to polit-ical or regional economic events, a cultural shift in global economics, or even a sign of something else. We're pretty sure it's not a cultural shift, at least not entirely, but what it *is,* we don't know. Our meeting this week was an informal gathering to discuss the possibilities."

"Who organized it?" Jake said.

"My colleague, Yoshi Saito, brought us together. I can give you the list of the other attendees if you like?"

"And did Yoshi Saito also choose the meeting location?" Alexis asked as she slid a pad of paper and pen over.

Charlotte shook her head as she started to write down all the names of her colleagues. "No, that was Victoria Korey. She's an economist based out of Los Angeles. I've known *of* her for years, but only met her in person a few years ago. She's attending the summit next year and wanted to see the place. She has some mobility issues and wanted to get the lay of the land—so to speak—while fewer eyes could watch her."

"And what about your friends with the boat?" Beni asked.

"What about them?"

"You told us their occupations, but what are their names and how long are they in the islands?"

Charlotte looked at Beni for a moment. The team was obviously exploring the idea that either her friends or her colleagues were behind this, which was patently ridiculous. Not that she was naïve enough to think people didn't lie, but her colleagues had nothing to gain from killing her—they knew everything she did about the situation they were discussing. And as for her former professor and his daughter, well, she'd known Simon O'Conner since her first day of college nearly twenty years ago, and his daughter just about as long. But still, the faster the team ruled them out, the faster they could get on to other possibilities. Whatever those might be.

"Simon O'Conner is a retired professor. He lives down here October through June. You can probably still find him on his boat somewhere around the islands. If he's not docked at his marina," she added. As she spoke, she wrote down his name, his daughter's, and the name of the marina.

"Mira O'Conner is his daughter. Like I said, she works for the World Bank but was down here on vacation for a couple of weeks. I think she's supposed to head back tomorrow or the day after." When she finished speaking, her stomach grumbled loudly.

"Any chance Damian has toast or anything like that? I can make it, but I don't want to go..." her voice trailed off, not wanting to say aloud that she didn't want to go rummaging around his house when she wasn't wanted.

"He keeps bread in the freezer that I can toast and has some peanut butter. Will that work?" Jake asked.

Charlotte nodded, and the man left the room to make her breakfast. It felt odd having people wait on her, she wasn't used to it and didn't like it, but since Damian was already struggling with having her in his space, she didn't want to invade it more.

"You said you are looking at arrivals in the past week," she said, eyeing Dominic's open laptop. "That seems a monumental task."

He lifted a shoulder. "Not as hard as you think. We're assuming he traveled here on his own, and there aren't a lot of single men entering the island unless they live here or have family that lives here. And for those who live here, we're only looking at ones who moved recently."

"Because of the lack of knowledge about the tides," Charlotte said, recalling what Damian had told her.

Beni nodded. "Absent a big storm, which we haven't had in weeks, the currents around the shores, especially this bay," she said with a nod toward the ocean visible through Damian's front windows, "wouldn't be strong enough to pull a body out."

"And then, taking into consideration that you identified him as a blond, white man; the pool of potentials isn't small, but it's not huge either," Dominic finished.

"What if he lives here full time? Or he entered the island by boat, and I don't mean a cruise ship. It's easy to slip on and off of the islands, and bypass any customs, if you're familiar enough with them," Charlotte said.

"We'll run checks on known criminals residing on the island," Alexis said. "But given that most of your life is based in

DC, it's likely that whatever you did or know originates from there."

"And so whoever attacked me yesterday must have traveled here too," Charlotte finished Alexis's logic.

"How many people knew you were coming here?" Jake said as he re-entered the room and set a plate in front of her. The smell of peanut butter wafted toward her, and for a moment, she was five again. Back then, peanut butter had been a special treat. It felt almost the same way now.

"Not many," she answered before taking a bite. Once she'd swallowed, she continued. "My mom and best friend knew, but I don't recall mentioning it to any colleagues."

"You scheduled a week-long boat trip with a friend in the Caribbean and didn't mention it to anyone other than two people?" Beni asked, her eyebrow arched in disbelief.

Charlotte met her gaze. "I'm not much of a sharer on my most extroverted days and given the ultimate reason for my visit—to meet with Yoshi and my colleagues to discuss anomalies we weren't sure we were seeing—no, I didn't feel the need to say anything to anyone other than that I was taking some time off."

Beni's hazel eyes held hers for a long moment, and then, to Charlotte's surprise, her lips kicked into a smile. "I bet that made for an interesting relationship. Rodriguez is the biggest sharer I've ever met."

Except when he wasn't. Of course, no one ever saw that side of him except for Charlotte because she'd been the only one who had ever tried to pry underneath his happy-go-lucky exterior. He clung to that façade—the façade of being an open book —so strongly. And in the end, it had been more important to him than she was.

"May I move around?" she asked, instead of responding to Beni's comment. "I know the wound is going to hurt for a while, but the rest of my body is sore, and I think moving around a little will help." She took the last bite of her toast as Beni slowly nodded, feeling the eyes of the rest of the team on her. She'd wager that they were all fully apprised of her past relationship with Damian—because, of course, Damian-the-sharer would feel obligated to tell them. But that didn't mean *she* had to discuss it.

"Feel free to move around as much as you're able," Beni said. "You don't seem the type to push yourself just because, so I'll trust you to take the rest you need when you feel you need it."

Beni had barely finished her statement and Charlotte was on her feet. She picked up the glass of juice she hadn't touched yet and walked toward the front windows. Dominic began typing away on his laptop again and the other three started talking, but Charlotte tuned them out.

Standing in front of one of the two large picture windows, she took in the expansive view. It would be even better from the porch, but for now, it would do. It would ground her in something bigger than herself. It was a trick she'd learned as a child. Living in the projects outside of New York, back when they were far more violent than they were today, she'd learned that if she found something bigger than herself to focus on, feeling insignificant had a way of also making her feel powerful.

It was an odd correlation, she knew. But knowing that she was little more than a blip on a blip in history reminded her that her life was her own. It didn't lessen the pain or reduce anxiety, but it did put them in perspective. She'd survive, even thrive in some ways, like people had been doing for thousands and thousands of years.

"Are you okay?"

Charlotte turned to see Jake at her side. Instead of answering right away, she pondered the question. *Was* she okay?

After a few seconds, she shrugged. "I'm sore, but my body will heal."

"Not what I meant," he said with a soft chuckle.

"You must have missed the part where I said I wasn't much of a sharer," she replied.

"You must have missed the part where we don't give a damn," he replied, his voice carrying his smile. "Not a single one of us will be put off by any walls you put up. The only reason we might not break through them is if we don't want to."

Charlotte studied the former pro-surfer as she thought about all the risks he'd chosen to take in his life—and the patience it must have taken to do what he'd done. She wondered how many hours he'd spent on a surfboard waiting for the perfect wave, how many hours he'd spent learning his craft. She didn't doubt he was sincere in his belief that he could wear her down if he put his mind to it. But the fact of the matter was, he was no match for a girl from the projects who'd learned from the cradle to keep her thoughts to herself because sharing her thoughts could have very well been a death sentence.

"So why did you and Rodriguez break-up?" he asked.

She chuckled at his tactic and let her gaze drift back to the expanse of the deep blue ocean. "You'll have to ask him."

"I'm asking you. I want your side of the story."

"There are a lot of things in life we want, but very few we actually need, and you don't need to know the answer to what you're asking," she said.

"Maybe I do. Maybe it's relevant? Maybe you hired someone to stab you so that you could inveigle your way back into his life." He sounded like a mystery writer testing out a new plot.

Her laughter quickly morphed into a wince as she turned to face him. "Look, I'll give you some points for trying and ask you this: is there anywhere else I can stay?"

Jake cocked his head and studied her.

She let out a deep breath. She wasn't about to let him into all her secrets, but she could give him a little something. "Me being here obviously makes Damian uncomfortable. I think we both know it wasn't Alexis that dropped that glass—"

"That's because he thought you'd hopped on a boat with another man for a week," Jake interjected.

"I *did* hop on a boat with another man for a week. But Damian didn't stick around long enough to hear the rest, did he? Regardless," she said, not wanting to go any further down that rat hole. "I make him uncomfortable. I'm not stupid enough to think I can go back to my room at that resort," she said, pointing toward her former lodgings, the eastern edge of which was visible from where they stood. "But there must be some other hotel or resort I can go to? This is his home; he deserves to feel comfortable here."

She held his gaze as he regarded her, and as often happened in tense situations, weird details seemed to pop out at her—like the fact that Jake's eyes were such a dark blue, they were almost slate grey.

"Hey guys," he said, breaking eye contact with her and speaking loud enough to get the attention of his team.

"Charlotte wants to move out. Says she makes Rodriguez uncomfortable. What do you think?"

"I think you're a bit of a bastard," she muttered just loud enough for everyone to hear.

"I think that whether I'm uncomfortable or not isn't Charlotte's call to make," Damian said, stepping into the dining room from the kitchen. Startled at his appearance—she hadn't even heard him come in—her gaze flew to his. Guilt pricked at her, but she wasn't sure why—she was suggesting leaving for *his* sake. Okay, maybe a little for hers, but *mostly* for his.

Silence fell in the room, and Damian held her gaze. She didn't miss the challenge in his eyes, or his stance. She was the first to look away.

"Beni, can you help me with one of those waterproof bandages? I'd like to take a shower if I can?" she asked.

A beat passed, then the woman answered. "Come on, and I might even help you with your hair. You've been hiding it well, but your body was hanging by one arm for at least thirty minutes yesterday, your shoulder has got to be killing you."

Grateful for the lifeline Beni had cast, Charlotte excused herself and quickly ducked into Damian's room and out of his line of sight.

CHAPTER SIX

DAMIAN WAS SITTING on his couch, feet propped on the coffee table, and laptop on his lap, when Charlotte finally emerged from his room. After her shower, she'd been exhausted—no surprise, really—and had decided to take a nap.

His teammates had stuck around long enough to make a plan. Dominic would keep culling through the files of the men who'd arrived on the island while Beni would see what she could find on the security footage from the resort, as well as pick up Charlotte's laptop and computer and see if they'd revealed anything during the forensic scan. Jake and Alexis returned to the office to be the agents on duty and he, well, he sat on his couch fighting off jet lag while reading through the files Dominic deemed interesting enough to warrant a more thorough review.

He didn't rise to greet her, but he did turn in his seat. "How are you feeling?" he asked.

She bobbed her head, "Been better, but better than a couple of hours ago, so moving in the right direction."

She hesitated in the middle of the room, and he watched her, curious what had her worked up, even though he had a pretty good idea.

"Look, Damian," she started. "What I said before is true. I think it might be better if I go stay somewhere else."

He dropped his feet to the floor and rose. "Because you think your presence here makes me uncomfortable," he said as he stalked toward her. Her watchful eyes followed him, but she didn't back down.

"I *know* my presence here makes you uncomfortable. And to be honest, knowing that makes *me* uncomfortable."

"Bullshit," he said. Her eyes flared, but still, she didn't move. Not even when he stopped a scant two feet in front of her.

Alexis had told him about the man she'd traveled with, her professor, and yes, he felt a bit like an ass for assuming what he had and for reacting to it the way he'd reacted. But he didn't believe her desire to leave was based solely on what she thought he felt about her being so near.

"I think you're uncomfortable because you're at a disadvantage here, with me. You don't know why what happened happened, you're injured, and on top of that, *I* was the one you came running to—not the hotel security, not the police. Now you have to rely on me, which was never your strong point, was it, Charlotte?"

Her jaw clenched and her nostrils flared as she inhaled sharply, no doubt reaching down into the near bottomless pool of calm she kept in reserve. One breath, then another. Then she spoke.

"There was a time when relying on you was effortless, Damian. You always showed up when you said you would, did the laundry, cooked, humored me about going to the movies, and you even held my purse at a few of my work events. But when things got real, when the chips were down and it wasn't about whether or not you'd remember to pick up the dry cleaning, but about sharing your life, you weren't so reliable then, were you?"

She let the question hang in the air for a moment. A moment when the thudding of his heart seemed to ripple through his body and his blood thickened and slowed.

"I trusted you with everything I had, Damian," she continued. "And if I was going to do that, if, for the first time in my life, I was going to take that chance, I damn well wasn't going to waste it on someone who wasn't willing to do the same. So yes, I find it hard to rely on you because when I really needed you, you weren't there. Not even when you knew how much it cost me."

"I trusted you, Charlotte. Not once did I ever doubt you—"

"March thirteenth and November twenty-second," she said, cutting him off. To anyone else, those rattled off dates probably sounded meaningless. To him, they sliced through the tightness that had been squeezing his chest as she'd spoken and stabbed at him like a knife.

"What do those dates mean to you, Damian?"

He took a step back and crossed his arms, not caring that his position would communicate just how defensive he felt. "You're not going to stay anywhere else," he said. "At least you can rely on me to keep you fed and safe."

Frustration flashed across her expression, but really, it was the disappointment that punched him in the gut. Like he'd just killed what little hope she'd had for them—which meant she'd actually had hope for them, even after a year apart.

"Fine," she said with a little shake of her head. She might have rolled her eyes and muttered "whatever" too, but it was hard to tell since she pivoted on her heel and stalked to his kitchen.

He listened to her rummage around and considered offering his help, but he knew Charlotte well enough to know that she was likely working out some of her frustrations by figuring out the puzzle a new kitchen presented. It was a diversion—discovering where everything was in the new space—and it would take her mind off what had just transpired, and that was a good thing. For both of them.

He was back on his computer when she wandered into the room, carrying something that looked suspiciously like a cocktail in one hand and a cheese sandwich in the other. He glanced at the clock.

"It's three o'clock," he said.

"It's five o'clock somewhere," she said. "Isn't that the motto down here?"

"Maybe if you're vacationing,"

She meandered over to the window in front of him and stood facing out. "Which I was, before this happened."

"It may not be good to mix those with your pain relievers," he pointed out.

She ignored him and took a sip of her drink. Fine, if that's the way she wanted it to be, it wasn't like he didn't have work to do. Work that he promptly went back to. And re-read the same file he'd been reading since she'd left the room.

Annoyed with himself, he opened another file and started to peruse that one. He was barely past the man's name when Charlotte's movement caught his attention. She was swaying slowly from side to side as she gazed out the window. He didn't know if she did so because she heard music in her head or if maybe she was trying to keep her body moving a little bit to ward off stiffness, but the results were distracting. Exceedingly so.

It didn't help that Alexis has provided her with nothing but skirts, summer dresses, and shorts. Charlotte had donned a pair of cut-offs earlier that day, and the sight of her long bare legs had thrown him back into memories that he hadn't been prepared for. Now, dressed in a sundress with slim straps crisscrossing across her back and a hem that landed several inches above her knees, he was mesmerized by the gentle movement of her hips.

An urge to rise and go to her, to put his hands on her waist and dip his lips to that spot where her neck met her shoulder, gripped him fiercely. It wouldn't be welcome, hell, it wouldn't be a good idea for either of them—he no more wanted to revisit their relationship than she did—but he also knew that the chemistry between them was something that had never died. All he'd have to do was dip his lips to her neck and whisper her name, and they'd both be in his bed probably before he got her dress off.

A dress she was wearing because his teammate had had to buy her new clothes because an unknown assailant had stabbed her for unknown reasons. Yeah, that train of thought effectively doused his lust.

He was about to suggest she sit down and rest when she spun and faced him. Her sandwich was nearly gone, but the light pink drink looked barely touched.

"I know Beni said that whatever reason someone had for attacking me is probably something that followed me from DC, but I'm not so sure about that," she said.

"What are you thinking?" He gestured toward a chair as he spoke, but she shook her head and remained standing.

"What I pointed out earlier is true—how much of your life isn't documented in your laptop or phone or some other device? I'd say next to nothing unless you're intentionally trying not to leave a trail. If that were the case, meaning if there was something I was intentionally trying to keep undocumented, I'd know about it and I'd know it would be something you and your team would probably want to know. But seeing as that's not the case, I find it hard to believe that whoever did this to me wouldn't also be concerned about my phone or computer. It just doesn't make sense."

He had to admit, she had a point. The fact that her computer and phone remained in her room was a piece of the puzzle that bothered him.

"Maybe they couldn't get into your room," he said.

She shot him a flat look then took a seat and set her drink on the coffee table. "I had my key with me. He would have had to have known that, otherwise how else would I have gotten back into my room? And you saw those pants; it wouldn't have taken him long to find it. There's only one pocket in the left leg."

Well, damn. Again, she had a point. "So, tell me more." He leaned forward and snagged the drink. "It's five o'clock somewhere." He took a sip then grinned when she glared at him.

"I was completely off the grid when I was out with Simon and Mira. Is it possible that I spoke to someone or saw something during that time that is behind all this?"

He pondered her words as he savored the drink. He wasn't quite sure what she'd added—maybe a little of Alexis's juice, definitely some gin, but he couldn't quite place the other flavor.

"It's possible," he said. "It seems a stretch since it means that whoever went after you must have already been following either the three of you or someone you talked to. But then again, this whole thing seems a little surreal, so you're right, it's worth looking into."

She finished her sandwich and held her hand out for her drink. He passed it over and she took a sip. Leaning back against the overstuffed cushion of the chair, she let the glass dangle between her fingers as she stared off into nothing.

"What are you thinking?" he asked. Charlotte was one of the smartest women he knew—yes, she was a whiz with numbers, and her faculty for understanding the economies of just about every country in the world was astounding. But what most people didn't know was that her ability to read people, cultures, and systems was born from having grown up in—and having survived—one of the most dangerous neighborhoods in New York City. And it wasn't just luck that had kept her alive until the age of thirteen, when she and her best friend, Matty—and their mothers—had been plucked out of that particular hell. No, cunning, intelligence, adaptability, and the ability to read situations had been vital to her survival.

"Do you know where Simon is? I don't think he was supposed to be back on Tildas Island until next week, but maybe he's nearby?" she asked, referring to her friend that she'd been boating with.

He shook his head. "I left that to Beni to look into. I can call her, but what did you have in mind?"

"I meant to give her a list of the places where we stopped while out on the boat, but I didn't get around to it. I think it might be worth talking to Simon—and Mira if she hasn't left yet —to see if, between us, we can come up with something. If he's nearby, maybe we can get him to come into port for a day. And before you say no," she said, raising her voice to talk over the objection hovering on his lips. He snapped his mouth shut; they'd had enough conflict for the day. The least he could do was listen. "I know you're worried about someone recognizing me. You and Beni made it clear enough that you want me to stay dead, which wouldn't work if I were seen out and about. But I can wear a hat, and if you don't have an extra pair of sunglasses, we can pick up a pair. And if I go out like this," she said, gesturing to her dress, "I'll look just like every other tourist on the island. No one will recognize me."

Damian couldn't help it; he let his gaze drift down the expanse of her bare legs that were propped up on the coffee table. Her toenails were painted a gunmetal grey. Charlotte's style tended toward a more classic look, maybe even a little retro, but what Alexis had brought her was a little more on the fun and flirty side.

"Damian."

He raised his gaze to meet hers. She looked a little exasperated with him, but not in the bad way. He grinned, which led to her rolling her eyes and shaking her head at him.

"So what do you think?" she asked.

"I don't like it."

"I didn't think you would, but that doesn't mean it's not a good thing to do," she countered, arching an eyebrow at him. And damn it, she was right. Provided, of course, Simon was on island or nearby.

He snagged his phone from the table and called Beni, who confirmed Simon had docked that morning. He filled her in on Charlotte's theory, and, after a bit of back and forth, Beni came around and agreed that it might not be a bad idea to meet with him. Two heads were often better than one, and together, Charlotte and Simon—and maybe Mira—might come up with something that would give them a clue as to what was going on.

After he hung up, he helped Charlotte to her feet—apparently, sitting down was a lot easier than getting up—and they headed toward his jeep. Snagging a baseball hat hanging by the door on their way to the car, they also let Steve, who'd decided to nap with Charlotte and was still in the house, out.

When they reached his car, Damian helped Charlotte into the passenger seat, taking a moment to admire the slide of the sundress up her thigh. Before his mind started going places it shouldn't, he reached into his glove compartment and pulled out a pair of sunglasses.

"They might be a little big, but they should do," he said, handing them to her.

By the time he rounded the car and climbed behind the wheel, Charlotte had settled in her seat, hat and glasses on. He paused and took her in—he couldn't ever remember seeing her in a ball cap. Distracted by how different she looked, it took him a minute to realize she'd gone a little pale and was taking deep breaths as she stared straight ahead.

Well, fuck him, with their fight and subsequent conversation, he'd almost forgotten that just over twenty-four hours ago, she'd been stabbed.

"Hold on. I'll be right back," he said before jumping out of the car.

Three minutes later, he slid back into his seat and handed her a bottle of ice water and a pain killer. "This could be a tough conversation; you don't need to make it any harder by ignoring your pain," he said.

He couldn't tell what she was thinking, not with the sunglasses hiding her expression, but after a beat, she took both from him and swallowed the pill down.

"Thank you," she said quietly, wrapping her hands around the bottle and cradling it against her chest.

CHAPTER SEVEN

CHARLOTTE KEPT her face turned toward the window as Damian navigated his steep driveway out to a main road. Although calling it a main road was probably a bit of an overkill, but it was paved.

Each pothole and rough surface jarred her body, but she did her best to shut out the pain and focus on something—anything —else. Damian shifted as they climbed a hill and flashes of color peeked out from the heavy green foliage. Ferns crowded the sides of the street, alongside bushes with elephant ear leaves and trees with brilliant orange flowers. Gardening had been a refuge for her and Matty after they'd been moved from the projects to DC by Matty's previously unknown—and very wealthy—grandmother at the age of thirteen. But she didn't recognize any of the plants she saw, not specifically anyway. Several looked related to those in the garden of the DC mansion where she'd resided until she'd turned twenty-two, but she couldn't identify any by their exact name.

She shivered against the blast of cold air from the vents that seemed to kick in suddenly, and Damian reached over and turned the fan down. Of course he did.

"Sorry," he said. "It's a quirk of the car."

She lifted a shoulder in response and kept her attention on the road that seemed to wind continuously uphill until it disappeared from sight. She had a fleeting thought that perhaps, when they reached the top, they'd just tip over the other side. And it startled her how much that thought didn't seem to bother her.

"You okay?" Damian asked.

She nodded. "Just feeling a little, I don't know..." Only she did. Growing up the way she had, shutting her emotions down had been a survival mechanism. Years of therapy and several good friends had helped her realize that. But she'd thought she'd outgrown slipping into that coping strategy and it surprised her that that wasn't, in fact, the case.

She supposed it made sense that if anything were going to trigger her, it would be a violent attack on her body by someone unknown and for reasons unknown. But still, she didn't like that numbing herself emotionally was where her mind had taken her.

Not that she'd say anything to Damian about it. He knew about her life in the projects, knew about the bullets she'd dodged, the friends she'd seen killed and assaulted, the lives wasted. But she'd shared all that with him back when they'd been a couple, back when they shared just about everything. Or she'd thought they had.

"How big is the island?" she asked, not wanting Damian to pick up on her mood.

"It's just under a hundred square miles. A little bigger than St. Croix. Did you get around it at all before yesterday?"

She shook her head. "Simon dropped me at the resort, and I hadn't left until this," she said, gesturing to her side. "Where are we going? Relative to the layout of the island?"

"The marina where Simon docks his boat is on the east end in a little hamlet called Marysville. It's about twenty-five minutes from the airport which is on the south side of the island. Havensted, the main town, is about another twenty-minutes west, past the airport, still on the south side."

"And where is your place?"

"Northside," he said. "Most of the resorts are either on the northwest or south side, but Hemmeleigh, where you were staying and where the summit will happen next year, is the only resort on the north, northeast side. I happened to find a rental basically next door and so it seemed like a good idea to snap it up."

As he spoke, they reached the rise and the car dipped and started its descent. Only they didn't descend far. About a half-mile down, Damian turned and started heading east.

"This is Center Road," he said, navigating the turns like he'd been doing it his whole life. "It, quite literally, runs down the center of the island from east to west. There are lots of roads off of this one, both paved and not, and then a road that more or less runs around the full island closer to the shore."

"Practical," Charlotte said, her gaze touching on a hillside filled with the same orange colored blooms she'd seen leaving Damian's. As they rounded a bend, the ocean came into view, setting off the flaming color and giving them a new vibrancy.

"It does make it relatively easy to navigate the island if you stick to the main roads. But of course, there are lots of side roads and private and semi-private roads that seem to head in one direction, only to end up somewhere completely different. Even in the short time I've lived here, I've realized there are two versions of this island—the one the tourists see and experience and the one the locals live in."

The jeep started climbing again, not quite as big a hill as the first, but certainly not one she'd want to run up, not even before she'd gotten stabbed. "I thought there was a lot of agriculture on the island?" she asked as she took in the peaked and steep hills around her. Dense green foliage covered most, with the occasional colored roof of a house dotting the landscape.

"Westside has all the ag land," Damian said, following a hairpin turn that ended abruptly at a stop sign. Charlotte glanced behind her. She had to give Damian props for driving a manual; the hills could compete with those in San Francisco.

"The eastside is, well, you can see for yourself," he continued as he navigated through the intersection and took another turn that looked as though it would lead them down to the water. "This is the rain forest side of the island. There are some great hikes up into these hills. Unlike many of the other US islands in the region, there's fresh water here, so we have a few rivers and waterfalls and things like that. It's also the much quieter side of the island and has a more bohemian vibe to it than the glitzy Havensted."

They rounded yet another bend, and in an instant, Charlotte felt as if she were somewhere otherworldly. The sharp rise of the mountains gentled and sloped down toward the eastern shore of the island. Small valleys tucked into the hills broke up the continual fall of the landscape, giving it depth and a bit of mystery—who were those people who lived in those little vales?

Beyond the deep green of the island, the Caribbean stretched before them, dotted with islands rising sharply from the sea. There were at least four she could see from their vantage point. With the clear blue skies and the neighboring islands filling her vision as far as the eye could see, she couldn't help but wonder what it must have been like to sail into these waters for the first time—either as one of the native tribes that had inhabited the islands or as one of the European explorers who'd ventured here hundreds of years later. Either way, she felt in her bones that what she saw now, the awe-inspiring beauty, hadn't changed with the passage of time and somehow, if she let it, it would connect her to a past, and maybe even a future, she hadn't ever contemplated.

"My favorite view on the island," Damian said, his voice soft. "It's almost beyond comprehension, isn't it?"

"There's a hike, called the Elskasti trail, that starts about a half-mile from here and goes to the top of that mountain," he said, gesturing to their right. "You can see even more islands from there."

Charlotte has seen plenty of beautiful places during her week on the boat, including several places where she was sure Disney must have filmed scenes from Pirates of the Caribbean because they were impossibly picturesque; but seeing it all from this angle was different—it was like seeing the forest for the trees.

"I hadn't intended to leave the resort once I arrived here," she said. "I figured I'd have my week of fun with Simon and Mira, then a few days of work, then home again. Don't get me wrong, I'm not happy about being stabbed or anything like that, but I have to admit, seeing the island like this is a hell of a silver lining."

Damian chuckled. "Depending on how long you're here and how you're feeling, I'll show you around a little more. The team has been here long enough that we're starting to find our favorite places—our favorite beaches, our favorite hikes, restaurants, that kind of thing."

The idea of spending time exploring the island with Damian held more appeal than it should; so instead of responding, she changed the subject.

"Where is the marina?"

"You can't see it from here, but it's on the other side of that point," he said, pointing to a jut of land than curled back toward the island, creating a protected harbor. She could make out the tops of a few tall masts, but other than that, it was little more than a lush spit of land against the blue ocean.

"Did Beni talk to Simon? I didn't think he was going to be

back for another week or so. I was surprised to hear he was on island," she said.

"No, she didn't talk to him. They tracked his boat to the marina a little earlier this afternoon."

Damian's voice held a hint of strain she hadn't heard since they'd first gotten into the car, and the potential meaning of it hit her hard. "Do you think something might be wrong?" If someone had gone after her for something that had come up while she and Simon and Mira had been together, could they be targets too?

Damian didn't answer right away. "I don't think so. Beni may not have gone to talk to Simon, but she does have eyes on the boat. If something were wrong, she would know about it."

"But you *are* worried," she pressed.

He inclined his head. "Simon and Mira were with you the whole week. If all this has to do with something you learned during that time, we'd be crazy—and negligent—not to consider their safety as well."

Not what she wanted to hear. She would have much rather Damian tell her she was worried about nothing or that he wasn't worried at all. But then again, Damian wasn't one to cage the truth—he might not have always told her things, but when he had, it had always been the unvarnished truth. It was one of the reasons he'd been able to earn her trust three years ago when they'd first started dating.

They rode the rest of the way in silence. First winding down the hill, then turning right on what must be the ring road because it followed the shoreline, before finally turning left and heading out toward the marina.

The parking lot was mostly empty, and Damian pulled into a spot close to what looked like a clubhouse—or maybe a bar for the boaters. She'd just released her seatbelt when Damian opened her door and held out a hand. She eyed it for a moment, but knew, despite not really wanting to touch him, she'd be cutting off her nose to spite her face if she declined his help.

Taking a deep breath of the heavy, salty air, she placed her hand in his, shifted her legs out the door and slid to her feet. He stayed where he was, holding onto her, until the worst of the pain passed.

After a couple of breaths, she eased her grip on his hand and he let her go, taking a step back.

"You sure you're okay?" he asked.

She nodded, not at all sure she *was* okay, but trusting that neither Beni nor Damian would have let her leave the house if her injuries had been life-threatening. The pain was intense—like nothing she'd ever experienced before—but she could deal with it.

Damian eyed her but then took another step back. She started toward the main gate to the dock as Damian locked the car before joining her.

"I think I may need to call him. I'm not sure there's anyone to buzz us in," she said, stopping at the locked gate.

"Do you actually know his number?" Damian asked, handing her his phone. She could hear the humor in his voice. After all, how many people remembered people's phone numbers anymore with everything programmed into some device or another?

"It's a number, of course I remember it," she said with a half-grin as she took his phone. Economics wasn't *all* about numbers, but numbers were definitely her thing.

Simon was surprised to hear from her, but less than five minutes later, she and Damian were boarding his boat.

"Everything okay, Simon? I thought you weren't going to be on island until next week?" she asked as she settled on one of the seats at the back of the boat. Yes, she knew it had a name, but "front" and "back" just seemed easier. "Where's Mira?"

"Change of plans," Simon said, popping the top on a beer as

he spoke. He'd offered one to both her and Damian, but they'd declined. "She had a work thing come up, and I dropped her on St. Thomas day before yesterday so she could fly home. I was going to continue on, but then I had a problem with my pump, so came back to get it fixed before I head out again. I'd ask how your meetings are going, but since you're sitting here with your ex-partner who is also an FBI agent, I think something must have happened?"

"I was stabbed," Charlotte said, figuring it was easier to rip the Band-Aid off. She gave a brief version of the story—not that it was that long of one to begin with—and by the end, Simon had dropped into a seat and his beer dangled between his fingers as he gaped at her.

"So you think someone we spoke to or something we saw while out on the boat might have been the reason you were *attacked*?" The question was half inquiry and half statement.

Charlotte nodded. Simon's gaze flitted to Damian, looking for confirmation.

Damian gave a small nod. "It's possible. At this point, we don't know, and so Charlotte thought it might be worth meeting up with you to see if two minds are better than one."

Simon rose then disappeared into the galley. He returned a minute later with a notebook that looked a little worse for wear. "I keep pretty detailed logs of where I go in the boat. I had a fuel gauge break on me once and ended up somewhere between Virgin Gorda and Anegada with no fuel."

He set the book down on the table and as he flipped to a page, Charlotte scooted closer. Finding what he was looking for, he turned it so they could both read.

"We should start here," Simon said, pointing to an entry. "This is the marina I docked at close to the airport the day you arrived. We left there at three-fifteen and headed over to Peter Island."

"We had dinner there, but I don't recall talking to anyone

other than the waitstaff," Charlotte said. Simon nodded, and they continued through the entries from the few days that followed. Damian remained silent, but she could hear him writing things down as she and Simon spoke.

They'd just reached day three of the trip when Simon's phone rang. He excused himself into the galley to take the call, and Charlotte turned to Damian.

"I guess it was wishful thinking that I might have an 'aha' moment and suddenly, everything would make sense?" She gave him a wry smile, and the expression in his eyes softened as he met her gaze.

"Everything is worth trying at this point," he said. "And we still have four days of the trip left to—"

His voice cut off when Simon returned. The phone hung from between his fingers and he braced his other hand on the doorway.

"Simon," Charlotte said, rising quickly to go to his side. A shard of pain pierced her side, but she ignored it. "What's happened?"

Simon's face had lost its color and his head moved in a continual, subtle back and forth, as if in denial over something.

"Simon?" Charlotte said, reaching out and touching his arm. She cast a glance at Damian, who was standing now as well.

Finally, Simon's gaze came around to hers. It was filled with so much confusion and fear and pain, that Charlotte's heart leaped into her throat.

"That was the DC Police. It's Mira," Simon said, his voice a scratchy whisper. "She's been in a hit and run accident, and they don't know if she's going to make it."

CHAPTER EIGHT

DAMIAN ALREADY HAD his phone in hand when Charlotte turned toward him, her eyes appearing even darker against her pale face. Her mind was a beautiful thing, and she did not disappoint. He could see from the panic in her expression that she grasped the full implication of Simon's statement.

"I need…I need to get on a plane. I need to get to DC," Simon muttered, spinning to head back into the galley.

"Damian?" she said.

"The team has access to a jet; I'll make arrangements. You go take care of your friend," he said.

She blinked back tears, then nodded and disappeared into the galley while he called Alexis.

"Rodriguez," she answered. "Everything okay?"

"No, it's not." He filled her in on Charlotte's theory that maybe she'd seen or heard something while in the Caribbean and explained they were currently sitting on Simon O'Conner's boat.

"I know Charlotte doesn't think the work she does could draw the wrong attention, but I *know* otherwise," he said. "I know her clearance levels and I know some of the projects she's worked. So while I was happy to take a road trip to meet with Simon and test her theory, I didn't really think it would come to anything."

"But it did?"

"How do you and Jake feel about flying up to DC? Simon's daughter got called back a few days early, and he just got a call that she was in a hit and run. It may be a coincidence, but I'm not willing to take that chance," he said.

"And if they went after Simon's daughter, he could be a target too," Alexis added.

"That's my thinking."

"Hhmm, yes, I think I agree," Alexis said, distractedly.

"Lex?"

"I'm just texting Jake to meet me at the airport. I'll pilot and he can act Simon's bodyguard. I'm on board with this, Rodriguez, mostly because Steve seems to like Charlotte, and I know you do too, but you should be prepared to convince Director Shah that we aren't spending a shit ton of resources on this just because you have a crush."

He bit back a "fuck off" that hovered on his tongue, mostly because Alexis was right. All they really had was a non-fatal stab wound and a hit and run—yes, the women were connected through friendship, but with the events occurring in two different locations, there was little more than his gut telling him the attacks were tied together. But even if they were tied together, there was still no reason to make this an FBI case and certainly no reason to bring it into the purview of their special task force.

"Fuck," he muttered.

"She'll be in meetings all day today in Atlanta. She won't be back on island until tomorrow afternoon. You have twenty-four hours to find a reason to make this our case," Alexis said.

"I shouldn't ask you and Jake to fly or travel with Mr. O'Conner," Damian admitted.

"We can get around that," Alexis said. Through the phone, he heard her close a car door, likely on her way to the airport already. "Professor O'Conner is Ambassador O'Conner, former ambassador to the UN. We're extending a courtesy to a diplomat."

It was a stretch, but it would work.

"Thanks, Lex," he said. "I appreciate it."

"Stop calling me 'Lex,' and Jake and I will be ready when you get to the airport." She disconnected the call just as Charlotte and Simon stepped back out onto the deck. She shot him a questioning look, and he nodded.

"Ambassador O'Conner, my colleague, Alexis Wright, will fly you up to DC, and Agent Jake McMullen will accompany you," he said.

Simon drew up short, his key still in the galley door. He eyed Charlotte then fixed his attention on Damian.

"You think this might be related to what happened to Charlotte, don't you?"

Damian thought about couching his response, but two things stopped him. First, this man had been an ambassador, and he'd spot bullshit a mile away. Second, his daughter might be dead by the time he reached her bedside, and he deserved the truth.

"We think there's a strong possibility of that," Damian said.

"Who's we?" Simon asked.

"I'm part of a five-person special task force stationed on the island until the summit next year. My team knows what happened to Charlotte yesterday, and I just told them about Mira." At the sound of his daughter's name, Simon flinched, then quickly finished locking up.

"Take the log, Charlotte," Simon said, pointing to the book that still sat on the table. "Comb through it and see if you can find something. Anything. It won't help Mira now, but if we can find the reason, then maybe we can stop whoever is behind this from hurting anyone else."

Charlotte scooped up the book as they exited the boat. Damian was conscious of her struggling to keep up with Simon's long strides as they made their way back to his jeep. Thankfully, Simon tossed his bag over the front seat and climbed into the back alongside it. Charlotte had a hard enough time getting into the passenger seat that Damian wasn't sure what she would have done if Simon had taken it. Scratch that, he knew she would have gritted her teeth and climbed into the back of his two-door, but he was grateful she didn't have to.

There were no multi-lane highways on Tildas Island and so he drove as fast as the roads and the traffic let him. No one spoke in the twenty minutes that they curved around the south side of the island toward the airport. He glanced to his right a few times to see Charlotte, her face grim, staring out the window. He wanted to take her hand in his and assure her that he and the team would figure this out, but he'd lost that right over a year ago.

Entering the tarmac through the private gate, the guard checked his ID then waved them on. He pulled directly into one of the five hangers that dotted the tarmac—Tildas Island was a playground for the rich and had enough private planes to fill the buildings and then some. He didn't know how Director Shah had managed to commandeer one for the duration of their stay on the island, or how she'd finagled a private jet for that matter, but he was grateful for it.

"Will you stay here?" he asked Charlotte as he climbed from his seat to let Simon out.

She hesitated, then nodded.

The sense of relief that he felt at her acquiescence was out of proportion to the request. "Thank you," he said, then he shut the door, leaving her safely inside, and led Simon over to meet Jake, who was jogging down the stairs of the jet.

"Ambassador O'Conner," Jake said, shaking the man's hand. "Why don't you go get settled inside. Agent Alexis Wright is our pilot today. She's just doing a final instrument check, and we're cleared to be wheels up in about fifteen minutes."

Simon gave a sharp nod and made his way toward the plane. Pausing at the bottom of the stairs, he turned. "Damian?"

"Sir?" he said.

"Find out what this is all about," Simon said.

"I plan to, Sir."

"And take care of Charlotte, will you?" he asked. "I'm not going to say you broke her heart, but something inside her changed when you two ended things. She needs physical protection now, but please guard her heart too. It's bigger than any of us give her credit for."

Damian glanced at Jake, who was watching him with unabashed interest. He shot a quick glare at his teammate before responding. "I'll protect her with my life, Sir. There's never been any question about that."

Simon held his gaze for a moment, then abruptly continued up the steps and disappeared into the galley of the plane.

"You'd die for her, but would you kill for her?" Jake asked, grinning at Damian's cliché response.

"Fuck off, McMullen."

Jake snickered in response. In the dossiers Director Shah had provided each of them about the other members of the team, she'd noted that Jake might very well have a death wish. She hadn't been exaggerating.

"If you wouldn't mind returning to the task at hand," Damian said. To Jake's credit, he instantly sobered.

"I'll stay with Ambassador O'Conner the entire time," he said. "Once Alexis gets the plane all tucked in for the night, she'll join me and we'll trade off duties. We have Mira O'Conner's address and will confirm her father plans to stay there when not at the hospital—"

"Assuming Mira lives," Damian interjected.

"She'll live," Jake insisted. "We're in touch with the hospital already, and she's in surgery now. We don't have any indication that she's succumbed to her injuries yet, so until we're told otherwise, I'm going to assume she's going to live."

Most people would assume the worst and prepare themselves for that eventuality. And then if they were wrong, they could be happy about being wrong. But that wasn't how Jake McMullen rolled. In the short time Damian had known him, Jake's approach to life mirrored what he'd just set out as his approach to Mira O'Conner's situation—always plan for the best and if the best doesn't happen then, and only then, do you deal with the alternative. More than once, Damian recognized the strength of character it took to live that way—to always look on the bright side and to know you have the fortitude to survive anything and everything else.

"I'm sure the ambassador will appreciate that. While you and Alexis are in DC, I'll work with the others to see if we can figure out what's going on. If you learn anything while you're stateside, call Beni, she'll be coordinating."

"You aren't taking the lead on this?" Jake asked, not bothering to hide his surprise.

Damian shook his head. "You heard me. My priority is Charlotte. Say what you want about how pathetic it is to feel so protective of someone who more or less kicked me out of her life. But I can't change how I feel and I don't have the inclination to anyway. If nothing else, if she walks away again when all this is over, at least she'll be *walking* and not being taken away in a coffin, which isn't something I could live with."

Jake studied him for a moment, then clapped his hand on Damian's shoulder. "You're a helluva man, Agent Rodriguez, and for what it's worth, I think Charlotte knows it too."

Damian wasn't so sure about that, but at the end of the day, it didn't matter—all that mattered was keeping Charlotte safe.

Alexis popped her head out of the door, saving him from having to say any more. "Time for taxi, McMullen," she said. "Twenty-four hours until Director Shah is on island, Rodriguez. I think you better hop to." She accompanied her suggestion with a sympathetic smile. "Let us know if there's anything we can do from DC," she added.

When Director Shah had approached him about joining the special task force, he'd been contemplating leaving the FBI. But watching his two new-ish teammates jump into action, and knowing that Beni and Dominic would be on their way to his house as soon as he asked, he knew he'd made the right decision to give the Bureau at least another eighteen months of his time. It might be an unconventional team, but his teammates were all damn fine people.

He lifted a hand in a goodbye gesture, and she gave him a mock salute before shutting the door. Fifteen seconds later, the hangar doors slid open, and the plane's engines came to life. He moved to stand in front of his car as Alexis taxied the plane out on to the tarmac. They were making their way to the end of the runway when the automatic doors closed again, leaving him in a sudden and deafening silence.

For two beats, he just stood, preparing for what was to come. Then, taking a deep breath, he pulled out his phone and made a call.

Less than four minutes later, he and Charlotte drove past the security and turned toward home. It wasn't far to his house, less than eight miles as the crow flies, but close to twenty-five minutes on the windy Tildas Island roads. And as each minute ticked by, Damian grew more and more worried about his passenger. Since rejoining her in the jeep, Charlotte had said nothing other than a comment about being surprised Alexis was a licensed pilot.

He chanced a glance at her only to see her huddled close to the door, staring out the window.

"Talk to me, Charlotte," he said, knowing there was a 50/50 chance she actually would.

He'd almost given up the ghost when she started speaking. "I can't for the life of me figure out why this is happening," she said, her voice barely audible over the sound of the jeep. "Aside from worrying about Mira and Simon, there's a sense of...I can't really explain it, other than to say that it's reminding me a little too much of the years Matty and I spent growing up in the projects."

There were a lot of reasons for Charlotte to feel pensive and concerned, but the reason she'd given him wasn't one he'd contemplated, much less thought she'd share.

"Our moms did what they could to create some stability for us," she continued. "But ultimately, we lived in a community where violence was as commonplace as breathing. And as a child, it felt so chaotic. With a few exceptions, we never knew when the violence would occur or why or who would be the target. And the helplessness that comes with living like that is something I'll never forget. Always on edge, always just a little bit afraid, and always just a little bit angry that we had to live that way." She paused, and despite their history, or maybe because of it, he reached across the console and took her hand. It was cold in his—and delicate—but she didn't pull away.

"It felt like everyone had abandoned us, and we'd been left to kill or be killed. As if we didn't matter," she said. "I know this is different. I know I'm not that child anymore, and regardless of our history, Damian, I know you won't abandon me. And because you won't, your team probably won't either. But it's still hard to beat back those demons that seem to want to come to life and pull me back down into the same despair that I felt as a child. And it's especially hard to focus on what it is I *can* do when I have no idea what that is."

He wanted to have an answer for her; he wanted to assure her that everything would be fine. But the thing about Charlotte was that she'd seen more of life than most people, especially as a child, and she well knew that even despite doing everything right, sometimes things *didn't* turn out fine.

And so he said the only thing he could say with absolute honesty. "When we get back, we'll start going through Simon's notebook to see if that triggers anything for you, and even if it doesn't, we still have avenues open to us to explore. We have CCTV of the resort, Dominic's search for likely suspects in the airline and cruise lists. And trust me when I say that Beni probably has a good dozen other ideas. I don't know which, if any, will pan out or lead to something, but chances are at least one will, and if nothing else, at least we *will* have things to do."

For the first time since they'd left the airport, she looked at him. A small, fleeting smile flashed across her lips, and to his surprise, she squeezed his hand. "Despite our past and everything we said—and didn't say—to each other, you're a good man, Damian Rodriguez. I know you know that, but I don't know that I ever said it, and for that, I'm sorry."

Her words affected him in a way they shouldn't have if he had any intention of protecting his heart from the hell it went through when she'd pushed him out of her life. He didn't fool himself into thinking that they might go back to what they were, but the question of whether or not they might find something new hovered in his mind as they made their way to the north side of the island.

By the time they turned onto his driveway, the energy between them had shifted. Neither of them mentioned it, but he knew Charlotte felt the same—her demons weren't banished, and they still had their past to deal with, but something had changed.

"Who's here?" she asked as they pulled up next to a car parked beside his house.

"You were right about my team not abandoning you. Jake and Alexis will protect Simon and Mira and Beni and Dominic are here because I asked them to come so we can formulate a battle plan, for lack of a better term."

Charlotte stared at the car for a moment, then turned and grinned at him. "I don't know, I kind of like the idea of having a battle plan."

CHAPTER NINE

DAMIAN HELPED her out of the car then, with a hand on her back, ushered her toward his front door. Something had changed between them in the short car ride from the airport to the house. What that meant she didn't know, and she didn't want to look at it too closely, but she felt it just the same.

"You doing okay?" he asked quietly from behind her.

On autopilot, she nodded. She hadn't been in a hit and run and she wasn't fighting for her life. In relative terms, she was doing just fine. In reality though, every step she took jarred her body and pain lanced through her side. And if she were being honest with herself, which she had no intention of doing, she was exhausted. The outing of less than two hours had wiped out any reserve energy her body might have had.

She was saved from saying any more by the presence of Dominic on Damian's porch.

"You look like a gorgeous kind of hell," he said with a mischievous grin.

She couldn't help but smile. "Thanks?"

"Meant as a compliment. Not many people would look as good as you a day after being left for dead."

"Yet another thing to add to my resume," she said as she climbed the steps and passed him on the way to the door. Damian muttered something to his colleague that she couldn't hear, but whatever it was, Dominic's rich laugh followed her inside.

As Charlotte walked in, Beni looked up from where she'd been studying something on the table and it didn't take a genius to figure out that Beni Was. Not. Happy.

"What?" Charlotte said.

"You look like hell. Go take a nap," the agent said. Charlotte opened her mouth to protest, but Beni cut her off. "There are pain killers beside the bed. I even left you a glass of water and a glass of Alexis's magic juice. You were supposed to die yesterday, Charlotte. Go be grateful that the sleep you get to have today is a choice. When you wake up, Damian, Dominic, and I will update you on anything we discover. Then we can talk about what we might want to do next."

Charlotte gaped at the woman, even as she felt Damian come up behind her. Very rarely, if ever, did anyone other than her mom tell her what to do. But as Beni's brusque words sunk in, Charlotte had to admit, they held some truth—okay, a lot of truth. She was exhausted, and while she knew she could power through, she couldn't power through forever. If she napped now —took care of her body and let it heal—then she'd be better able to contribute when the team had real leads to follow.

"Fine," she said, turning on her heel toward the bedroom. She didn't miss Damian's quiet exhale of relief. Without her around, he and his team would be able to do their thing, whatever that might be.

"You need anything from the room before I go lie down?" she asked him. He shook his head.

"You going to be okay?" he asked.

She nodded. "I hate to admit it, but Beni is right. A little nap might do me some good. I don't know if this will help, but I think you should take it," she said as she handed him the spiral notebook she and Simon had been going through when he'd gotten The Call. The same notebook that she'd kept a death grip on since Simon had handed it to her on the boat.

Damian took it from her. A look she couldn't discern flashed in his eyes, but it was gone as quickly as it had appeared. "Holler if you need anything," he said.

Not knowing what else to do, she nodded and made her way to the room, but she paused at the door. "May I borrow your phone? I'd like to call Matty," she said.

This time she recognized the look he gave her. She'd just spoken to Matty yesterday, but for good or for bad, they were each other's safety blankets when things got hard or scary or confusing. Damian knew this, and because she'd had to ask for his phone to make the call, he now had a pretty good idea of just how shaken up she was.

He walked toward her holding out his phone. "Of course," he said. "The code is 1015."

Her gaze jumped from the phone to his. "1015?" she repeated, taking the device from him.

For a moment, his attention skittered away from her, but on a breath, he raised his eyes back to her and nodded. "You remember?"

She didn't have any words, but she nodded. She supposed that the date of their first date was just an easy code for him to remember, but she didn't think that's why he'd chosen it. Damian also wasn't a masochist; he wouldn't have chosen those numbers as a way to punish himself with something he didn't want to remember.

"Go call Matty," he said. "Just set the phone on the bedside table when you're done, and if I need it, I'll come in and grab it. I'll try not to wake you."

Still reeling from the knowledge that even after a year, even after their break-up when they'd each said things she preferred not to remember, he still held onto that date—it still had meaning to him—she managed to nod again before walking into the room and shutting the door quietly behind her. She stood in the cool dimness for a moment, letting her thoughts filter and fall into place. She'd had a lot of doubts in the year since they'd ended things but had always reasoned that they'd done the right thing because he'd never reached out to her since she'd walked out of his apartment that night. Yes, she could have reached out to him, but that was the crux of the matter—she'd trusted him with *everything*, and he hadn't returned the sentiment.

There was never any doubt that Damian was loyal to her or loved her in his way, and it wasn't that kind of trust he failed to show her. No, despite what he showed the world, Damian had demons. But unlike her, he refused to share them. And with her past, the fact that he hadn't trusted her when she'd exposed all of her own, had been like a punch in the gut. Or more precisely, he'd broken her heart. He hadn't understood why it bothered her so much and she hadn't understood how someone who could love her the way he had—who she had loved like no other —didn't see the chasm his holding back from her caused. Perhaps if she hadn't grown up in the environment she had, it would have been different and she would have been able to let it go, but as it was Damian had *been* to her therapist with her, he'd *known* everything about her triggers, her insecurities, her trauma, and yet, he'd still chosen to protect himself rather than share with her.

That was what had hurt the most. He'd chosen himself over their relationship.

With a sigh, she tossed the phone on the bed, grabbed one of Damian's white t-shirts from his closet, and made her way into the bathroom. After using the facilities, she washed her hands and face and slipped out of her sundress, which thankfully slid off her shoulders and down her hips.

Gingerly pulling on the t-shirt, she walked back to the bed, picked up the phone, then hesitated. If she called Matty now, Matty would know something was up—something more than just what had happened with Simon and Mira. She was staring at the screen, debating whether to call, when it lit up with Matty's name.

Charlotte frowned and hit the answer button as she climbed into bed. "Why are you calling Damian's phone?" she said when the call connected.

A beat passed. "You said yours was left in your room at the resort, and so I was calling to check in on you," Matty said. "Why are you *answering* his phone?"

Charlotte pulled the lightweight blanket over her legs. "Just a second," she said, then set the phone down and reached for the pill Beni had left her. After swallowing it, she picked the phone up again.

"I was just getting ready to call you," Charlotte answered then proceeded to tell her about Mira and Simon. When she finished, Matty was uncharacteristically quiet. For all of five seconds.

"What the hell is going on? Did you meet anyone on your trip that maybe you shouldn't have?" she asked.

Charlotte snuggled down against the pillows. "I've been wracking my brain on just that question, but I really can't think of anyone."

"Is it work related? I know sometimes Mira uses you as a sounding board for the work she does at the World Bank."

Charlotte thought about this for a moment. Much as Simon had been *her* mentor, she'd mentored Mira here and there as the young woman grew her career at the Bank. Because Charlotte herself often did consulting work for them, Mira felt comfortable sharing the projects she was working on and tapping her for advice. But they hadn't talked about work during the trip. Or had they?

"Nothing comes to mind, but we were together for seven

days, we *must* have talked work at some point. I'll have to think about that a little more."

"There's not much I can do from up here in New York, but if there is, you'll let me know?"

"Of course," Charlotte said immediately.

"Now, how are things going with Damian?" Matty asked. If Charlotte hadn't been so sleepy, she would have smiled at Matty finally getting to the real reason she called. To be fair, Matty's priority probably *was* to check in on her, but this was a close second.

"Fine, he's doing his FBI-thing. His team seems great. Actually, he seems great. Aside from having me suddenly drop in on his life, I think he likes it here."

"That's not what I was asking," Matty said.

"Matty, it's water under the bridge, you know that," she responded.

"It's not, and *you* know that. Have you talked about anything?"

"Yes, a lot of things."

Matty sighed. "Stop being difficult and obtuse. You know I will wear you down anyway, and you'll spill it all, so could we skip the formalities and get to the important stuff?"

Charlotte debated hanging up on Matty, but she knew two things: first, Matty was right, and second, if she did hang up, Matty would keep calling back.

"His phone code is the date of our first date," Charlotte said.

"Is it a new phone or an old one?"

At that, Charlotte chuckled. "Are you asking whether he was just too lazy to change it?"

"It occurred to me."

"It's new. It's the same model as mine. So yes, I know what that means. It means he's chosen to be reminded of that date."

"And how do you feel about that?"

Charlotte rolled onto her good side. "You sound like you've been hanging out with a psychologist," she grumped.

"I have, both as a friend and my own therapist. Answer the question," she said.

Now it was Charlotte's turn to sigh. "I don't know, Matty. I honestly don't know. I miss him. God, I miss him. But after the things we said, the year that's passed, I don't think we can ever go back, and I'm not sure I want to."

"It's not about going back, Char," Matty said. "You've both had time to think and reflect on what happened. Maybe things would be different moving *forward*."

"I asked him again," Charlotte said. "About those dates." Those two dates that were a mystery to her. The only thing she knew about them was that in her two years of dating Damian, on each of those days, he had turned into someone she didn't know. Never one to drink heavily, he'd gone far beyond a buzz on those days. But even more perplexing was how combative he'd gotten. He'd picked fights, slammed doors, and, eventually, walked out. Each time, he'd returned the next day—from god knew where—apologized, then went on with life as if nothing had happened. She'd asked him about it then—of course she had —but each time he'd just shaken his head and changed the subject.

"And?" Matty asked.

Pain twisted in Charlotte's chest. "He shut me down. Again."

Matty paused before speaking again. "Listen, Charlotte, you know I support you, and you know I think Damian should have come clean either by talking to you or by telling you why it's something he didn't feel comfortable sharing. But have you also considered that maybe you were looking for a way out because it wasn't *him* you didn't trust, but yourself?"

Matty's words took Charlotte by surprise, so much so that she had to take a minute to let them sink in. As if sensing her need for time, Matty continued.

"There was a time when I first met Dash that I tried to push him away. I gave him all sorts of reasons—I didn't trust him, I was only visiting the area, I wasn't planning to stay. You name it, I threw it at him. And Dash being Dash just called bullshit on the whole thing. He was right; it was *me* I didn't trust, not him. My situation was a little different than yours, but what I realized, with time, was that I didn't trust that I could truly love someone the way I knew he deserved to be loved. Our moms did their best and created an oasis for us, but they couldn't protect us from everything, and we grew up believing things like love and true friendship were dangerous because people would use them against you. And so, outside of the four of us, we never really learned how to feel those things, let alone how to navigate them in a relationship with people who didn't, or couldn't, understand where we came from.

"You know I have your back, Charlotte. Always. But that's also why I'm telling you this now. Maybe Damian isn't the love of your life. But maybe he is, and maybe that scares you in ways you haven't let yourself explore because it's easier to pin the destruction of your relationship on one specific thing. One specific thing that doesn't happen to be your fault or isn't something you have to own."

There was so much in Matty's words that Charlotte wanted to reject, but one of the things she'd learned about herself was that when she felt a strong denial rise so swiftly, that that was exactly the time when she needed to take a step back and think about her reaction.

"I like how you lay this on me the day after I get stabbed," she grumbled.

Matty laughed. "Nothing like a best friend—"

"To ruin your day," Charlotte finished, smiling at the saying they'd learned from Matty's grandmother more than twenty years ago.

"Just think about it, Charlotte," Matty said. Unnecessarily, Charlotte thought—they were hardly words she could ignore.

"And get some sleep," Matty added.

At the suggestion, Charlotte yawned. The day had definitely taken its toll on her.

"Aye, aye, captain," she said. "Love you, and I'll call you later."

"Love you, too, and you better."

Charlotte ended the call then rolled over to set the phone down on the bedside table. She paused before rolling back to her side, and her gaze drifted to Damian's closet. It was a little thing to have this view of his intimate space, but her eyes lingered there. She took in his shirts and pants hanging neatly in rows and wondered what they looked like on him. Good, no doubt. Damian was an attractive man who kept himself fit, both for the job and because it was his nature. She bet he looked damn good in bathing trunks.

She groaned at her pining thoughts and rolled over. She would *not* think about Damian in a bathing suit.

Really, she wouldn't.

CHAPTER TEN

"What did you give her?" Damian asked Beni. The sun had set an hour ago, and Charlotte still slept.

Beni didn't bother looking up from where she was reviewing CCTV footage of one of the bars Charlotte, Simon, and Mira had visited. "She needed to rest and didn't look like she'd do it without a little help. I changed her pain killer to one that would have the same impact on the pain but would make her a little sleepy as well."

"Is that even close to ethical?" Dominic asked from where he sat on the couch, going through his own footage. While some of the locations had requested warrants, several had been happy to let the FBI view their video. Unfortunately, there were a few in the British Virgin Islands that would require cooperation from their British counterparts, but as they didn't yet have grounds for even making the case a federal one, the request for assistance would have to wait.

"Probably not," Beni answered. "But it was still the right thing to do. So what are you going to do about her, Rodriguez?" she asked.

The abrupt question caught Damian off guard and he accidentally started fast-forwarding his video. Scrambling to stop the feed, he ignored her until he was back where he needed to be, watching Simon, Mira, and Charlotte have dinner at a table for three. So far, no one other than the waitstaff had spoken to them, but he kept his eyes trained on the rest of the customers, looking for anyone who might be paying a little too much attention to the threesome.

"Well?" Beni asked.

"Leave the man alone, Ricci," Dominic said. Silently, Damian thanked the man. "Love is a complicated thing for a man like Rodriguez. You know, being all likable and all, it's probably really confusing for him why she's not falling at his feet."

Not so silently, Damian cursed the man, making Beni chuckle.

"How close are Alexis and Jake to touchdown?" Damian asked.

"I would have expected better avoidance techniques from you, Rodriguez," Dominic said. "But I guess, being a Ranger and all, subtlety isn't in your nature."

Damian gave Dominic—a former pararescuer—the finger and turned to look at Beni.

"It's a four-and-a-half-hour flight time. They'll be landing in about an hour," she answered.

"I wish we had more to give them. If whoever went after Charlotte is the same person who went after Mira, he's probably still in DC knowing Simon will show up," Damian said.

"And I'm not getting shit off these videos," Dominic said. "I haven't seen them have more than a fleeting conversation with anyone, and no one in the background is making the hairs on my neck stand up."

"You and me both," Beni said.

"That makes three of us. We need to find another lead. I don't think we should give up on this altogether, but we need something else," Damian said, setting his computer to the side and rising from his seat. He stalked over to one of the big picture windows that looked out onto the ocean. The view during the day never failed to inspire him, but at night, especially when the moon was bright, it brought on a different kind of awe. Like Charlotte had mentioned that morning on the way to the marina, there was something about the islands that made it easy to forget that time was linear. Maybe it was because, for the most part, the islands weren't very developed. But especially on nights like this, with the moon hanging over the horizon, it was easy to slip into the distant past and *know* that what he was seeing, and what the view made him feel, was something shared over centuries with all the others who had ventured to this place.

He shoved his hands into his pockets and, bringing himself back to the here and now, he mentally went through everything they knew, which, admittedly, wasn't very much.

"Dominic," he said, turning to face his colleague. "I know you were looking for passengers who landed on the island in the week Charlotte was here. Have you cross-referenced that against passengers who left the island yesterday or early today?"

Dominic shook his head. "I stopped the program when we left the office this afternoon, but I'll start it up again," he said, typing the commands into his laptop as he spoke. "When I left, there were forty-seven men who fit the criteria of traveling alone, not islanders or family of islanders, and who arrived by plane within the week Charlotte was here. I'll add departure date to the filter and see if we can narrow the list even more."

"There's still the possibility that he arrived on the island by boat, but if he showed up in DC the day after Charlotte's attack, I'm betting he flew here," Beni said.

Damian nodded. "Let's get that list finalized and then see if Charlotte recognizes any of the faces."

"What faces?" Charlotte said as she stepped out of his bedroom, wiping sleep from her eyes. Her hair had come loose from its braid and she wore the cut-offs she'd had on earlier and one of his white t-shirts. The fierce need that erupted in his system—need and hunger that he could do nothing about—froze the breath in his lungs and made him want to growl, or howl, in frustration. Instead, he did the only thing he could to salvage his emotions. He left.

"I'll go pick up some dinner," he said. "Beni, Dominic, you can walk Charlotte through what we've been doing." He didn't wait for a response before walking out the front door.

CHARLOTTE CAST a wry look at Beni and Dominic. "Was it something I said?"

"Nah," Dominic responded. "You just walked out of his bedroom looking all—"

"Do *not* finish that sentence, Burel," Beni said, cutting her colleague off. The two shared a look, and for a moment, Charlotte thought Dominic might not heed his teammate's warning —not that he needed to finish what he'd been about to say because Charlotte had a pretty good idea of what was about to come out his mouth—but after a beat, he grinned and gestured her to a seat at the table.

"Can I offer her a drink, Ricci, or would you advise against it with that pill you gave her? She drugged you by the way," he added, flashing a got-you grin at Beni.

"You are such an asshole, Burel," she muttered. "I didn't drug you," Beni said to her. "I just gave you a slightly different pain killer that also contained a muscle relaxant. It wouldn't have made you sleep if you hadn't already been exhausted."

Charlotte frowned at the agent. "So you *did* drug me?"

Dominic snickered, and Beni glared at him. "Go grab some beers out of the fridge. The pill was short-lasting; she can drink if she wants to."

Dominic rose from his seat and arched an eyebrow in question at her. Charlotte nodded, a beer might be good. It would be even better if she could drink it while kicking back on Damian's porch. But alas, that was not in her future. Well, as Matty's words whispered in her mind, she allowed herself a correction —it was not in her *near* future.

"If Damian has any more of that juice, will you bring me some of that, too?" she asked.

"On it," Dominic called back from the kitchen.

"So, what faces were you talking about when I came in?" Charlotte said, directing her question to Beni.

While Beni updated her, Dominic returned from the kitchen carrying three bottles of beer and a glass of juice. When he was seated at the table, he typed a few things into his laptop and waited for Beni to wrap up her update.

When she finished, he spoke. "It looks like there are thirty-eight men who fit the criteria. I'll pull pictures of each, but while I do that, you should have a look at this," he said, gesturing to what appeared to be a map of the area and all the islands in it. Crisscrossed with lines and locations noted with numbers, it took her a moment to realize that the team had mapped out the journey she, Simon, and Mira had taken.

She stood to get a better look, her eyes tracing her seven days at sea laid out on sheet of paper. As she traveled from the first location to the next and so forth, memories of the places sifted through her mind. Unfortunately, while they were good memories—memories she'd cherish—none of them struck her as being particularly helpful to the situation.

But then her eyes caught on their eleventh stop, an independent island nation to the east and south of the British Virgin Islands. Without thought, her finger traced the path from Virgin Gorda to the location and hovered there.

"We wondered about that stop," Beni said. "It's a little different than your others."

It was. The island was stunningly beautiful and achingly poor. The World Bank had funded an infrastructure project based on the premise that with an improved infrastructure—roads, utilities, sewers, and water—the island could start to take advantage of the tourist trade. And they hadn't been wrong. After ten years, the project had just recently been completed and the tourism numbers were already creeping up—slowly, but increasing nonetheless.

Mira had been the Bank liaison for the last few years of the project. And having spent a significant amount of time with it in her portfolio, she'd wanted to stop by and see it for herself.

Charlotte relayed all this to Dominic and Beni as Matty's words—not those about Damian but those about the potential reason for their current situation—turned over in the back of her mind. Had that stop triggered something? If so, what? Charlotte and Mira had chatted about it but hadn't discussed anything in detail. What Charlotte had taken away from their brief talks was that the project had been one of Mira's favorites, and she'd grown close to a few members of the onsite crew over the years. There'd been nothing nefarious or suspect in their conversations.

But still, Charlotte couldn't discount the fact that out of the seven days they'd spent on the boat, this one trip—an afternoon on the island, an evening dinner at a local beach bar, then overnight moorage in one of the bays—*was* the outlier.

"Tell us about it," Dominic said, sitting back in his chair, beer in hand.

"There's not much to tell," Charlotte started. "We arrived early afternoon and moored at the main township. Mira had arranged to meet some of her colleagues—two men and a woman, I believe. They'd known each other for years via email, but they'd never had the opportunity to meet in person. She was excited and headed off pretty quickly. Simon and I wandered around town for the afternoon, had lunch at a local bar, I did a little shopping for my niece and nephew," she said, referring to Charlie and Daphne. Having finished her juice, which Dominic had thoughtfully mixed with sparkling water, she took a sip of the local beer. The light flavor washed over her tongue as she tried to remember anything from that day that might give them an idea of why first she, then Mira, had been targeted.

"We did a little snorkeling, and when Mira came back, probably around six or so, we boarded the boat and moved to the other side of the island where there was a restaurant Simon wanted to try. We moored in the bay and the water taxi brought us back and forth from the boat to the restaurant. We didn't talk to anyone at dinner other than waitstaff and Mira seemed fine, or at least not like she'd learned anything that concerned her.

"After dinner, we returned to the boat, had a relatively early night, then untied the next morning and headed back to the BVI," she finished.

"Do you know who she met?" Beni asked.

Her answer was interrupted by Damian walking through the front door carrying a couple of bags.

"Oh good, you got everyone drinks," he said. "I picked up rotis for everyone." He placed the two bags on the table, then disappeared into the kitchen.

"Looks like you got more than rotis," Dominic said, digging through one of the bags and handing out the burrito-like wraps that Charlotte knew would be filled with chicken, potatoes, a curry sauce, and likely a few other vegetables thrown in.

"I might have gotten some plantains and peas and rice. The latter of which isn't peas at all, but beans," he said to Charlotte as he rejoined them in the dining room with small plates, forks, and a bottle of beer for himself.

So, they were going to pretend he hadn't hightailed it out of his own home like the devil was on his heels? Well, Charlotte could go for that.

"Sounds good. Thanks for making the run. I was just telling

Beni and Dominic about our stop here," she said, pointing to the island. As they dug into their food, she gave him a summary of what she'd just told his colleagues. "Beni asked if I knew the names of the people Mira had met and I have to admit, even though I know she was excited to meet them, I didn't pay too much attention. I think one might have been named Tim and I think Sophie was the woman, but I can't remember last names—if she ever told me—or the name of the third person. Still, it probably wouldn't be too hard to find out. The project was big. Their names will be all over the reports."

"Is that something you can help us find?" Damian asked.

She nodded and swallowed a bite of her roti, which was the perfect blend of sweet, savory, and spicy.

"Yes, I can pull the reports and see what I can find. It shouldn't take me long, but I will need a computer. The only catch is, depending on who the people are, their names might not be in the public reports. If they're not, I'll need to use my credentials to log into the internal system. If that's not a problem for you, then I'm happy to do it, but I know you all wanted me to stay *dead*, and if I'm logging into the World Bank, it might be pretty obvious I'm not. If anyone is paying attention, that is."

Charlotte forked a fried plantain from the box they had come in and popped it into her mouth as the three agents seemed to have a silent conversation. Finally, Damian nodded and turned to her.

"Let's see what you can find in the public reports, and depending on how that goes, we'll go from there."

She nodded, then took a sip of beer. Caribbean food was an amazing mix of cultures and flavors, but sometimes it was a little heavy and the crispness of the beer offset the richness of the food.

She'd just taken another bite of her roti when Beni's phone dinged. The agent tapped a few buttons and read the message.

"Alexis made good time. They landed in DC ten minutes ago, and Jake and Ambassador O'Conner are already on their way to the hospital. Alexis will join them once she has the plane serviced and fueled."

"I can't believe this isn't the first thing I asked when I woke up, but is there any news on Mira?" Charlotte asked.

Her heart stuttered at the grim look on Beni's face. Mira was a lovely person who should have a long life ahead of her, and Charlotte didn't want to think of the pain her death would cause Simon. Mira's mother had died a month after Mira's birth, and the father and daughter were closer than most.

"It's still touch and go," Beni said. "She did make it out of surgery, but she hasn't woken up yet. It's a good thing her father is there."

Charlotte nodded and set her roti down, no longer hungry.

"You need to eat, Charlotte," Damian said, pointing his fork at her food. "You won't help anyone if you stop eating."

Rather than debate with Damian, she turned her attention to Dominic. "May I use your computer?" she asked. "I'd like to see if I can find who Mira was meeting with."

Dominic flicked a glance at Damian, but Charlotte didn't bother to look at her ex; she didn't have it in her to try to reason with him tonight.

Finally, Dominic sighed and handed over his laptop that had been sitting beside his food. "It's unlocked and already connected to Damian's WiFi. Let us know when you find something."

Charlotte gave him a grateful smile as she rose from her seat and took the device from his hand, avoiding Damian's scrutiny altogether. "If you don't mind, I think I'll go sit outside." Without waiting for a response, she grabbed her still mostly-full beer and headed out, computer in hand, to Damian's porch.

CHAPTER ELEVEN

"Wow, you just got burned," Dominic said as all three of them watched Charlotte through the picture window. She set her beer on a small side table, then sank onto one of the chairs. Propping her feet on an ottoman, she set the laptop on her lap and went to work.

"Fuck off, Burel," Damian responded, his eyes still on Charlotte.

"She's going to get eaten alive out there," Beni said. The lure of sitting outside under a tropic moon on a warm night was a rather romantic notion, and he knew better than anyone how alluring his porch could be. But the truth was, the humidity would have her sweating in no time, and the mosquitos in the tropics were relentless assholes.

"Is there a breeze at all?" Dominic asked. The trade winds were sometimes—but only sometimes—the only thing, other than navy grade radioactive repellent, that could keep the bugs away.

"Not much of one," Damian answered. "At least not when I came in twenty minutes ago."

"I give her fifteen minutes before she's back in," Beni said.

Damian snorted. "You clearly do not know Charlotte Lareaux very well," he said. "She's stubborn as all get out. She won't come in until she's done, and since she's decided she doesn't want to talk to me, she probably won't be done doing whatever she's doing until she's ready to go to bed."

"There might not be much left of her by then," Dominic commented. He'd suffered the worst from the mosquitos when they'd all first arrived on Tildas Island. It seemed that no repellent existed that would keep them away from him. Thankfully, after about a month on the island, something happened, though no one knew quite what, and the mosquitos didn't seem to bother any of them anymore.

"Maybe I should go talk to her," Damian mulled out loud.

"Don't," Beni said. "It's been weird enough between the two of you tonight and I don't want to have to witness another awkward scene."

"Amen to that," Dominic interjected.

"I'll just take her some of that bug spray, the Bureau provided us as part of our kits," she continued, rising from her seat.

"I have some in the kitchen. Second drawer to the left of the stove," Damian said. He wanted to be the one to take it to her. Hell, he wanted to take it to her, along with his drink, and have a little sit down on the porch, and maybe a chat. Like normal people. But he knew Beni was right. It was probably better to let her take it out.

Beni walked back into the dining room with the small canister in hand, and passing him without a word, she slipped out onto the porch. He watched the two women interact; Charlotte reached for the spray and Beni held the computer while Charlotte applied it. Then to his surprise, Beni sat beside Charlotte, and the two put their heads together, obviously looking at something on the screen.

"Well, will you look at that," Dominic said. "Do you think

Beni will come back in, or should we just continue on like two old bachelors?"

Damian rolled his eyes at his colleague as he started to gather up their empty plates. "Help me clear this mess up and then we can continue on as two old FBI agents and pull that list of travelers together. It would be good to have it for Charlotte by the time she gets in."

"You mean we can't just sit here, drink beer, and scratch our balls?"

"You touch your balls in my house, you are a dead man, Burel."

DAMIAN AND DOMINIC had just finished putting together the file of pictures for each male traveler on the watch list when his printer came to life, startling him.

A page fed onto the tray and, in the corner of his eye, movement at the window caught his attention. Beni and Charlotte were headed inside. Finally.

The two women stepped into the air-conditioned house, both looking a little flushed from the humidity, but pleased with themselves. Charlotte shut the door behind her, laughing at something Beni must have said. She raised her hands to tame her hair into a ponytail, and the movement pulled her—his— shirt tighter across her chest. With the sudden coolness of the air and the way the cotton clung to her curves, it was abundantly clear that she wore no bra underneath. Underneath *his* shirt.

Dominic cleared his throat, and Damian yanked his eyes away to find his teammate staring at him with one eyebrow arched. "Eyes in your head, Rodriguez," he muttered too quietly for either woman to hear. Thankfully.

"What are you printing?" he asked, dropping his gaze back to the first picture in the file they wanted Charlotte to go through. She hadn't seen her attacker, so they weren't pinning too many hopes on her identifying him, but hope springs eternal, especially when hunting an attempted murderer.

"Charlotte found the names, addresses, and contact of the three people Mira met. But before we go over these," Beni said, holding up the documents from his printer. "We need to talk about what we're going to tell Director Shah tomorrow. Officially, this isn't an FBI case, but I think we all agree we need to make it one."

"The problem is, it doesn't fit our mandate," Damian said to Charlotte. "We, our task force, was created specifically to get a handle on criminal activities in the Caribbean prior to the summit next year. While your attack falls into criminal activity, the question is, and I don't mean this to be dismissive—"

"Does it rise to the level of requiring your involvement," Charlotte finished. Reluctantly, he nodded. He hated that anyone might view her life as "not worth it,"—especially after what she'd said earlier about what it had been like growing up—but he worked for a federal agency, and resourcing and procedure were unavoidable components of that.

"It's a thin argument, but what about organized crime?" Dominic said. "We don't have any hard evidence of that yet, but we do have a crime here and what appears to be a related crime in DC."

"Actually," Beni said, holding her finger up as she seemed to be pondering something. "I don't think you're far off, but rather than organized crime, we frame it as a major, cross-border crime. Given that a valuable asset to the World Bank was attacked here on the island, and the following day, another employee was also attacked, I think it's a fair argument to say there's the potential for a major crime incident."

"Especially if we think the ambassador might be at risk too," Dominic interjected.

"If we argue this, and I think it's a good strategy, could we get the Diplomatic Security Service to sit on Simon and Mira and get Alexis and Jake back here?" Damian both asked and suggested.

Charlotte's eyes bounced between him and his two colleagues as they each silently weigh the pros and cons of that approach. Then one by one, they each nodded.

"I'll draft up the request for resources," Beni said. "We'll still need to keep Charlotte's survival quiet, but I don't doubt Director Shah will be on board with that. Now," she said with a grin, "let's get onto the good stuff. Charlotte, do you want to tell them what we found?"

Charlotte laughed at Beni's dramatic pronouncement. "We didn't find much more than what Beni already told you," she said. "But besides the names, addresses, and contact information for each of the three, I was able to track down their ages and their tenure with the Bank. I could probably find out more, but I'd need to log into the internal system, and Beni and I decided to wait until tomorrow to see if that was necessary." As she spoke, Beni handed out the information they'd printed.

When it was clear she had no more information to share, Damian slid his laptop in front of her and showed her how to go through each of the images he and Dominic had pulled together. Then leaving her to focus on the task, he and the others began tidying up.

"These are good images," Charlotte called out after a few minutes at the screen.

"Thanks," he and Dominic said at the same time. They'd captured clear images of each man as he'd passed through security on his way off the island. And those that hadn't been clear enough, they'd run through a program to re-pixilate.

It took her about twenty minutes to go through all the files, and by that time, the three agents were back seated in the living room.

"I cut the list down to about half," she said, handing the computer back to Damian. "I went based on height and build," she paused, then gave them a rueful smile. "And strangely, the color of their arm hair. I never thought I'd pay such close attention to the color of a man's arm hair," she said, making a face. "Also, I don't know how you would find this out, but remember, the man who came after me had no thumbnail on his left thumb and he's right-handed."

"We might not be able to find that out, but we'll do our best to see if we can," Damian said, typing a few commands into his device and sending the file to Dominic.

"Now," he said, shutting his computer down. "I know you didn't wake up all that long ago, but are you tired enough to go back to bed? Tomorrow could be a long day. And I suspect Director Shah will want to meet you."

CHAPTER TWELVE

CHARLOTTE WASN'T sure what to make of the idea of meeting Damian's boss. But she supposed if she were in Shah's shoes, she'd want to meet her too if for no other reason than to verify the situation.

"Of course," Charlotte said in response to Damian's comment. "I'm not that tired, but if you have a book or something, I can just read until I fall asleep."

Damian's eyes held hers and there was no way she could miss the naked hunger in them. It would be such an easy thing to give into, but the thought of making that leap had her stomach doing acrobatics. And not in a good way.

Once again, Matty's words came back to mind, and she suspected, though she'd have to give it a little more thought to confirm, that being with Damian again scared her. And although she didn't doubt it would be amazing to connect with him again in that way, the fact that something was holding her back, even if she couldn't name it, was enough for her to back off.

Thankfully, he broke eye contact first and turned to say good night to his teammates. She joined him and thanked them for everything they'd done. After she'd given them both hugs, Damian said he'd walk them to the car. He was obviously trying to avoid her, and a small part of her was grateful.

After the three had left the house, she quickly perused Damian's bookshelf and grabbed a copy of The Master and Margarita —not exactly lite reading, but the Russian satire/social commentary would take her brain to a different world if even just for a short time.

She was climbing into bed when she heard Damian come in again. Expecting him to knock on the door, she was surprised when she heard him walk into the kitchen, or perhaps the small laundry room that adjoined it, then head out again through the kitchen door. She hated that she made him uncomfortable, that he felt he had to leave his own home because she was there, but they'd already had that argument and he was a grown adult. If he wanted his house back, he knew she was willing to move, so all he'd have to do is say something.

With a sigh, she decided not to get lost in the book she held in her hands, and instead, she set it down on the bedside table. If she woke in the middle of the night, she could always pick it up. Rolling to her good side, she studied the shadows cast by the light of the moon shining through the shutters. There, staring at the vertical lines, she willed herself to sleep.

Because the very least she could do was stay out of Damian's way as much as possible.

———

DAMIAN JOGGED down the path from his house to the beach below. The events of the past two days and jet lag had caught up to him, and he was exhausted. But he knew if he were in the house when Charlotte was awake, he'd never be able to sleep. So he planned to take an easy two or three-mile jog along the beach and hope that by the time he got back, she was fast asleep.

He started with a slow pace, this run being more for his mental health than physical health, and focused on the feel of the sand between his toes. He'd taken to running barefoot in the packed sand about two weeks after he'd arrived when he'd realized that he got a much better work out, with much less distance, than if he ran on the roads.

He carried on for a short while. The air was still thick and salty although a slight breeze had picked up in the last half-hour or so—not enough to cool him, but definitely enough to keep the worst of the heat from gathering on his skin. As he jogged toward the Hemmeleigh resort, the dock where Charlotte had been attacked came into view. He hadn't had the time to come down and look since she'd shown up on his doorstep, and he found his gait slowing now.

Moving from a jog to a walk, he approached the wooden structure that jutted out into the bay. He drew to a stop where the sand met the dock and, for the first time, really looked at the setup. Oh, he'd seen the dock many times and even been out on it, but he'd never surveyed it from the perspective of planning an attack on someone.

There were two directions from which someone could approach; the way he had come or from the resort. If the man had come from the resort, chances were that Charlotte would have seen him. But if he'd come from the direction Damian had come from, he would have either had to come around the rocky point or down one of the paths that led from the houses on the point—like his—to the beach.

He studied the steep rise of the mountain from the beach. There weren't many paths down. His house had one, but only two others did as well. And he knew both of those owners, neither of which he had any qualms about eliminating as suspects.

So how did the man get to the dock without being seen?

Slowly, he turned in a circle until his attention fell to the thick jungle that lined this part of the beach. The roads to the resort came in from the other side of the bay, it was unlikely that he'd meet up with any Hemmeleigh land if he ventured into the dense foliage. Or any managed land, anyway.

It was too dark to explore the area further, but he made a mental note to come back in the next day or two to check it out. Who knows, maybe if they were lucky their assailant dropped a cigarette or something. That thought made him smile, it was never as easy as that, but it was fun to think it might be. But the smile died on his lips when he turned his attention back to the dock.

The place where Charlotte was meant to die.

He forced himself to take a step forward, then another until he was standing where she'd stood when the attack had happened. And he knew exactly where she'd been because even in the dim light of the moon, he could see dark stains on the sun-bleached wood from where her blood had fallen before her assailant had tossed her in the water.

It took all his energy not to drop to his knees at the thought of how close she'd come to dying. Since she'd arrived on his doorstep, he'd been able to keep these particular emotions at bay, focusing only on the investigation. But at the sight of her blood, all thoughts of the investigation fled and all he had left was the gut-wrenching reality that Charlotte had almost *died*. And it hadn't been him, or even Beni, who'd saved her. No, it had been nothing but pure dumb luck that her arm had gotten caught on the piling. If not for that, she would have been gone from this world—gone from his life—forever. A thought that didn't bear thinking.

He managed to stay standing, but he couldn't stop the tears that gathered in his eyes. When they'd broken up a year ago, he'd thought his world had shattered. But those feelings were distant and minuscule compared to the crushing despair he felt standing where she'd nearly lost her life. What would he have done if she'd died? What if her arm hadn't caught on the piling, what if his flight had been delayed and he hadn't been home when she'd all but crawled back into his life?

Those thoughts were big, almost too big for him to contemplate, and after a long moment, he turned and started back toward his house, no longer feeling the need to stay away. Vaguely, he was aware that the enormity of the feelings he was experiencing meant something. Of course they did. Coming this close to having to mourn Charlotte's death rather than being in a position to protect her, humbled him. And with that realization, his pride seemed to fall away like the tears he'd shed on the dock. He didn't quite know what to make of this jumbled mass of emotions or what to do with it, but her narrow escape did bring clarity—things had to change between the two of them. *He* had to change.

And he knew exactly what he needed to do.

CHAPTER THIRTEEN

WHEN CHARLOTTE AWOKE the next morning, the first thing she saw were the sun's rays casting shadows across the ceiling. She lay still for several moments, allowing her mind and body to wake, as she traced the lines with her eyes and thought about the day before her.

Damian had returned not long after he'd left. She had no idea where he'd gone, but she'd been awake with her back to the door when he'd quietly come into the room to take some clothing from his closet and then just as quietly, he'd closed the door behind him and left her alone. He'd paused for a moment before leaving and it had taken all her will power to keep her breathing even and her body relaxed and still. But she'd kept her back to him, doing her best to give him some freedom that might come with thinking he didn't have to deal with her.

After he'd left the room, she'd tossed and turned, metaphorically, if not literally, most of the night. And now that the sun was shining, she was exhausted. Awake, but exhausted. The good news was that at least she'd had time during the night to formulate a plan that she intended to propose to Damian that morning.

But not wanting to intrude as Damian slept, she remained in bed until she heard him rise. He padded to the kitchen and into the half bath. The walls were sturdier than the floors, and she heard nothing more until he stepped back into the kitchen and, judging by the sounds of the water filtration system that came on whenever someone used any water, started making coffee.

Rising, she quickly slipped into another sundress that Alexis had left her—one that crisscrossed across her breasts then fell from the empire waist to three inches above her knee. She almost laughed at the image of herself in Damian's full-length mirror. Never in her life would she have bought a dress like this. To her, clothes had been a means of projecting the image she needed to project as a minority woman working in international business. Her clothes conveyed power—tailored to her body—and were, perhaps, a little more on the retro-classical side. Yes, she had more pencil skirts and high heels in her closet than any sane woman should, but they looked damn good on her.

But this dress did, too. Charlotte's smile died a little when she realized that somewhere along the way, she'd forgotten to have a little fun with her body; she'd forgotten that sometimes she didn't need to *project* anything. She just needed to be comfortable. As she stood there looking at herself, she knew she hadn't *forgotten* anything—she'd never learned in the first place.

Like Matty had said, there were a lot of things that, as children, they hadn't had the luxury of learning and having fun and being frivolous were two of those things. And even when Matty's grandmother had moved them into her mansion and eventually into private schools, they'd both thrived academically, drinking in everything they were taught. But "fun" had never been her focus because despite her successes, Charlotte always, always harbored a little part of her that felt she just wasn't good enough—wasn't good enough for the school, wasn't good enough for the scholarships she'd earned, wasn't good enough for her Ph.D., or her first consulting gig.

She *knew* she was. She knew she'd earned every bit of her success. But that was the thing about trauma, it often didn't respond to reason. And so, more angry with herself than with the circumstances that led to her self-doubt, she donned her armor every day in a picture-perfect image of a successful businesswoman.

A knock at the door startled her, and she spun as Damian popped his head in. He paused and his eyes swept over her then lingered on her face.

"You okay?" he asked.

She started to nod, then stopped herself. "I don't know why, but this thing," she gestured first toward her wounded side then toward the general direction of the dock, "is bringing up a lot of stuff for me. More than just what I mentioned yesterday. And it's not very comfortable."

He opened the door fully, strode in, and came to a stop behind her. She looked at the image of the two of them in the mirror.

"I've never seen you wear a dress like this," he said. "Not even when we vacationed in places like this."

She gave a soft self-deprecating laugh. "I know, that's exactly what I was thinking about when you walked in. I *like* this dress—"

"It does look good on you," he interjected with a smile.

She playfully elbowed him before continuing. "But I never would have bought it because it doesn't project the image I need the world to see. It's more an I'm-going-to-dance-around-a-bonfire-on-the-beach-while-drinking-rum-out-of-plastic-cups than I'm-a-successful-business-woman-on-vacation. I don't like that a simple dress has made me question why I've felt the need all these years not to let that façade down. Why haven't I been strong enough to say 'yes, I'm a successful businesswoman, but

I'm also someone who likes to dance around bonfires and drink rum'?"

He set his hands on her bare shoulders, the most he'd touched her since she'd arrived at his house, bleeding and nearly dead. His thumbs played over the top of her shoulder blades.

"First, being a successful businesswoman isn't a façade you need to drop or pick up. It *is* who you are and don't belittle everything you've done to build the incredible life you have. But it doesn't have to be *all* you are. Maybe it's not a question of strength. Maybe it's a question of whether or not you've ever asked yourself the question."

"What question?" she held his gaze in the mirror.

"What else do you *want* to be other than a successful businesswoman?" he said. "You are one of the strongest, smartest women I know, Charlotte. I don't have any doubt that if you decide you want to be the kind of person who dances around a bonfire drinking rum after holding all-day conference calls with the ministers of several countries, you'll be that woman. You just have to ask yourself what you want."

The truth of his words sank deep into her soul. She didn't have an answer now, but he was right, she'd never asked herself that question. All of the opportunities Matty's grandmother had offered her had been such largess that she'd focused only on one —excelling in the business world. It had become both her anchor and her lifeline—the one thing to cling to when much of the rest of the world hadn't made much sense.

But she didn't need to cling to it anymore. She'd proven herself—to herself most of all—so maybe it was time to start asking what *else* she wanted out of life.

"You're pretty damn smart yourself," she said with a smile.

Damian's smile widened and he dropped a kiss on the back of her head before stepping away. "Beni texted this morning and wants us to meet at the office in about an hour. Director Shah will be there by ten and we need to get all our ducks in a row. I don't think she'll disagree that we should take the case, but we want to make the decision easy for her by making sure she has all the information she needs."

"So, after all the revelations this little dress has just caused, I probably shouldn't wear it?"

Damian laughed. "That's your call, Charlotte. She's well aware of who you are because you're one of the advisors for the summit, and she isn't the kind of person to judge you based on your clothes. But even if she were, is that something you want to care about right now?"

Charlotte rolled her eyes. "Point taken, Rodriguez," she said as she started to gather her wayward hair into a ponytail. She'd taken a quick shower the night before to wash off the radioactive bug repellent, and her hair now resembled a bird's nest. The good news was, she could lift her arms enough to manage it with relatively little pain.

"Let me just get my hair under control, and I'll be right out," she added.

Damian nodded and started to leave but paused in the doorway. "Out of curiosity, *would* you like to dance around a bonfire drinking rum?"

She held his gaze for a moment, then smiled. "I think I might. Especially if the music was any good, and I was dancing with the right person."

A beat passed, then Damian grinned. "That's good to know."

DAMIAN LEANED against the wall and watched Director Shah and Charlotte, still in her sundress, discuss the upcoming summit. It had taken their boss all of fifteen minutes to sign off on the case and then another fifteen to arrange for the Diplomatic Security Services to relieve Alexis and Jake, who would be arriving back on island that evening. Now the two women were going over the list of summit invitees. Director Shah knew the dossiers of each, but Charlotte had met—and worked—with many of them, and his boss was not one to waste an opportunity to obtain insider information.

"She's amazing," Charlotte said, pointing to a name on the list. "Put her next to Stephen Hamish at the resort because if things start to go off the rails, you'll want them close to each other. They have the power and influence to bring things back under control and if they are neighbors, they'll have more of an opportunity to make plans, if needed."

Director Shah made a note, then pointed to another name with her pen. "And him?"

Charlotte all but snorted. "He's way out of depth with this group. I'm sure you know he was only invited because his aunt is the Prime Minister. In fact, I just spoke to her the other day, and I think even *she's* surprised the ministry decided to send him. She thinks they were trying to curry favor with her, but she doesn't hold her nephew in very high regard, so I wouldn't be surprised if he's pulled before the final confirmations."

And so it went for another forty minutes. Damian considered joining his teammates as they dug into the lives of the men Charlotte hadn't eliminated from the airport footage, but the truth was, he was enjoying himself too much to leave. Watching Charlotte with Shah was a beautiful thing.

"I think that's it for now," Director Shah said, closing her notes and gathering the invitee list. "If you think of anything between now and the summit, you'll let me know?"

"Of course," Charlotte said as she rose from her seat. "There are advisory committee meetings every month until the event, and assuming I no longer have to play dead, I can touch base with you after each if there are any developments?"

"I'd appreciate that, and I anticipate this situation will get resolved quickly enough so that you can return to your normal life. Isn't that correct, Agent Rodriguez?"

"Yes, ma'am," he agreed. Because one did not disagree with Sunita Shah.

"Excellent," she said with a smile. "What now?"

Damian opened his mouth to update her on the progress his teammates were making, but Charlotte spoke first.

"I meant to ask Damian about something this morning, but got distracted."

Shah's eyes flickered to him and damned if he didn't feel a little heat creep up his neck. *Nothing* had happened between him and Charlotte, but Charlotte's inadvertent choice of words implied otherwise.

"Yes?" Shah said, returning her attention to Charlotte.

"I'd like to go talk to Mira's friends. The ones she met with from the World Bank project. Assuming they aren't suspects, they might be able to shed some light on what they talked about and give us an idea if that's a lead the team should follow. I know it's possible to talk over the phone, but I find people to be more forthcoming in person. But that would, of course, entail traveling to the island."

"Not a good idea, Charlotte," Damian said. Her eyes flew to his at his abrupt response, then narrowed in question. "You were barely able to make it through the day yesterday," he said. "And you were stabbed not forty-eight hours ago. Hopping on a plane or chopper and being gone all day doesn't seem like something that might be good for you right now."

She studied him for a long moment before turning back to Shah. The silent conversation the two women seemed to be having did not do good things to his stomach. Especially not when Shah smiled.

"Have Harvey fly you over," she said, referring to the helicopter pilot they kept on stand-by. "I'll call my counterpart on the island and let him know we'll be there. The three aren't suspects so he shouldn't object to a friendly chat."

Damian clenched his jaw to keep from arguing. It would be

futile, of course. Once Shah—or Charlotte for that matter—made up her mind, very little would change it, but that didn't mean he didn't want to try.

"Shall I call them to see if they have time today to meet, or do you want to?" Charlotte asked him, her expression full of innocence, but he could swear he saw a glint of smugness in her eyes.

"I'll do it. You're still supposed to be, well, you know." She might joke about playing dead, but he wasn't about to go there.

"Excellent, we have a plan then," Shah said. A clear dismissal. "Keep me posted," she added unnecessarily. Shah held the respect of her team, and they would always keep her updated, but she also had an uncanny ability to *know* things. It was part of the mystique that surrounded her within the rank and file of the Bureau.

Damian ushered Charlotte out, but before he could offer his opinion on her plan, she informed him she was going to check in with Beni and Dominic while he made his calls and she was gone before he'd even taken a breath. Smart woman.

Conceding defeat, he sat down at his desk, pulled the documents Charlotte and Beni had printed the night before and placed three calls. Sophie was off island, having gone to visit family in England, but Tim Waller and Ahmed Baloch, a couple in both life and work, were at home and happy to meet with them. As his call ended, an email from Shah came in confirming they'd received authorization to land on the island and talk to the two men.

The ride to the heliport was mostly silent and he knew Charlotte was doing her best not to rile him, but he wished she would because he was spoiling for a fight. Still, she held her tongue as they parked and said nothing as they checked in with security.

"It didn't dawn on me that Director Shah must have pulled some strings since my passport is still in my hotel room," Charlotte said when the security agent disappeared into the back office to check the documents Damian had provided him, compliments of Shah.

She was leaning casually against the counter and something in her stance finally triggered him and he couldn't take her blasé approach anymore.

"You almost died two days ago, Charlotte," he said, stepping into her space. She remained leaning against the counter though her eyes locked on his. "How can you possibly think that flying off to another island for a day trip is a good thing?" He was inches away from her and he curled his hands into fists so as not to reach out for her.

She shrugged. "But I didn't die, and now it looks like Mira is going to pull through too," she said. Jake had updated them that morning on Mira's status and though both of her statements were true, neither changed how he felt. And she really shouldn't have shrugged. As if her nearly dying wasn't *that* big a deal.

It was the shrug that got to him and he snapped.

His hands came up and he slid them into her hair as he pulled her toward him, closing those last few inches. It had been just over a year since he'd kissed her—kissed anyone—and if he'd given it any thought, which he had, this wasn't how this kiss was supposed to be. But he couldn't help it; he couldn't help invading her space and crushing his mouth to hers. But what had started in anger, in frustration and fear, erupted into something entirely different when she opened up to him. Their tongues danced with each other as she took a step and pressed herself flush against him, her hands coming to his waist.

Cupping her face, he tilted his head and deepened their connection even more. He felt Charlotte's hands still on his body for a split second, then suddenly they were under his shirt and her short nails were biting into the skin of his lower back.

Maybe he could convince her that they had better ways to spend their day than flying to another island. Maybe they'd even make it to his bed before he was inside her, though with the fierce need coursing between them, he wasn't going to place any bets on that.

"Charlotte," he said, pulling back just enough so he could suggest they ditch the helicopter ride.

But then sound of a throat clearing filtered through the fog of lust that had engulfed him, and though he didn't step away from Charlotte or take his hands off her, he did ease his body back. Charlotte started to lean toward him again when the official cleared his throat again. She froze, then her eyes widened. Licking her lips, lips he'd just kissed the devil out of, she stepped back. Their hands fell away from each other and instantly, he missed the contact. Charlotte must have too because even though she took one more step away, she reached for his hand and entwined her fingers with his.

"Your papers are in order," the official said, his tone giving no indication of what he'd just witnessed. "Harvey is waiting for you. Have a nice trip, Agent Rodriguez."

The man looked at them expectantly, waiting for them to head toward the helipad. But the feel of Charlotte against him again, after so long apart, fogged his brain, and for a long moment, he simply stood there.

Then Charlotte tugged his hand.

"We should go," she said, gesturing with her head toward the helicopter.

"It's a bad idea, Charlotte."

"I know you think so, but I promise I'll take it easy tomorrow."

His lips flattened as he tried to think of a way to persuade her not to go, but she wasn't having any of that, and before he knew it, she was pulling him along toward the helicopter and Harvey was handing them both headsets.

And five minutes later, they were airborne, racing across the clear blue of the Caribbean.

CHAPTER FOURTEEN

TIM WALLER and Ahmed Baloch were not quite what Charlotte had expected. She knew they'd been married eleven years and she knew their ages and work history, but the two wiry men who greeted them at the beachside bar where they'd agreed to meet, both dressed in tie-dyed shirts and shorts that had seen better days, did not align with her image of World Bank employees. Then again, she supposed her expectation was what came of only working with the administrative part of the organization and not the field.

The four seated themselves at a table in the far corner of the bar, away from the three other patrons. After ordering a light lunch and Painkillers all around—the regional rum drink, not a pill—Charlotte got down to business.

Both men appeared genuinely shocked to hear about the attack on Mira and relieved to know that it looked like she would pull through. When Charlotte laid out why she and Damian wanted to talk to them, they were as bewildered as she was by the idea that Mira might have learned something during their get together that had led to the situation.

They each picked through their food as Charlotte walked

through a series of questions she'd thought of the night before, hoping to find something to give them a clue.

"Where did you meet Mira? I know it was in the township, but walk me through your day," she said.

Ahmed and Tim shared a look, then Tim spoke. "We picked her up outside the post office and drove around the island a bit. She wanted to see some of the actual projects we'd completed. We talked work the entire time. It was fun to have her here. We'd been communicating over email for a few years and always enjoyed working with her. And it's not often we get people from HQ who come to visit the sites for any reason other than to inspect or audit. But Mira just wanted the opportunity to see how the loan had benefited the island. She asked a lot of questions, but most had to do with how we managed the project, not from an audit-like perspective, but things like how we found contractors, how equipment and materials were delivered, if we encountered any resistance from the community. Those sorts of things."

"More project administration questions than economic or 'World Bank' questions," Ahmed interjected. "Almost as if she was considering moving into the field herself."

That was news to Charlotte, Mira had never mentioned anything like that before. "Do you think she was considering that?" It would be an unusual move for someone with Mira's background to make.

Ahmed shrugged. "Hard to tell. She could have just been excited at learning something new. She's definitely someone who loves to learn."

Charlotte smiled at that as she took a sip of her drink. The fruity concoction slid down her throat and though it was a little sweet for her, she could see making a version more suited to her tastes. And then maybe lying out at the beach all day drinking it.

"I'll make you one tonight," Damian said, gesturing to her drink. "If you use fresh coconut water, it's less sweet."

She blinked, wondering how he'd read her mind. But then she gave a little shake of her head. Damian had always been very good at reading people, especially her.

"He's right," Tim said. "The bars use canned coconut water because it's easier and cheaper, but if you use real coconut, then it's a truly decadent drink."

Charlotte murmured something about looking forward to trying it then returned to the reason for their visit. "So, after you toured the island, what did you do?"

"Came here, actually," Ahmed said. "They have the best fish tacos on the island, and the four of us had a leisurely late lunch before we returned her to the township."

"And what did you talk about over lunch?" she asked.

"The conversation veered to the more personal," Tim said. "We talked about the boyfriend Sophie had left behind in London and whether or not she should get back together with him."

"The resounding vote was no," Ahmed said. "He wasn't at all supportive of her career, and Sophie not only loves what she does, but she's damn good at it too."

Tim nodded and continued. "We talked about how Ahmed and I met on a project in northern Africa and all the places we've lived."

"We covered Mira's love life—"

"Which was sadly lacking," Tim interjected.

Ahmed nodded. "For such a lovely young woman, we were surprised to hear she wasn't seeing anyone. Not that she needs to by any means, but she seemed to *want* to."

That was something Charlotte knew all about. While she was Mira's professional mentor, she was also her friend.

"And was there anything during the conversation that struck you as odd? Or different?" she asked.

Both men shook their heads, but then Ahmed stopped. "There was that one comment," he said.

It could mean nothing, but Charlotte found herself sitting forward in her seat, and she sensed Damian come to attention, too.

"What comment?" Tim asked.

Ahmed frowned. "That's right, you weren't there. Sophie had gone off to use the restroom and you'd gone to pay the bill, but Mira asked why we'd considered switching contractors for the roads project halfway through."

"And?" Damian asked.

"Our roads contractor was great. We never considered replacing them," Tim answered. Then looking at his husband, he asked, "Why would she think we'd considered switching contractors?"

Ahmed shook his head. "I didn't get to ask. You came back to the table, then Sophie did, and we never revisited it."

Both men looked at her and Damian. Charlotte glanced over at Damian, too, and he gave her a nod to take the lead.

"I know that the Bank is more diligent now than they used to be in terms of conducting anti-corruption audits, but tell me the process for getting contractors approved," she said.

"At a high level, it's not that complex. Once the project is approved, we put it out to bid. A panel selects the winning bids, and then we submit the names to the Bank to run the checks they need to. Once the Bank clears the contractors, we award the bid."

"So, you can't award a bid until then?" Damian clarified.

Tim and Ahmed nodded. "If we need to replace a contractor, it can be the death knell for the project because we have to go through the same process before awarding the work to the new contractor, which can put all other work on hold if one is dependent on the other."

"But that didn't happen on this project?" Charlotte asked.

They each shook their head. "Not for the roads work. We did have to replace the sewer contractor about a year in, but that was the only major contractor we had any issues with," Ahmed said.

"So when you sent your reports to Mira, I assume there were line items for contractor expenses, but did they include the names of the contractors?" Charlotte asked. She'd done a lot of consulting with the World Bank, but the level she worked at was far higher than the day-to-day work Mira did.

"Actually no, not the monthly summary reports. But the formal annual reports would have included the names of the contractors as we have to disclose the major recipients of the funds," Tim said.

"And who sees those annual reports?" Damian asked.

Both Tim and Ahmed laughed. "Probably no one. I'm quite convinced that the only people who see them are the people who create them. And maybe our liaisons if they care to look," Tim said.

"And do you think Mira looked?" Charlotte asked.

"She's one of the few who probably did," Tim said. "As we've mentioned, she likes to learn. She probably went through it with a fine-tooth comb to ensure it aligned with her summary of the monthly reports."

"But you think she was the anomaly?" she asked.

Ahmed nodded. "Definitely. For most of the projects we work on, the liaisons use the monthly summary reports to create the annual report because weirdly, although the Bank requires that we submit *our* annual reports in a specific format, the annual report that people like Mira have to submit up *their* chain, is more closely aligned with the information provided to them in the monthly reports."

"So it's actually more efficient for the liaisons to use the information that they have from the monthly reports to create the annual reports that the Banks want, than it is to use the actual annual reports the Banks makes you provide," Damian said, sitting back in his chair.

Tim nodded. "A vagary of the World Bank," he said.

"A way to keep the bureaucrats employed," Ahmed corrected. Tim inclined his head in agreement.

"Is it possible to get a copy of the reports you sent to Mira?" Damian asked. "Both the monthly ones and the annual ones?"

"I wish," Tim said. "Mira can likely provide them to you, but we had a break-in a few months ago."

"Six months ago," Ahmed said. "A few months after the project ended. They took all our electronics, even our old record player."

"And you have no backups?" Charlotte asked. She was fanatical about backing up her documents and couldn't fathom people who operated otherwise.

"Our connection to the Bank servers is sketchy at best. And so it's standard practice in the field to rely on the liaison to manage the backup," Ahmed said.

Well, that was some good news. Charlotte was certain Mira would have taken the appropriate steps to secure the documents. Now they just had to wait until she was well enough to access them.

The waitress came over and cleared the plates. Charlotte thanked them for meeting with her and Damian on such short notice, and they chatted about lighter topics while they waited for the check to arrive. Once Damian had paid, they said goodbye to the couple, thanking them again, then hopped into a cab to head back to the heliport. All in all, by the time they returned home, the trip would be less than four hours. A little more strenuous than the day before but not by much and she had to admit to feeling a little smug about it.

"That went well, don't you think?" she asked. Damian, who'd just finishing texting Harvey to let him know they were on their way back, slid his phone back into his pocket and took her hand in his.

"Don't be so self-satisfied," he said, "We aren't home yet."

She chuckled then leaned her head against the back of the car seat. They rode in silence for the ten minutes it took to get to the helipad, and all the while, she simply enjoyed the feel of his hand surrounding hers.

With the kiss—that one explosive kiss—things had changed between them. She'd given Matty's words a lot of thought during her sleepless night, and she knew her friend was right. If she and Damian were going to have any chance at a future, being together again couldn't be about going back to what they were. It had to be about moving forward to what they wanted to be.

CHAPTER FIFTEEN

ALEXIS AND JAKE were an hour out by the time Damian and Charlotte returned to the office. Damian took a few minutes to fill Beni and Dominic in while Charlotte immediately went to the public website for the World Bank to see what kind of full reports on the project she could download.

Unfortunately, as the final project audits tended to take more than a year, there wasn't much available yet, and certainly nothing as detailed as the list of contractors Tim and Ahmed had managed. Charlotte printed off a few documents that he and the team reviewed while she continued to dig into the Web to see what else she might be able to find.

Soon enough, Jake and Alexis strolled back into the office.

"That looks good on you," Alexis said to Charlotte with a nod to the dress.

"Thanks, you have a good eye. Better than anything I would have picked out," Charlotte responded, her eyes returning to the computer.

Alexis took the compliment as her due and promptly took a seat at her desk. "Talk to us," she said.

Perched on the edge of his desk, Jake chimed in. "Beni's been keeping us updated about the traveler watch list, but how did your lunch go?"

Charlotte didn't look interested in filling in the gaps, so Damian took on the task while she continued working. By the time he'd given them the summary, she'd sat back from her chair and had been glaring at the computer for at least a minute.

"Is there a problem, Charlotte?" he asked.

She turned toward the group, and her eyes bounced between the five of them. Finally, they landed on him. "There's not enough about the project in the public domain yet to give us any indication whether or not the question Mira asked Ahmed means anything to our current situation. I need either Mira or her computer," she said. "But I can't have either and I'm getting irritated."

He couldn't help the smile that tugged at his lips. He always kind of liked seeing Charlotte irritated—when it wasn't directed at him.

"I think her computer might still be on the ambassador's boat," Jake said.

"What?" Charlotte demanded as all eyes fell on the man.

"Simon mentioned it on the flight," he said. "He said his pump was giving him problems, but he'd been planning to come into the marina anyway because he needed to overnight Mira's laptop to her. In her haste to leave, she'd left it behind."

"And, with his mind on other things, he didn't think to pick it up when he packed," Alexis said.

Jake shrugged. "Probably."

"Can you get a key to his boat?" Damian asked Charlotte.

"I think he has a hidden one on the boat," she said tentatively. "But I don't remember exactly where. Maybe if we went to look, it would come back to me?"

"Better than nothing," Damian said, rising from his seat. "Anyone want to join us?"

"I'll come," Dominic said, while Beni opted to stay back and finish up the research into the travelers, and Jake and Alexis declined in order to catch up on paperwork and email. But they all agreed to meet at his place that night and a few minutes later, he, Dominic, and Charlotte were in his jeep on their way to the marina.

Damian listened to Dominic give Charlotte a running tour of the town and island as they drove. Pointing out a few historic spots, a couple of good restaurants, and even a few dance clubs. The latter of which somewhat surprised Damian. Dominic was a social creature—he and Jake competed for the most social of the team—but Damian had never heard him talk about going dancing before. He knew the clubs would all serve rum, maybe he should find out if any had beach access.

Forty minutes after leaving the office, they pulled into the marina where Ambassador O'Conner kept his boat.

"I'll kick it out here," Dominic said, making it clear he intended to watch their six from the parking lot while they searched the boat. Damian nodded and he and Charlotte went in search of the harbormaster; without Simon to buzz them in, they'd need someone with an access key.

It took a little convincing, but eventually, the man let them through the gate, and he and Charlotte made their way to Simon's boat.

As he expected, she paused before stepping onto the deck, likely recalling her memory of the boat as she'd seen it on that first day. He waited patiently, knowing she'd remember where Simon had hidden the key if given enough time. And sure enough, a full two minutes passed, but then she stepped on the boat and went directly to the far storage unit. Reaching under the latch, she pulled out a key. To his surprise, she didn't use it on the unit or galley door, but rather went to a small cabinet that lined the top of one of the windows. Standing on a bench, she used the key to open the drawer, then punched a code into an even smaller box and withdrew yet another key.

"This is it," she said, stepping down from the bench. "Mira's cabin was toward the front and to the left. I'll go check there and be right back."

He nodded as she unlocked the galley door then disappeared inside while he fixed his attention on the surroundings. The marina was fairly quiet this time of day and only a few people puttered around their boats, all several docks away.

"Charlotte," he called, when he realized five minutes had passed and she hadn't returned. Boats had lots of small spaces for her to search, but there weren't *that* many.

"Still looking," she called back. "It wasn't in her room, so trying to think where it might be," she added.

There wasn't any reason for him to be anxious, but suddenly, the hairs on his neck stood on end. Sweeping the area, he took in the people still working on their boats, a sailboat just coming into the harbor, and a small motorboat on its way out.

"Charlotte," he called again. "I think we need to hurry it up." He didn't know why and maybe he was overreacting, but he'd rather overreact and find he'd had no reason to than not react at all and regret it.

"I think I found it. In Simon's cabin," she said, her head popping out of the galley. "He must have put it there to remind himself to send it. Here," she said, holding the device out to him. "I just need to lock up."

She was sliding the key into the lock when Dominic came charging toward them, waving his arms in the universal sign to clear out.

"We have to go now, Charlotte," he barked, reaching for her. She stood just far enough away that his fingers came away with nothing but air. "Now, Charlotte!"

Dominic was coming closer and they could hear him shouting for them to get clear of the boat. For a split second, Charlotte froze, and his heart stuttered.

He was not going to lose her now.

Dropping the computer onto the dock, he leaped onto the boat, as Charlotte came out of her panic. She let go of the key and reached for his hand.

Closing his fingers around hers, he pulled her toward the edge of the boat as Dominic reached them.

"Get the computer, Dominic," Charlotte shouted as they leaped from the boat to the dock. Without breaking his stride, Dominic swooped down and grabbed the device, then, grabbing Charlotte's other hand, he dragged her toward the end of the dock.

"Sorry about this," Dominic said. It took Damian a moment to understand what Dominic meant, and not a second later, the three of them were sailing through the air and plummeting into the cloudy, dark marina waters. But the darkness was fleeting and before they'd sunk under the weight of their jump, a ball of fire rolled over the surface and the water roiled, buffeting them against each other. Damian's training kicked in and he relaxed his body so as not to fight the churning currents. The only part of him he did not relax was his hold on Charlotte. There was little he could do for her now, not with debris raining down on them, but he damn well wasn't going to let her go.

When he started to worry that she might lose consciousness, he dragged her up, hoping the worst of the debris had already landed. His head breached the surface and a split second later, he tugged hers up too. On her other side, Dominic's came into view as well.

"We need to get her out of the water," Damian said. Charlotte's eyes hadn't opened and she didn't seem to be responding to the change of circumstances. But he refused to think beyond what he knew he had to do next.

Dominic slipped below her and got her in a lifeguard hold. "That boat looks relatively unharmed and has a ladder. Climb up and I'll hand her to you," he said, gesturing to a small yacht ten feet away.

Damian was loathe to let go, but he knew Dominic's plan was for the best, and so he released her, and in two strokes, was at the ladder that led to a back diving deck. Wrenching himself up, he turned just as Dominic reached him. Positioning his arms under Charlotte's, he pulled while Dominic used the boat to give him more leverage and pushed her toward him.

After what seemed like ages—ages in which Charlotte had yet to open her eyes—he had her on the deck. Turning her on her side, he pounded her back, hoping that any water she might have taken in would come out. When nothing happened, he rolled her back over and placed his hands on her chest to start CPR compressions. He was just beginning to press when Dominic's hands halted his movement.

"She has a strong pulse, give her a minute," he said, rolling her back onto her side. Damian blinked at the man who had muscled him to the side and now held Charlotte draped over his forearm. Damian couldn't believe he'd forgotten to check for a pulse—not even in his most panicked moments as a Ranger had he gotten so flustered.

With a shake of his head to clear it—now was not the time for self-recriminations—he grabbed Charlotte's hand and squeezed.

"Come on, Charlotte. We know you're there, fight for this," he said. When nothing happened, Dominic once again pounded on her back.

"Dom?" he said, not bothering to hide the fear in his voice.

"She's got this, Rodriguez. Just give her a minute," he repeated. And then, as if on command, Charlotte came coughing to life.

Water poured from her mouth as she coughed up all she'd swallowed, and through it all, Dominic held her body while Damian held her hand and whispered words of encouragement. When it looked like she'd finally rid her system of everything, Damian gently took her from Dominic and pulled her onto his lap as he leaned against the rail of the boat they'd taken over. With his arms wrapped around her, she tucked herself against him, and for the life of him, there was nothing else in the world he could do.

He heard the sirens, he felt Dominic leave to meet the fire crew and paramedics, and he heard his teammate barking orders to the EMTs to treat both him and Charlotte. He didn't know how much time had passed, but soon two men and a woman were leaning over him, gently trying to take Charlotte from him.

He glared at them all and refused to give her up.

"She needs medical attention, Rodriguez," Dominic said. Slowly, Damian's gaze focused on his colleague. "You need to let her go. They're here to help," he added quietly. Damian's gaze dropped to the three EMTs, and numbly, he nodded. Before he'd even finished, they were taking her from him.

"Go with them, Damian," Dominic said, holding a hand out. "She won't want to be without you any more than you want to let her go alone."

Damian took Dominic's hand and pulled himself up. His clothes felt heavy and uncomfortable, but he'd deal with that later. Right now, he just needed to be beside Charlotte as they wheeled her away toward the ambulance.

CHAPTER SIXTEEN

A CHILL WHISPERED across Charlotte's skin, and she frowned. She hadn't been cold since she'd landed in the Caribbean, why was she cold now? And where was she? The bed she was lying on was stiff and uncomfortable. Not like Damian's cozy king-sized bed with decadent cotton sheets.

Her eyelids felt heavy and she tried to open them.

"Come back to me, Charlotte," she heard Damian say.

She frowned again. Had she left him? Again? She remembered leaving him a long time ago, but hadn't she just been with him? Yes, she had. They'd just been together when—

Adrenaline shot through her and her eyes flew open. "Are you okay?" she said. Or "croaked" probably would have been a better word.

The chair Damian had been sitting on scraped across the floor as he rose, his hand holding hers.

"You're back," he said, stroking her forehead.

"I never went anywhere. I held your hand the entire time," she said. Memories of the plummet into the marina waters and the explosion that followed flooded back. "Are you okay? And Dominic?"

"Everyone is fine," he answered. "It's you we were worried about. You lost consciousness for a little while. We finally got you to cough up all the water you'd swallowed, but then you were a little out of it when we brought you in. You've been sleeping for a few hours."

"Just a few hours?" she asked.

He nodded.

She tested her body, moving each limb just a tiny bit, and found she could feel everything. She was a little sore but not too bad. "I must be okay. I don't feel like I've injured anything."

Damian pulled his seat close to the bed and sat, keeping her hand in his. "You're fine. The doctor took some scans and no major injuries. You did stretch one of your stitches, but it didn't pull out altogether. She tightened it up, cleaned the wound again, and gave you some more antibiotics. They even said they'd discharge you once you'd been awake for a little while."

Charlotte let out a long exhale. Twice in less than three days, she'd almost died. And she'd only survived today because Damian had pulled her off Simon's boat and into the water on the other side of the dock.

She curled her fingers tightly around his and started to speak, but he cut her off.

"I never wanted to look too deeply at myself," he said.

Charlotte had no idea what Damian wanted to say to her but she sensed it was important and so she stayed silent as he struggled with words. Finally, he took a deep breath and spoke again.

"When I was a Ranger, so many of my friends and brothers suffered physical injuries or different kinds of trauma, that it felt wrong that I pretty much always just walked away—away from every mission, every tour, and eventually the Army itself. I was grateful, of course, but there was always a little part of me that wondered *why* it was so easy for me to walk away, why I didn't end up with PTSD or something similar. Did the things that we saw, or did, not bother me as much as they should have?

Was there something wrong with me that I could walk away and not *feel* much of anything? It didn't seem fair or right," he added quietly.

"Survivor syndrome," she said, her voice soft in the quiet room. She knew a thing or two about that.

Damian inclined his head. "I'm sure that's part of it. But sometimes it felt like more than that, like maybe there was something wrong with me in that I just didn't have the ability to feel things deeply." He paused and traced the line of her thumb with his forefinger. "And that maybe, it was this defect in me that made it possible for me to escape some of the problems my fellow Rangers experienced. I know that sounds crazy—"

"It doesn't," Charlotte cut him off. What he felt was real, and he needed to hear that.

He gave her a half-smile, then continued. "I appreciate that, but that question is always there, lurking in the back of my mind—is there something wrong with me? Am I a heartless monster or some kind of sociopath who is incapable of empathy? I know that intellectually my thoughts don't make sense. I know different people experience and process life differently. But we both know that what we *know* doesn't always matter. And over the years, the thought that maybe there *is* something wrong with me has festered. If it's true, then it's something so big and ugly, that I'm not sure what I would do with it. And so it's become easier to not ask the question, it's become easier to just be Mr. Congeniality and everybody's friend. Because if I am, then I don't have to contemplate whether or not I have the capacity to feel real human emotions. But I can't do that anymore, Charlotte."

He paused and ran his palm over his face, then squeezed the bridge of his nose with his thumb and forefinger, and his gaze dropped to the floor. Finally, he looked up.

"I almost lost you, really lost you, twice. There's no question in my mind now just how deeply I can feel things—at least things like absolute panic and terror. And love."

His gaze came up and met hers, and the emotion she saw in his eyes brought tears to her own. He reached out and brushed her cheek.

"You have every right to know what you've asked so many times about those two dates, Charlotte. And the only reason I couldn't bring myself to talk about them was because I was afraid if I did, you'd see me the way I always feared I was—a man without true feeling, someone cold and, ultimately underneath it all, heartless. And of all people, if you reacted in a way that confirmed my worst fears, I'd be forced to admit to myself what I never wanted to face, that I was a monster, a fraud, and an imposter. And worse, I'd be someone unworthy of any love, especially yours."

Charlotte could no longer be still, and so she did the only thing she could while lying in a hospital bed. She brought his hands to her lips and placed a kiss on his knuckles. There was nothing in the world that could lead her to believe he was heartless or unworthy of her love, but she also knew that saying this wouldn't make him believe it.

And so she had her own confession to make.

"I don't need to know about what those two dates mean to you anymore, Damian. Not because I think it will change how I feel about you, because it won't, but because it was never fair of me to give you that ultimatum in the first place—give me your truth or our relationship is over?" She'd never stated it so baldly before, but at the end of the day, that was the choice she'd given him. And it had been grossly unfair in so many ways.

"You saw so much of me," she started to explain. "And I don't mean how much time we spent together. I mean that you *saw* me. You talked to me about my childhood, and you went with me to my therapist, you helped me manage my trauma. And you did it all with this bottomless well of generosity and love.

"You aren't perfect, but our relationship felt so perfect to me. Yes, we bickered and yes, we had our moments, but I'd never, ever been as close to someone as I was to you, not even Matty in some ways. But then the doubts started creeping in, the demons from my past that insisted nothing good ever lasted. And I became a cliché." She offered him a rueful smile and he pulled her hand back and kissed *her* knuckles. Keeping her hand wrapped in his and pressed against his cheek, his gaze urged her to continue.

"I got scared," she said bluntly. "And because I was scared, I started to look for things that were wrong. I started to look for reasons why you couldn't or didn't love me as much as you said you did or as much as your behavior showed me. And so when you refused to tell me about what those dates meant to you, I took it as a sign that you didn't really love me because if you did, you would have trusted me. But the truth is, if you'd told me, I would have just found something else to pin my fears on. With my obsession with those dates, I'd put us in an untenable position, and I now know that's because I never asked myself the most important question of all—how best *I* could love *you*.

"I had made it all about how much you did or didn't love me when I should have been focusing on how much I did—do— love you. And because I couldn't bring myself to focus on *that* question, everything that comes with love—mainly respect—I withheld from you too."

Again, he brought her hand to his lips and held it there. She curled her fingers around his more tightly, and for a moment, they simply existed together. Their truths were big, they were hard, and they weren't very pretty, but despite the weight of them, Charlotte felt a burden ease between them.

"I love you, Damian. And I respect you," she said. "I don't ever need you to tell me about those two dates unless you want to. I care because I know they are something painful for you, but I don't want to be the kind of partner who makes demands on your pain, and I can't tell you how sorry I am that I *was* that person.

"I trust you, more than anyone else I know, and I trust that you love me—that you truly, deeply, and honestly love me," she said, echoing the words he'd used earlier. "And it might have taken some drastic circumstances for me to figure this out, but just as importantly, I finally trust myself. I trust myself to be strong enough to love you without conditions and without fear."

At her words, Damian bowed his head, still holding her hand tight in his. After a moment, she untangled her fingers from his and cupped his face, bringing it up so that his eyes met hers. In that moment, she wished she were more mobile. She wished that she could rise from the bed and pull him to her and hold onto him, feel him holding her. But though her mind and heart were willing, her body had a few objections. And so instead, she offered him a tremulous smile.

His dark eyes studied her for a moment, and then he turned his lips to touch her palm, then brushed the backs of his fingers across her cheek.

"So we're in this together? For keeps this time?" he said.

She didn't bother to stop the tear she felt tracking down her face. She nodded. "For keeps this time," she said.

Slowly, he leaned forward and touched his lips to hers. A promise, sealed with a kiss. When he pulled back, they stared at each other for a long moment, and slowly, they both began to smile. Big, goofy, happy smiles.

"Well, that looks promising," Dominic said as the door flew open and he entered the room with Jake trailing behind.

"It is," Charlotte said, enjoying the look of surprise her answer brought to Damian's face. She was usually the more circumspect of the two, but things were going to change. At least in some ways.

"Excellent, so glad you're awake," Jake said, handing her a laptop.

"She's barely awake, McMullen," Damian groused when she pulled her hand from his and took the device.

"'Barely awake' is still awake," he countered. "Now, can you help us with the password?" he asked her.

She glanced at the computer. "I don't even know whose computer this is."

"It's Mira's," Dominic said, not a little smug.

"You saved it?" she asked, taking another look at the device and the quirky, cartoon holographic sticker Mira had put in the upper left corner at some point.

"I tossed it onto a nearby boat when we jumped into the water," Dominic said. "It was a little shaken up, but if we can get into it, our tech guy thinks he can probably repair anything that might have come loose."

"Why on earth would you think Charlotte would know Mira's password?" Damian demanded, still sounding grumpy.

"Try this," she said, handing the device back. She had a good idea of the code, but she'd rather the computer stay in FBI control. "132724575990," she said.

"You got that?" Dominic asked Jake. In response, Jake tapped his head and recited the numbers back.

"Why in the world would you know that?" Damian said.

Charlotte shrugged. "I don't, not for certain. But it's the same code Simon had on his key box and it's the birth days of Mira, her mom, and Simon along with each of their birth years. Mira is a bit sentimental and I know she would have had to change her password when she logged on from an unknown WiFi, so I'm just guessing she used the same one as her dad."

"And she did," Jake confirmed, having opened the computer as she'd been speaking and typed in the code.

"Good, now you can leave," Damian said. "Charlotte needs to rest."

"I don't need to rest. I want to know what happened. How did you know something was wrong?" she asked Dominic.

He opened his mouth to respond, but before he could, a woman walked in. She drew up short when she saw Dominic and Jake, and after staring at them for a moment, her gaze bounced to Charlotte, then to Damian, and then back to Dominic and Jake. Both of whom grinned at the attractive nurse.

"Good lord," she said, turning her attention to Charlotte and waggling her eyebrows. "I would not at all be surprised if you're a bit hotter than normal right now." As she spoke, she walked to the bedside and shoved Jake and Dominic aside so she could take Charlotte's temperature. When she finished with that, the nurse took her blood pressure and examined her eyes.

"The doctor said all your tests and scans look good. You might feel a little nauseated—"

"Is she pregnant?" Jake asked.

"You're such an ass, McMullen," Damian muttered.

"What? Look at you both. You guys would have beautiful babies," he said. Then with a grin, he turned to the nurse. "Don't you think they'd have beautiful babies?"

She rolled her eyes and shook her head, making Charlotte laugh. "Should they chose to go that route, I'm sure the baby or babies will be darling," she said, reaching for Charlotte's chart. "Now, as I was saying. You might feel a little nauseated from all the water you took in today, especially since it was saltwater. But just try to eat light and keep something in your stomach. It should pass in a day, no more than two. The doctor gave you another shot of antibiotics, and we'll send you home with some pills. The doctor will need to take one more look at your chart, but if she agrees with me that all looks well, we'll discharge you, and you can go rest at home."

Everything the nurse said sounded good to Charlotte, especially the part about being able to be home in Damian's bed and she gave his hand a little squeeze.

"When will the doctor be in to check?" Damian asked.

"Not too long," she responded as Alexis and Beni walked in. The nurse hung the chart on the end of the bed, and again, her gaze bounced between them all. It didn't take an FBI agent to see she was wondering who all these people were. But she held her curiosity in check and the only thing she said before leaving them alone was to issue a warning not to tire Charlotte out.

As soon as the door closed behind her, Alexis held up a bag. "I picked up some clothes from Damian's for you."

Damian rose and took the bag from Alexis with one hand as his other stroked her hair. "Since I doubt any of you are planning on leaving anytime soon, why don't you use the time between now and when the doctor discharges Charlotte to fill her in so that when she gets home, she can rest?" he said.

Charlotte shot each of his teammates an apologetic look. Yes, she understood he was feeling a little tetchy right now, but he didn't have to take it out on them. Thankfully, none of them seemed to mind, and Beni perched on the end of her bed while Dominic and Jake pulled a couple of chairs over and Alexis leaned against the wall.

"So how did you know something was wrong, Dominic?" she asked. "And thank you, by the way, for saving us." Damian's hand paused mid-stroke, but then he continued. She was pretty sure his hesitation had come from the reminder of just how close they'd come to dying rather than from any objection to her praising Dominic for saving them, when *he'd* been the one to pull her from the boat.

"I started chatting with the harbormaster after you guys went through the gate," Dominic said, leaning back in his chair. "We chatted about the weather and other inconsequential things, and then he asked about Ambassador O'Conner. He said the other law enforcement guy had told him about Mira and he was genuinely sorry to hear about her accident.

"As you can imagine, that caught my attention, and I asked him who had stopped by earlier. He didn't know the guy's name but said he thought he was FBI like we were. I asked him to describe him and he said he was Indian—or of Indian origin, to be more precise, because he had a West Indian accent—but that was about all he remembered. That was also all I needed to hear before deciding you two needed to get off that boat. I knew none of us had been by and the only two other agents on the island aren't Indian. Nothing ever good comes when someone is impersonating law enforcement." Dominic shared a look with each of his teammates. Charlotte supposed being able to read situations, the way Dominic had, was part of their training, but even so...

"You knew there'd be an explosion just by hearing that some guy came by and claimed to be law enforcement? What if he actually was? I mean you guys aren't the only game in town," she pointed out. "The island does have a police force."

"He wasn't in uniform and the police officers all wear uniforms," Dominic answered.

"What if he were a detective," she countered.

"Are you seriously arguing with Dominic's instinct when it saved your life?" Alexis asked, sounding more curious than annoyed. Which, on reflection, would have been a reasonable response from them all.

"Sorry," she said, casting him an apologetic look. He shrugged and smiled at her.

"I'm just glad I was right," he said.

"Contrary to how I might have just sounded, so am I," she said, reaching up and taking Damian's hand in hers. It didn't escape her notice that four sets of eyes watched her movement.

"I'm grateful for your instinct, but I am curious how you went from knowing something *could* be wrong to believing strongly enough that it was a bomb, that you pulled us both into the water," she asked Dominic.

"I didn't know at first, but honestly, it's what I would have done. If whoever is behind this came after you and Mira, it's only logical they'd come after the ambassador next. It would be unlikely, with the Diplomatic Security Services all over him now, that they'd ever get to him in DC, so that leaves getting to him when he came back," he answered.

"By doing something like setting a bomb to go off that was triggered by, for example, unlocking the galley door," Charlotte finished the train of logic.

"Beni did say you were a smart one," Dominic said with a wink.

Charlotte laughed and shook her head. "I grew up around some of the worst examples of humanity you can imagine, but I'm not sure even I would have made the leap from an unknown law enforcement officer to a bomb."

"To be fair, I wasn't a hundred percent sure it was a bomb until I got close and heard a couple of telltale clicks," Dominic said.

Damian squeezed her hand. Thank god Dominic hadn't hesitated.

"So not to state the obvious," she started, "but this means that at least two people are involved, doesn't it? Because whoever attacked me most definitely wasn't Indian and we don't know who attacked Mira, so maybe there are even three?"

"I'd wager there are even more than that," Jake chimed in. "The man who attacked you and the man who set the bomb may be the only enforcers, but if this has anything to do with something going on at the World Bank, I'd bet my pension there are more than a few people involved."

"Which brings me to my next question," Charlotte said. "What *do* you think is going on? Because I sure as hell have no idea."

Beni shrugged. "Right now, neither do we. But now we have Mira's computer. Maybe it will shed some light on the discrepancy she mentioned to Ahmed, and maybe that will give us something. And even if it doesn't, knowing what leads *not* to follow can sometimes be more valuable than knowing which ones *to* follow."

Silence fell on the group and in the momentary stillness, she rubbed her thumb along Damian's hand just to absorb the feel of him. But as she did, a dark thought slithered up her spine.

"It didn't occur to me, probably because I didn't want it to, but do you think Ahmed and Tim might be behind this and if so, was it monumentally stupid of me to insist on speaking with them today?" she asked, directing the question to Damian who still stood by her side.

"I mean, if it was something Mira said while she was visiting with them that caused the first domino to fall, was going back..." She had to face the possibility that her insistence on talking with Mira's friends might have tipped their hand. Before today, they'd thought she was dead. But now, if Tim and Ahmed were involved, then they not only knew she was alive, but they knew Damian was involved as well, and that meant they knew that the FBI now suspected something to do with the project might not be what it seemed.

"Tim and Ahmed weren't the only ones Mira saw that day," Damian pointed out, gently. "Sophie was there as well, and it's possible, though we didn't ask, that they ran into others while they were out and about."

"And while Director Shah is scarily cunning," Jake weighed in, "She's not about to dangle one of her people out for bait, let alone a civilian. If she thought Tim and Ahmed were involved, she wouldn't have agreed so readily."

"But it *is* possible," she half asked, half insisted.

"Yes," Alexis said, as blunt as ever. "It is. Both of the men have solid records of working in the field and both are very well regarded. But they are also both inching toward retirement so their priorities—and loyalties—might be changing. We're already looking into them."

Charlotte didn't like the idea of two people Mira considered friends involved in anything meant to harm her, but she'd seen enough people turn on each other to know that when power and money were involved, friendship could often fall by the wayside.

"So what now?" she asked.

"Now we head back to Damian's while you wait for the doctor to discharge you," Beni said, rising from her position at the end of the bed. "We'll do what we do best and continue digging. The good news about the bomb is that there are a couple of businesses nearby that have CCTV so we may get something on those feeds."

"That's our Beni, always with the silver lining," Dominic said, pushing to his feet. "And if you were wondering," he added, turning to Charlotte with a grin, "that was sarcasm."

Charlotte rolled her eyes. "Yeah, I got that. But I'll take blunt honesty over fluffy appeasements any day."

"That true, Rodriguez?" Jake asked, even as he shuffled everyone toward the door.

For the first time in what felt like too long, Damian chuckled. "I tried fluffy compliments once. She almost threw a drink in my face."

Charlotte laughed at that. "We were at some stupid political event and you told that sheik that I was the sunshine to your flower petals," she said with a playful punch.

Damian gave her an unrepentant grin. "He seemed the sort to appreciate the poetry."

"That wasn't poetry," Alexis said, trailing everyone out the door, their laughter filling the hallway. "That was some serious eighth-grade angsty shit."

"Nah," he said. "It was *at least* high school angsty shit."

"I wrote better lyrics when I was ten," Alexis called back just as the door shut behind her and the others, leaving her and Damian alone.

"Lyrics?" Charlotte raised a brow in question at Damian.

"I'll only mention this because I know you've met kings and queens and such and so won't freak out, but her dad is Jasper Wright."

Charlotte's mind immediately started to place the name, and when it did, she drew back. "You're kidding me?"

Damian shook his head.

"Huh," she said, sorting through her few interactions with Alexis with this new lens. "I guess that explains a lot," she said. And it did. Having your dad be one of the most famous R&B performers of the past several decades probably tended to make one cautious about just who you invited into your life and how much of your life you shared with others. It also explained her excellent fashion sense. Sometimes, but not always, money did buy taste. Especially when your mother was a former supermodel.

It did not, however, explain how she ended up being an FBI agent.

"How…"

"We have no idea," Damian said, anticipating her question. "Jake asked her once why she applied to the academy. Being the excellent agents we are, we all know there's more to it than what she'd told us—"

"Which was?"

"That she needed to do something useful with her life."

Charlotte snorted at that. "There are lots of ways to be useful in the world that are far less demanding or specific than joining the FBI. I'd give anything to see her application," she added. Most applicants were law enforcement or former military, but Damian hadn't said she'd been either, so there must have been something else that had caught the attention of the review committee.

"As would we all. I wouldn't mind seeing Jake's either. He went from being a pro-surfer to joining the academy. At least Beni, Dominic, and I had some experience with criminals and terrorists."

Charlotte started to ask about Jake, but cut herself off when the doctor walked in. Fifteen minutes later, the doctor walked out and Charlotte had her discharge papers.

"Ready to go home?" Damian asked, holding up the bag Alexis had brought.

Their gazes caught and held. His question held more meaning than just the words. They would be going *home*. She may not live here on Tildas Island, but together, they had a *home*.

She nodded. "Help me change?"

Slowly, a lascivious grin spread across his face. "It would be my pleasure."

CHAPTER SEVENTEEN

DAMIAN ALREADY KNEW his teammates were waiting for him at his house, but if he'd needed any warning other than the cars in his drive, Steve—who only showed up when Alexis was around —was also waiting for them at the top of the porch steps. His eyes, a bright yellow against his long, black fur, followed them as they approached. He remained sitting, though, with his tail curled around his paws.

"Is he here because Alexis is here?" Charlotte asked as they made their way up the steps.

"Of course. I have no idea how he knows when she's here, but I'm kind of surprised he hasn't made his presence known to her already," Damian said, pointing out a few scratches the seventeen-pound beast had left on his front door from prior visits. His hand was on the knob when he looked over to see Steve winding himself between Charlotte's legs.

"Then again, maybe he had a reason to stay outside and wait," he added.

Charlotte bent down to stroke Steve as Damian opened the door. Immediately the smell of bay rum and spice wafted toward them. The cat perked his head up, then bolted inside.

Charlotte laughed as she stood. "Does he think he's going to get some of whatever it is that's cooking? And what is it that's cooking?" she asked, stepping through the door and into the house. "It smells amazing," she added.

Beni, Alexis, and Jake were all sitting around his dining table —Beni and Jake each had a bottle of beer in front of them while Alexis had a tumbler of whiskey. But it was Dominic who answered.

Walking out of the kitchen, he beamed at Charlotte. "Just a little island-influenced Cajun jerk chicken and rice. It will be ready in about five minutes."

"I have no idea what 'island-influenced Cajun jerk chicken means,' but I'm all for giving it the old college try," she said, taking a seat beside Alexis. Steve jumped onto Alexis's lap and walked in circles, looking for the perfect position to lie down.

"None of us does, but we've stopped asking," Jake said. "I think the only thing he's ever made that wasn't worthy of seconds was that weird banana flan thing."

"I like that weird banana flan thing," Beni said.

"It was the texture, more than anything. The taste was good," Alexis weighed in.

"But don't let them fool you, between the five of us, we ate the whole thing," Damian said as he came out of the kitchen and set a bottle of beer on the table in front of Charlotte. He didn't think she'd last very long before needing to head to bed, but he at least wanted to keep her up long enough to have some dinner.

"We couldn't let it go to waste," Beni said.

"And you got used to the texture after the second helping," Alexis said.

"And I'm not the kind of guy who turns down any sweets," Jake weighed in.

Charlotte laughed at his teammates, and Damian smiled.

Joining the special task force had been the right decision for him, but with Charlotte in his home, with her back in his life, he knew it had also been a good decision. Yes, if he hadn't joined the task force, he wouldn't have been anywhere near the island when Charlotte had been stabbed, but more importantly, he was pretty sure that he'd needed to shake things up in his life a little bit to be ready to have her back in it. He'd stagnated in his position in the DC office, and then breaking up with Charlotte had made him stall out even more.

Moving to the islands had been the first step in breaking free of the pattern he'd allowed himself to fall into. And working with his new colleagues—men and women who both challenged and supported him—had helped him start to look at, and live, his life a little more fully, a little more openly. And he knew, beyond a doubt, that his little life-course adjustment had changed him just enough to be open in the way he needed to be to have Charlotte back in his life—back in his life in a way that was deeper and steadier than before. And while there might be some awkward moments in the coming weeks as they re-familiarized themselves with each other, their roots were firmly and irrevocably intertwined now.

A few minutes later, the chatter died down as Dominic brought out a large pot and placed it on a trivet in the middle of the table. Steam poured out when he removed the lid, carrying with it smells more subtle than—but just as enticing as—the bay rum.

Everyone seemed to take a moment to appreciate the presentation, but then all pretense was gone and they descended like locusts and devoured the meal.

By unspoken consensus, no one discussed work—or their current situation or all the unanswered questions—while they enjoyed the meal. But as soon as they finished and began sipping on some after-dinner rum-based drink Dominic had concocted and picking at cookies Alexis had produced, Charlotte spoke.

"So did you find anything on Mira's computer," she asked as she sat back from her empty plate and rolled her glass between her hands.

"She'd only worked for the Bank for seven years, but she has a shit ton of files on her computer," Jake said before popping a little ball of coconut covered chocolate into his mouth.

"But she only took over as liaison for the project down here three years before it ended," Beni said, eyeing a cookie but not reaching for it. "So while she has a lot of files, we're only focusing on the ones she has related to the project Tim and Ahmed oversaw."

"Do you know who the Task Team Leader was?" Charlotte asked. "I forgot to ask Tim and Ahmed."

"What's a Task Team Leader?" Dominic asked.

Charlotte took a sip of her drink before answering. "The way the projects usually work is they have someone who oversees the entire project, like a CEO would, and everything related is their responsibility. That's the TL."

"Depending on the size of the project," she continued. "The TL will have people like Tim and Ahmed working more in a senior project management capacity—managing the actual work, dealing with contracts, tracking schedules, that sort of thing. Tim and Ahmed are kind of in the sweet spot as far as project organization is concerned because they have a tremendous amount of control but only over their sphere of influence whereas the TL, again, depending on the size of the project, has a huge sphere of influence but sometimes very little control."

Charlotte gave the team a wry smile. "And that, my friend was a long explanation for what essentially amounts to asking who Tim and Ahmed reported to."

"It's a good question to ask, but it seems like you might have had another reason for raising it other than just curiosity," Alexis said.

Charlotte finished her drink and set the tumbler on the table. Damian reached over and took her now-free hand in his as she answered. "There has been some trouble in the recent past with some TLs. Well, to be honest, I think the trouble was always there, but people are speaking out more, and the Bank's compliance programs are getting better. But while some of the instances I've heard of have been a little unfair, some have been legitimate concerns and I just wondered if the TL for this project has any kind of reputation we should know about."

"That information will likely be in Mira's files, right?" Damian asked. Charlotte turned to look at him and nodded. Then yawned.

"Need some rest?" he asked with a grin.

She shook her head. "I'm fine. I'd like to see some of Mira's files."

"You need rest," Beni said, pushing back from the table. "And don't argue, it's tedious. The 'I am a woman, and I can do everything' is just as much a cliché as the blond virgin in the horror movies. Do us all a favor and just go do what your body is telling you it needs. We'll cull the through data tonight and then we can all have a fresh look tomorrow."

Damian bit his cheeks to keep from laughing. He had no idea how Charlotte would react, but he was pretty sure that if Beni survived, it would only be because she'd had the good sense to sound practical rather than condescending.

"And we won't be at it very long," Alexis said. "We'll do the initial pass tonight, but since you, Mira, and the ambassador are safe for the moment, we'll all take the opportunity for a little sleep while we can."

Charlotte's gaze bounced around the room. Jake and Dominic were nodding at Alexis's statement. Beni was already seated on the couch with Mira's computer open on her lap.

"At least let me clean up," Charlotte finally said. Damian cast a questioning look at Dominic, who shrugged.

"Sure, go ahead," Dominic said.

Charlotte rose and walked into the kitchen. Dominic held up four fingers, then one by one lowered them. As if on cue, when the last one folded down, Charlotte reappeared in the doorway.

"There's nothing to clean," she said, glaring at Dominic.

"My mama is a chef," he said, his grin unrepentant. "Growing up, some kids got into trouble for not cleaning their rooms or for fighting at school, those kinds of things. In our house, if you wanted to see Mama turn red and steam come out of her ears—which mind you, after once or twice none of us kids did 'cause she's terrifying—all you had to do was leave a pot in the sink. Or worse, crumbs on the counter."

Charlotte smiled. "My mom is a cook. I know *exactly* what you're talking about." She paused and looked at everyone before her gaze fell on Damian, and he knew this was one of those awkward moments he'd been thinking about earlier.

"Why don't you head into bed? I threw some towels in the wash earlier, I'll bring some clean ones to you in a minute, in case you want to shower tonight," he said, giving her an opportunity to head to bed but also letting her know he'd be in to say goodnight—out of sight of his colleagues—shortly.

She nodded, "Thank you. After bathing in the marina today, I think a shower might be in order." She said goodnight to everyone then slipped into his room, closing the door behind her.

"Clean towels isn't the only thing you're going to give her, is it?" Jake said, waggling his eyebrows.

Damian opened his mouth to tell him to shut the fuck up, but Alexis beat him to it.

"I'd tell you to grow up," she said. "But most of the time, your juvenile sense of humor does a good job of cutting the tension that's a common part of the job. However, tonight, I will tell you to shut the fuck up. Rodriguez has nearly lost the woman he loves, not once, but twice. And to top it all off, we still don't know why, who's involved, or how to stop it. If he wants to go tuck her in for the night—hell, if he wants to stay there by her side all night while we go through the computer—then more power to him. Show some respect for the adults in the room, McMullen."

Jake stared at Alexis for a moment, his mouth hanging open. She didn't seem to notice, though, and she rose from her seat and joined Beni on the couch.

"Oh, snap," Dominic said, his quiet voice held just a little bit of awe too.

Jake's eyes flew to Damian and he could see the apology in them.

"You know I'd never—" Jake started, but Damian cut him off with a shake of his head.

"Don't worry about it," Damian said as he rose. "She's right, on all counts. We need your sense of humor, both of yours," he added with a nod to Dominic. "But she's also right about me needing to be with Charlotte tonight. I'll come back out and help you all with the files, but I need a little bit of time to be with her. To be grateful that she's here and that she's with me."

Jake nodded, and Damian left the room to retrieve the clean towels from the dryer. When he passed back through the dining room, both Jake and Dominic were standing and appeared to be waiting for him.

"Yes?" Damian said, giving them both an expectant look. He *really* wanted to be in with Charlotte right now.

"This isn't about having our approval or anything, because we know that isn't relevant," Dominic started. "But we want you to know that we like Charlotte, and as often as we might act like pubescent boys at times, it's clear to all of us that there is nothing childish about what the two of you have."

"And so," Jake interjected. "We may keep teasing you about it, because hey, a leopard can't change its spots, but she's one of us now. Not *literally* one of us," he said with a grin, "but you know, *one of us.*"

And Damian did know. Charlotte was more than just a civilian they had a duty to protect; she was part of their family. He'd had this kind of comradery with his Army brothers, but this was the first time he'd felt it since joining the FBI. And despite the relatively short time the group had been together, he didn't doubt Jake or Dominic's sincerity.

Something eased in his chest, a small weight lifted—he'd always known he could count on his team to do their job, but now he wasn't alone anymore in thinking of this case as more than just a case.

"Thanks," he said. "Both of you. There's a long history between Charlotte and me, but she means everything to me, and it's good to know that you don't just have my back, but you have hers, too."

For a moment, the three shared one of those manly-emotional moments where no one said a thing, but they all had the feels. Then Jake grinned and nodded toward the towels he carried.

"You better hurry. You wouldn't want to keep Charlotte waiting for her *towels.*"

Damian let out a snort as he pushed past his teammates. "Such an ass, McMullen."

He left the two men snickering as he eased the bedroom door open and stepped inside. He couldn't see Charlotte from where he stood, but he could hear the shower. God help him.

Taking one for the team, he entered the steamy room to find her standing under the spray, her eyes closed, her head tipped back. Water ran down the gentle curves of her body; the white waterproof bandage on her right side the only thing marring what Damian otherwise considered the most perfect sight he'd ever seen.

Moving as if she sensed his presence, Charlotte shifted her face out of the spray. Her eyelashes fluttered then opened, and she turned her head toward him. Their gazes held and in that long moment, a hunger rose up inside him, pulling the breath from his lungs. He wanted to bury himself inside her, he wanted to hear her call his name, he wanted to feel her skin against his. But more than all that, he simply wanted to hold her close—as close as two people could get in both body and soul—and never let her go.

Not that he'd ever really let her go before. Yes, they might have been physically apart, but without a doubt, his heart and his mind had been, and would always be, with her.

She held his gaze as she turned the water off. Then opening the glass door of the shower, she didn't bother waiting for a towel as she stepped out and walked to him. Her fingers were wet and warm as she cupped his face and drew him into a kiss. A kiss that took all his willpower to keep as just a kiss.

He loved her, he wanted her, and he knew she wanted him. But it wasn't going to happen. Not now. No, the first time he and Charlotte came together after the long year apart, it would not be a hurried affair with his teammates on the other side of the door waiting for him. And he knew, judging by the way Charlotte was careful not to press her wet body against his and soak his clothes, she knew it too.

Slowly, she drew back, and her dark eyes fixed on his. "I know you have work to do, but I just needed that."

That elicited a smile from him.

"I did too," he said, dropping all but one towel on the counter, then wrapping her up in the one he still held. When he had it tucked between her breasts, he handed her another one for her hair. "I *want* a whole lot more..."

Charlotte smiled. "So do I, but you have work to do." She swung her long black hair to the side and used the towel to squeeze water from it.

"We need to change your bandage," he said, taking a reluctant step back.

She scrunched her nose at his comment, but nodded. "Give me five minutes to manage my hair and brush my teeth?"

"I'll go get the stuff ready," he responded, not wanting to leave her, but knowing for his own sanity that it would probably be better to remove himself from the room.

But what little cooling effect the short distance had given him vanished when she walked back into his bedroom wearing nothing but one of his white t-shirts. "Are you trying to kill me?" he asked.

She smiled.

He reached out and pulled her to him. "You are, aren't you?"

Her arms came around his neck and her fingers dug into his hair. "I'm the one who's going to be lying in this bed with nothing to do. At least you'll be out being distracted by work."

"You need to sleep," he said, backing toward the bed and bringing her with him.

"I'm sure I will, eventually," she said, placing her lips against his neck as he sank onto the bed, her legs straddling his.

"Do you need some help?" he asked as hands inched up her hips and gripped her waist. Charlotte drew back to look at him just as he pulled her down and rocked against her. A surge of satisfaction washed over him when he heard Charlotte suck in a breath and her eyes closed.

"Your teammates," she said. She may be cautious, but she was still rocking against him.

"Can you be quiet?" he asked, nipping lightly on her ear lobe.

"Like 'in the coatroom of the Slovakian Embassy' quiet or 'in the bathroom stall of the Met' quiet?" she asked. He couldn't help it, but he barked out a laugh at the memory of those two encounters. Neither of them had ever been particularly demur when it came to sex but that she was now using those two instances as a yardstick struck him as *so Charlotte*. And so helpful.

"'Met' quiet," he said.

She made a humming sound as she worked her way with her lips along his jaw. "Yes, I can do that."

"Excellent," he said, then he cupped her face and pulled her in for a long deep kiss as his hand reached between them. It was the only word spoken for the next few minutes as he teased and pleasured her. And when Charlotte finally went rigid in his arms, and he felt her clenching around his fingers, he had to bite his tongue. There was so much he wanted to say—so many things he wanted to do to her—but it would have to wait.

When the tremors subsided, he slowly withdrew his hand as she slumped against him, her breath coming in warm puffs on his neck. He stayed that way for a moment, just holding her, but then the sound of Jake calling to the team from the kitchen to ask if anyone wanted any coffee, brought him back.

Gently, he slid Charlotte from his lap and onto his bed. She kept her languid gaze on him as he lifted her shirt and began the process of changing her bandage. When he was done, he pulled her shirt down over her hip and tucked the blanket around her.

She rolled to her back and placed her hand on his chest. "You'll come to bed, to this bed, tonight after you're done working?"

He nodded. Nothing was going to keep him away.

"I love you," she said, her eyes already drifting closed.

The simple statement brought a smile to his lips. He picked her hand up and kissed her knuckles. "I love you, too. And I especially love that I can still make you come in less than three minutes."

Her eyes were shut, but she smiled. "It's one of my favorite talents of yours, too."

He chuckled then leaned down to kiss her. "Sleep well. I'll be in later."

She mumbled something he couldn't make out. Placing another kiss on the palm of her hand, he set it down on her chest.

Rising from the bedside, he took one last lingering look at her then left to join his team. They had a criminal to catch.

CHAPTER EIGHTEEN

DAMIAN CRACKED his eyes open to see the sunlight filtering into his room. He looked at the clock and noted he'd had about five hours of sleep—not bad for when he was working a case. It was also not bad to wake up with Charlotte wrapped around him. He turned his head to look at her. Curled against his side, she had her head on his shoulder, an arm draped over his chest, and a bare leg flung over his. He smiled, for as reserved as she generally was in public, it had surprised him to learn all those years ago, that she was actually a big cuddler in bed. He was glad that hadn't changed.

He was also glad she was still asleep. She might have doubted Beni's assertion that she needed rest, but clearly, she had. After his teammates had left, he'd returned to the bedroom and found her sound asleep with the bedside light on. And she'd slept through the noise he'd made getting ready for bed and barely seemed to notice when he'd slid between the sheets and pulled her to him. At some point, her body must have recognized his next to hers, and she'd curled up against him like he was her personal pillow. Which he could think of a lot worse things to be.

Gently, he stroked her arm as he considered what he and the team had learned the night before, which was, admittedly, not as much as they'd hoped. Then again, had a smoking gun *ever* been dropped in his lap?

They hadn't found anything about a change in contractor in Mira's records, so either Ahmed had misunderstood the question, or it was something Mira had heard but had no record of. He supposed they just might not have *found* the record yet—they had a forensic tech person going over the computer this morning—but given how organized Mira's files were, it was hard to believe that if she had one, they wouldn't have found it already.

The only other potentially weird thing they'd discovered was that the original Team Leader on the project had been removed a little less than a year before the project had wrapped up. The original TL had moved on to manage a project in Senegal and so there wasn't anything to indicate there'd been an issue. But Damian still had a few questions to ask Charlotte about the inner workings of the Bank—such as, was it unusual to move someone so close to the end of a project, and how would the new TL have been selected?

One good note was that they *had* cleared Tim and Ahmed from any suspicion. Charlotte had been worried about that—about what that might do to Mira if it had been people she considered her friends behind the attacks, and so it was nice to at least be able to allay that concern.

As he watched the shadows shift on the ceiling, he considered Tim and Ahmed. The questions he'd planned to ask Charlotte were ones they could answer as well. They'd know as much as she would and would be able to give him and the team some insight into the TLs themselves. That way, Charlotte could continue sleeping.

With his mind on a new plan, he slid from beneath Charlotte

—not an easy task when she was so warm and pliant—and made his way to the bathroom to shower.

Fifteen minutes later, he walked back out, a towel wrapped around his hips, to see Charlotte sitting up on the side of the bed, her long legs curled underneath her, looking at him. Like she'd been waiting. She kept her gaze on him as she set a glass of water down. The reminder of her pain, and that she'd likely just finished taking a pain pill, should have doused the lust heating his blood, but it didn't. It didn't help that there was no mistaking the look she was giving him.

"You're injured, Charlotte," he said, staying where he was, five feet away.

"Then maybe you need to take care of me," she said.

One side of his lips quirked up. "Cliché, Charlotte. I think you can do better than that."

She held his gaze and, god help him, he could practically hear everything she wanted him to do to her. And he was on board with all of it. If only she weren't in pain.

"Charlotte." He tried to sound stern, or if not stern, at least cautionary. In response, she pulled the t-shirt slowly up and over her head, then dropped it on the floor.

At the sight of her, desire, lust, and *need* hit him so hard he physically jerked. Between that and his arousal, his towel fell to the floor. Charlotte's eyes dropped and lingered, as if remembering everything about how they'd felt—and could feel —together.

"You have two choices, Damian," she said, her gaze rising to meet his again. "Either I come to you and return the favor from last night, or you come to me and we take our time together."

As much as the idea of Charlotte kneeling before him held a huge amount of appeal, he knew his decision before she'd even finished her sentence. He'd been waiting too long, missed her too much, to do anything other than be as close to her as he could get.

In two strides, he was standing before her. Reaching his hand up, he drew his fingers over her cheek then through her hair, tugging her head back, so she was looking up at him. "We'll go slowly," he said.

"If you insist."

"And if you're in pain, or if anything hurts, you'll tell me right away," he insisted.

She gave him a cat-like smile. "Of course."

He didn't believe her. Not one bit.

"I don't have any condoms," he said, suddenly remembering. That took some of the gleam out of her eye.

"I hadn't," she paused, and her eyes dropped to the bed for a moment before rising again and meeting his. "I haven't been with anyone since we broke up, Damian. I don't know if you have—and I wouldn't begrudge you if you had—but I still have my IUD if you..."

He leaned down and kissed her, slowly maneuvering her back on to the bed until they were lying side-by-side. He drew away as he traced the line of her body—her collarbone, down over her breast and hip, then to her thigh and back again. Cupping her cheek, he bent down and kissed her again before resting his forehead against hers.

"There's been no one for me other than you, Charlotte." He kissed her again, and then, in between reacquainting his lips with her body, he added softly. "Since you walked into my life, there's never been anyone for me but you."

AN HOUR LATER, Charlotte was standing at the stove, stirring scrambled eggs, when Damian came up behind her, wrapped his arms around her waist—careful to avoid her wound—and dropped a kiss on her bare shoulder.

"I don't think I've ever seen you in cut-off shorts before this week," he said.

Wearing a tank top and with her hair up in a loose bun, he had easy access, but she tilted her head to give him more. Good man that he was, he obliged and traced a line with his lips up her neck to her ear where he nipped her earlobe.

"I don't think I've worn cut-offs since I was ten," she said, leaning back into him. "But I have to admit, they are pretty comfortable. I'm not sure if all cut-offs are this comfortable or if this is a result of Alexis's preternatural fashion sense, but I have to admit, all the hang-ups I had about them are slowly fading."

"They look good on you," Damian said, stepping away and opening the fridge. "Not that all the other things you wear don't look good on you, but there's something different seeing you like this. Like maybe we should skip the coffee and go have a rum on the beach," he added with a smile, reminding her of their conversation the day before.

She smiled. "How about I finish making these eggs, and you can spike our coffee then we can sit on your porch and eat. It's not exactly dancing around a bonfire and we'll need some of that radioactive mosquito repellent, but I'm game if you are."

He was up for it, but rather than spike their coffee, he made an executive decision to add a dash of rum to the juice Alexis had brought by. A few minutes later, they were sitting out on the porch, admiring the view of the vast Caribbean Sea. The mosquitos buzzed around but mostly stayed away.

Their peace only lasted ten minutes when a car pulled onto his driveway, and the security app on Damian's phone dinged. He glanced at the image on his phone, "Beni," he said, holding it up for her to see.

"And it looks like Alexis is with her," Charlotte said as the sounds of the car grew louder before finally pulling to a stop at the parking area beside the house.

They finished eating as the two women climbed out of the

car and joined them. Beni took a seat opposite them while Alexis leaned against the porch rail.

"I thought you were going to take that to the forensic tech person," Damian said, nodding to Mira's computer—with its distinctive holographic sticker—that Alexis held.

"How are you feeling today?" she asked Charlotte, ignoring Damian's question.

Charlotte shrugged. "Sore, but alive, and in the grand scheme of things, not too bad."

"Are you still taking pain pills?" Beni asked.

"I took one this morning when I woke up. I think all the retching yesterday did a little bit of a number on my stomach muscles."

"Charlotte," Damian said, not bothering to keep the exasperation from his voice. If she'd told him that an hour and a half ago, their morning would have turned out very differently.

She turned and gave him a cheeky grin. "Don't tell me it wasn't worth it."

He frowned at her. "Not when you're in pain."

She gave a little wave, brushing off his concern. "I assure you, *pain* was not the dominate feeling."

"Glad to hear the healing process is well underway," Beni interjected, reminding them both their conversation wasn't private. "And that you two seemed to have worked things out. In more ways than one," she added with a hint of a smile.

Damian slipped his hand into Charlotte's. "When we broke up, it sucked. Big time," he said. "But the thing was that at least I knew she was still out there, doing her thing, hopefully happy. These last few days made me realize what a chicken shit I'd been that whole time—"

"You weren't the only one," Charlotte said.

"I know," he responded. "You had your own stuff you needed to work through too, but that doesn't change the fact that there was so much I could have done in the past year to fight for you, fight for us. And I didn't do it. I'm such an ass that it took nearly losing you to wake me up to what was really important. I—we—have been given a second chance, and there's no way in hell I'm squandering that."

His words grabbed at her heart and pulled her close. There was so much to say between them and yet, in some ways, she thought they didn't need to speak at all.

Beni cleared her throat.

And maybe, they especially didn't need to speak too much when his teammates were around.

Charlotte turned and looked at Beni, who had an eyebrow cocked. "See, I told you. Not that you didn't know, but seriously, Rodriguez is the biggest sharer I know," she said, making Charlotte laugh.

"It's healthy, though," Alexis said. "And I might suggest that if it feels awkward just to *hear it*," she said with a pointed look at Beni, "then maybe that says more about the receiver than the speaker."

"Yeah, yeah, yeah, Wright," Beni said with a roll of her eyes. "I know I'm emotionally stunted." Then turning to Charlotte, she added, "She's been trying to get me to see a therapist since about the second day we met. At first, it pissed me off. Now I know it just means she cares. In her weird, disassociated way.

"Did you know none of us has ever been to her house? Damian's is like a second home to all of us. Dominic has a condo on the beach, so that's where we go when we want to be on the water. Jake lives on a boat, so while we've been there, we don't hang out there much, and I have a place in Havensted, so my place is always the meeting ground when we want to go out on the town. But Alexis is like a vault, none of us even have an idea of where she lives."

Charlotte glanced at Alexis, who was watching Beni. Then a small, rueful smile tugged at Alexis's lips. "It's way more interesting to think about other people's psychology than my own."

All three laughed at the uncomfortable truth of that statement.

"So can we be done sharing for the day? And get back to work?" Beni asked, gesturing to the computer Alexis still held. Alexis handed the computer to Charlotte, who reached out and took it.

"Like Damian said, we were going to take it to a forensic tech person, but then this morning, we both—independently—concluded that we wanted you to dig around in it first," Alexis said.

"Me?" Charlotte repeated at the same time Damian asked, "Why?"

Alexis's gaze bounced between the two. "Why," Damian repeated.

Alexis looked to Beni, who answered. "We don't have a concrete reason. We have no reason to suspect turning the computer over to another member of the FBI will pose a concern, but both Alexis and I had a strong gut feeling that Charlotte needed to look at it first, that maybe she'd see something we didn't. If we hand it over to a tech, it could be days before we get anything back. If Charlotte finds something now, then great, we have the information sooner rather than later. If she doesn't, there's no harm done and we'll take it to the tech tomorrow."

Judging by the way Damian had straightened in his seat, she could tell he wasn't happy with something, but Beni's explanation made sense to her. She wasn't sure she'd find anything, but she *was* more familiar with the work Mira did than the team, and if there were something out of the ordinary, she'd probably have a better chance of spotting it. Besides, Damian had told her about the timing of the TL change and it had struck her as odd, too. It wasn't as though changing out a TL that late in a project never happened, but it was unusual and she wanted the opportunity to see if Mira had any notes on the transfer.

"I'll set up inside," she said, rising from her seat and only wincing a little bit. "I just want to refill my coffee, and then I'll get started." Leaving Damian to his teammates, she made her way inside, setting the computer down on the dining table on her way to the kitchen.

Returning to the table, with a fresh cup of coffee in hand, she booted up Mira's computer and was gratified to see it was fully charged. And judging by the number of files she saw, Charlotte suspected she was going to need every minute of that battery life.

Glancing up through the front window, she could see Damian and Beni in a heated conversation while Alexis just looked on. She had no idea what the two could be discussing that would cause them to be snapping at each other—because based on their body language that was exactly what they were doing—but she figured her attention was better fixed on Mira's computer, and so she dropped her gaze and went to work.

Her first stop was to click open the file for the Caribbean project. True to Mira form, within the main folder were various sub-folders covering everything from monthly and annual reports to tourism stats. All told, there were about fifteen sub-folders, each filled with documents, spreadsheets, and even further sub-folders.

For a moment, Charlotte just stared at the list, the volume of data overwhelming her. But then, with a shake of her head, she dove in, opting to start with the sub-folder named "Transition Documents."

She lost track of time as she waded through the file. She heard Damian enter the room, but as she didn't hear Alexis or Beni, she assumed they must have left. Rather than join her, Damian took his computer and sat down on the couch. Propping his feet up on the coffee table, he set the laptop on his lap and proceeded to do whatever FBI agents did in the middle of a case.

As for her, she returned to the document she'd been perusing—the conflict of interest and anti-corruption checks the Bank had conducted on all the contractors who'd successfully bid for various aspects of work. Including the contractor for the roads portion of the project that Mira had asked Ahmed about.

Noting the name, Charlotte then opened the master accounting spreadsheet and tracked the contractor. Sure enough, KLJ Construction had won the bid and completed the project—one of only two contractors that looked to have done it on time and within budget, too.

Charlotte frowned. Why would Mira have thought they'd considered changing out that company? Where had she'd heard that? And most importantly, did it matter?

Charlotte sat back in her seat, but her eyes remained fixed on the open document. The truth was, there were a hundred-and-one places Mira could have heard that kind of rumor, but Mira also had enough experience to tell the difference between a rumor and statements based in fact. And she wouldn't have asked Ahmed about just a rumor. Which meant she must have seen it in a report or heard it from someone who knew first hand.

Charlotte drummed her fingers on the table as she thought through the problem. If it were something Mira had heard, there'd be no record. If she'd seen it in a report, Charlotte might be able to do a search and see if she could find the reference. But the overarching question was, did it matter?

"What are you thinking over there?" Damian asked.

She turned her head and looked at him. "I'm not sure."

"Talk to me," he said, staying where he was. Which was probably a good thing. She needed to concentrate and it would be easy to get distracted if he were too close.

"The question Mira asked Ahmed. It bugs me," she said.

"Tell me why."

She shook her head. "It could be nothing, just a misunderstanding. But Mira was good at what she did, and she wouldn't have asked the question if she hadn't either heard about it from someone she trusted or seen it somewhere. But, where I'm really getting hung up, was the question of whether or not it matters. Is it wasted time to try to track down the origin of Mira's information? It was such an innocuous comment, could it really be what triggered all of this?"

Damian rose and walked toward her, grabbing her empty coffee cup on his way into the kitchen. "More coffee?" he asked.

She nodded, and he put the kettle on then leaned against the counter. "There's something about it that's bugging you. Talk to me about that."

She sat back in her chair and folded her arms across her chest. "What's getting to me is the fact that that one question, as inconsequential as it might be, seems to be the only thing that seems out of place. Based on our conversation with Tim and Ahmed, the rest of the day was exactly what you'd think it would be, sightseeing and talking shop, so hardly likely to be anything that would raise a red flag. But since she only mentioned it to Ahmed, and both Ahmed and Tim have been cleared of any part of this, doesn't that argue for it being irrelevant?"

The kettle whistled, and she paused while Damian poured the coffee into the French press, his forearms flexing with the movement.

"You have the sexiest arms," she found herself saying. It was not the best timing she'd ever had, but judging by the glint in Damian's eye, he didn't seem to mind the leap in topic.

"Arms, huh?" he said, dropping her mug of well-sugared coffee on the table in front of her. He set his own cup down and placed one hand on the back of her chair and the other on the table. She tilted her head up, and he obliged her with a lingering kiss.

When he pulled back, she smiled. "Your lips are pretty nice too, but I have to say, there is something about your arms." She wrapped a hand around each of his forearms, appreciating the texture and flex of his muscles under her palms.

"You have no idea the kinds of things I want to do to you right now," he said.

She slid her hands over his shoulders, then cupped his jaw and pulled him into another kiss. "I think I have a pretty good idea, but unfortunately, we have a few other things to get to first."

He held her gaze for a moment, then sighed and straightened away from her. "You're right," he said, picking up his coffee. "So what would be the implications of changing a contractor mid-project?" he asked as he returned to his computer on the couch.

There were several, but as she opened her mouth to talk through a few, the security app on Damian's phone dinged, cutting her off. He picked up the device, glanced at the picture, then made a face.

"It's the whole team," he said. "I'm surprised they held off for this long. Ready for an invasion?"

"If the invasion means we resolve this soon, I'm all for it," she said. "The sooner we sort this out, the sooner we can get to important things. Like dancing on the beach and drinking rum."

"I'll hold you to that," he said, rising again from his seat to open the door. Two minutes later, his four teammates poured in.

"I'll make the coffee," Beni said, heading straight for the kitchen.

"More juice," Alexis said, holding up a glass jug as she followed Beni.

"And what do *you* have for us?" Charlotte asked Dominic and Jake.

"I have the identity of the man who stabbed you," Dominic announced.

"The fuck, you say," Damian said, reaching for the file Dominic held out. He opened it and started reading as he walked toward her.

Setting the file on the table in front of her, he continued to read over her shoulder as she glanced down, her gaze quickly catching on the picture paper-clipped to the inside. She scanned his name on the page below, Fredrick Althorp, then returned her attention to the picture. Fred was a big man. Judging by the mug shot, he stood a hair over six foot three, but he had a barrel chest and thick, hairy arms. Awkwardly, he was holding his arrest number so that his thumb was visible—his nail-less left thumb.

"Is it him, Charlotte?" Damian asked, his hand a reassuring anchor on her shoulder.

"It certainly could be," she said. "His thumbnail is one thing, but he seems the right size and has the same hairy arms."

"How'd you find him?" Damian asked, pushing away from the chair, leaving her to stare at the information.

"I took the shortlist of photos Charlotte went through the other night and just started digging," he said. "Some were easy to eliminate as the pictures from the airport included images of both hands, and when I enlarged them, I could see if he had all his nails. There were about seven that I couldn't eliminate, but Freddy is the only one with a record, and so I started with him and bam, he was nice enough to pose for his mug shot with his left thumb exposed."

Beni came over, unclipped the picture from the file, and held it up. "I wonder if the Alexandria police had him pose like that on purpose?"

The team murmured a few responses, but Charlotte dropped her attention back to the actual report Dominic had included. It appeared that three years ago, Freddy had been arrested by the Alexandria, Virginia police for threatening a congresswoman. His last known address was in a small town outside the DC beltway. He didn't appear to have any consistent source of income.

"He didn't just fly down here to stab me, did he?" she asked. The room fell abruptly silent.

Jake cleared his throat. "Uh, no, we don't think so."

"Someone hired him to do it," she clarified.

"We think that's likely," Alexis responded.

"So even if we get this guy," she said, pointing to the picture Beni still held, "it may not resolve anything."

"It might not, but it will be more than we had before," Alexis said. "Between Fredrick and the man who set up the bomb on Ambassador O'Conner's boat, we might get one of them to talk."

"And once we get one talking, we can start to unravel the threads," Damian said.

Charlotte held his gaze for a moment, then turned back to the file, her mind racing. She knew enough about how the criminal underworld worked—she'd grown up around it the first thirteen years of her life—and she knew that it was unlikely either Freddy or the bomber would talk. But even if they did, she doubted they'd have anything of real substance to share. That just wasn't how things worked. There would be many layers between the hired hands and the people directing them.

So where did that leave them? Until they knew what information Freddy and his cohorts thought she, Mira, and Simon were privy to, they'd be at risk.

Unless, of course, they weren't the only ones who knew it—whatever "it" might be.

"We need to go public," Charlotte said, rising from her seat.

"No," Damian said.

She appreciated his concern, but the silence of his teammates told her she wasn't the only one to be thinking along these lines.

"We do," she said, looking at Damian. "And you know it's the only way."

CHAPTER NINETEEN

"THERE'S STILL TOO MUCH we don't know," Damian said, his heart sinking at his teammates' silence. It didn't take a genius to sense they agreed with Charlotte and it didn't take a psychologist to know his reaction was purely emotional, but dammit, going public would expose Charlotte too much. As it was, there was a chance that Freddy and his cohorts still thought her dead —she hadn't given her name when they'd gone to Simon's boat to get the computer, and when she'd arrived at the hospital, they'd been careful to keep her a Jane Doe. Shah was handling the subsequent investigation of the bombing, liaising with the local police and continuing to keep Charlotte's name from the record.

"Rodriguez," Beni said. Her calm surety sent a bubble of rage through him, one he barely managed to contain. It was easy for her to agree; it wasn't someone *she* loved on the line.

"Don't," he cut her off with a glare. She narrowed her eyes at him but heeded his warning. The last thing he needed was a barrage of reasons from his teammates as to why going public with everything was a good idea.

"I'd like another twenty-four hours with Mira's computer,"

Charlotte said. If he could bring himself to look at her, he was sure he'd find her speaking to his teammates and avoiding his gaze.

"After that," she continued. "I think we need to let it leak that I'll be turning the computer over to the FBI."

"The less we say, the better, but what's the back story?" Alexis asked. "We need a plausible reason why it took you two days to turn the computer in after collecting it from Ambassador O'Conner's boat."

"She was still recovering from her attack when she was injured in the blast," Jake offered. "Originally, she was just going to pick the computer up and send it to DC. But then she started putting two and two together—her attack, the attack on Mira, and then the bomb on the boat, and she got concerned that there might be something on it worth killing for."

"And so she's now turning it over to the authorities," Beni finished. "It's a good story."

"Except for the part where we're basically taunting the fucking people who want to kill her," Damian bit out.

"I'm exposed anyway, Damian, and you know it," Charlotte said. He whipped around to face her. She didn't shrink from the angry glare he shot her way—not that he would have expected her to, after all, this was *Charlotte*.

"Chances are they already know I survived the stabbing, but even if they don't, I can't stay in hiding forever. I know that I'll be vulnerable in the time between when we leak the fact that I'm going to turn the computer in until the time that I actually turn the computer in, but that's the time that we need to give these people—whoever they are—to make a move. There are five FBI agents involved and I understand there are two more permanently stationed here. If we lay low here at the house, we should be able to keep both me and the computer safe."

"We already have a copy of everything on the hard drive, so

we don't actually need to protect the computer. We can keep our focus on Charlotte," Dominic said.

Damian forced himself to look at everyone. Five sets of eyes looked back. Five sets of expectant expressions.

"Fuck," he said, running a hand through his hair and turning his back on everyone. He needed a moment to accept what he already knew was the truth.

"Could you all excuse us for just a moment," he heard Charlotte say. Her request was met with a shuffle of feet and the sound of four people filing out his front door. From the corner of his eye, he saw Beni and Jake put their heads together while Alexis and Dominic strode off, most likely to double-check the extra security they'd put in place the day before.

"Damian."

He flinched when one of Charlotte's hands curled around his bicep and the other landed on his lower back. She pressed a cheek to his shoulder and stood there for a long moment.

"I wouldn't like it if it were the other way around," she said. "But you know this is the best way to ensure not just my safety, but Mira's and Simon's too. If we make a production about going to the FBI, then they'll have to assume that whatever we know, or they think we know, is no longer limited to just the three of us and then they'll have no reason to keep coming after us. And if we do it this way, if we lure Fredrick Althorp and whoever the bomber is out, then we might even get a lead on who's really behind this."

He turned and wrapped his arms around her, resting his cheek on the top of her head. "I know it's the best way. But I hate it. It terrifies me, to be honest." And it did. He didn't think his heart had stopped racing since Charlotte had first suggested the plan.

She leaned into him. "No one ever said the right thing was the easy thing, but I can promise to make it as easy on you as possible because, like I said, I would hate it too if it were the other way around."

"It would make it a hell of a lot easier if you said you wouldn't do it," he said, knowing full well what her response would be.

He felt her smile against his chest. "Not going to happen, Rodriguez. But I will promise to follow your every order or command or whatever, until this is over."

He couldn't help it, all sorts of thoughts—and images—flew into his mind at her words.

She chuckled and pressed against him. "So cliché, Rodriguez," reading his mind.

He didn't stop the laugh that rumbled out. "What can I say?"

"I know, you're a guy," she said. But she accompanied it with an eye roll and a little shake of her head.

He raised his hands and sank his fingers into her hair, tilting her head up. "For the record. I hate this."

"Duly noted. I'm not a big fan either. But I'm also not a fan of putting our life on hold and waiting for this to resolve itself."

He had to admit that she had a point. Of course he knew that the plan—as fucked up as it was—was the best way to ameliorate the risk, but more to the point, they wouldn't be able to get on with their lives, in the way they both wanted to, until this was over. And getting on with life—with *their* life—was something to fight for.

"I guess we can't really go dancing on the beach until this is all over, can we?" he said, dropping a kiss on her lips.

"Or travel to Charlie and Daphne's birthday, or go on a hike, or take a swim in the ocean—"

"I get your point," he cut her off. "Promise you'll do everything I say? Or everything my teammates tell you to?"

She nodded.

He held her gaze for another long moment, then inhaled

deeply. "I guess we better go round up the others and tell them it's safe to come in now?"

She grinned. "I don't think you'll need to do much rounding up."

He turned to look out the window only to see all four of his teammates standing in front of it, watching them.

"They are such assholes," he muttered, waving them in.

Charlotte laughed. "But admit it, you love them."

"I might *like* them. A little bit. But only a little bit."

"So everything good now?" Jake asked, leading everyone in.

"Everything is not good," Damian said. "But we'll deal with it."

"So, what's the plan?" Beni asked, taking a seat on the couch.

"I still need to find out who our bomber is," Dominic said, picking up Damian's computer.

"Any leads on that?" Damian asked, dropping another quick kiss on Charlotte's forehead, then moving to join his team in the living room area. He passed Alexis, who was leaning against the wall beside the window, and took a seat in a chair.

"And Charlotte?" he said, looking up. "I assume you're going to stay on Mira's computer?"

"After I get some of Alexis's juice," she said. "Anyone want any?"

There was a chorus of yesses from everyone except Alexis, who declined but joined Charlotte in the kitchen. Damian watched his teammate disappear into the room and wondered what she had to say to Charlotte. In many ways, the women were very much alike—strong, smart as hell, and innately distrustful. But Charlotte was starting to break down some of the barriers she'd put around herself, some of her self-imposed preconceived ideas about who and what she needed to be. Whereas Alexis still preferred to remain just a little bit apart from everyone. He had no idea why, and had no idea if he'd ever know why, but he hoped she wouldn't try to push Charlotte one way or the other. Not that Charlotte was easily pushed, but she was also dealing with a lot of shit right now and didn't need someone trying to dig into her head.

"Yo, Rodriguez."

Damian jerked his gaze from the kitchen door.

"You going to moon all day—"

"Not that Charlotte's not moon-worthy. I mean seriously, she's pretty smokin'," Jake cut Dominic off.

"Fuck off you two," he shot back and took the papers Dominic had been holding out to him. "What's this?"

"One of those could be our bomber," Dominic said, handing Damian back his computer and pulling his own out of his bag.

"Seriously, how'd you land her?" Jake persisted, his eyes on his laptop. "Smart, gorgeous, sexy as h—"

"I will kill you," Damian bit out, even knowing Jake was just trying to get a rise out of him.

"Can you all shut up and get to work," Beni said.

"Thank you, Ricci," Damian said.

Beni inclined her head, her attention on her screen but her lips twitched. "Although if I were into women at all, I'd *definitely* be into Charlotte."

Damian glared at all of them, trying to hide their grins behind their computer screens. "I hate you all."

CHAPTER TWENTY

LAUGHTER ERUPTED in the living room, drawing both Charlotte's and Alexis's attention.

"What do you think that's all about?" Charlotte asked as she pulled glasses from the cabinet.

"Probably something we—or you—are better off not knowing."

Charlotte arched a brow but conceded Alexis's point. God only knew what Jake and Dominic were saying to get a rise out of Damian. Not that he made it hard to do.

"He's a little sensitive," Charlotte agreed, though if asked, she'd admit that she liked that about him. He was easily riled—at least about her—but he was also quick to dish it back out and, at the end of the day, didn't take it too seriously.

"I imagine it's a little tough for him right now," Alexis said, putting some ice in the glasses. "First, you show up back in his life, then it turns out someone is trying to kill you, then you two work things out...you did work things out, right?"

Charlotte nodded as she poured some sparkling water into each glass. "We did. We've both had a few revelations in the past few days, and although the kind of hurt we inflicted on each other last year doesn't just go away, we both know what we have is worth fighting for."

Alexis smiled. "And he's rubbing off on you. Two days ago, you never would have said any of that out loud. Not to me, anyway."

"Two days ago seems like a long time ago, both emotionally and physically. But I suppose you're right. I definitely wouldn't have said it to you. Probably not even to myself."

Charlotte topped off each glass with some juice while Alexis refilled the ice trays.

"Are you really okay with this plan?" Alexis finally asked.

Pouring the last of the juice, Charlotte considered her answer. When she finished, she set the jar down and leaned against the counter. "Is that why you joined me in here?" she countered.

Alexis bobbed her head. "One reason, yes."

"And the other? Or others?"

"I'm curious what you think about the information on Mira's computer."

Charlotte stared at her.

"And I also wanted to let you know that I'll be picking up your stuff from the resort later. I know you were supposed to check out today. I'll tell them I'm your cousin."

"And that's it?" Charlotte asked.

Alexis nodded.

"So, first, thanks for picking up my stuff. Will you leave a tip for the cleaning staff? I'd give you cash, but you know, I don't have any until I get my stuff."

"You were there for less than half your stay," Alexis pointed out.

"Just because someone is trying to kill me doesn't mean the cleaning staff deserves to get shafted on their tips."

Alexis grinned. "Okay, consider it done."

"As for what I think about the information, I'm not sure yet, that's why I wanted another twenty-four hours," Charlotte said, and then proceeded to share with Alexis the same thoughts she'd already run by Damian.

When she finished, Alexis stared out the window, a thoughtful expression on her face. "Can you get back in touch with Tim and Ahmed? Since we've cleared them, it might be interesting to get their take on the second TL and to follow up on the contractor question."

"So you don't think I'm chasing rainbows?"

Alexis shrugged. "Maybe, but maybe not. Do you have anything else you could or should be doing?"

At that, Charlotte gave a rueful laugh. "Okay, good point. No, I don't. So I guess I keep looking into that anomaly until something else more promising comes along."

"And the plan. Are you really okay with the plan?" Alexis repeated her initial question.

Charlotte hesitated. "Honestly?"

"That better not be a real question."

Charlotte smiled. "Of course, you want my honest answer. I don't actually know," she said. "In theory, yes, I'm good with it. I think it's the best way to lure these people out into the open. Does the plan have holes? Yes, it does. What if we bandy about the story Jake and Dominic came up with and the people we want to hear it, don't? Assuming they think there's something on the computer, what if they don't believe that I haven't already gone through it? And last but not least, how do we ensure that they believe that Mira, Simon, and I are no longer the only ones who know whatever it is they think we know? And if they still want to come after me, how will they do that?"

"Those are big questions."

"Really? You've got nothing more to say than that?" Charlotte countered.

Alexis grinned. "They're all legit questions, and the truth is, we have no idea if the plan will work, but if it does, are you okay with what that might mean?"

"You mean, am I okay with knowing that if it works, Freddy or the bomber—or both—may try to get their hands on me *and* the computer? And if they do, they won't be looking to take me on a spa day."

"They definitely won't be looking to take you on a spa day."

Charlotte glanced down at her nails. Their words were gallows humor, but...

"I actually could use a manicure," she said.

"Focus, Lareaux," Alexis said. "And I'll take you to the spa when all this is over."

Charlotte sighed. "I don't want to focus on it, okay? It is what it is. I don't want to think about all the things that could go wrong, I don't want to think about any of us being put in danger over this. And I really don't want to think about what it will be like if something happens to Damian."

"Or what it will be like for him if something happens to you," Alexis added.

Charlotte crossed her arms over her chest. "I know it could happen. I do. I've seen enough violence in my life to know what people are capable of and I was with Damian for two years before we broke up—I know what his job entails. But it's still not something I want to think about, not in detail. For now, all of this is just something that needs to be done so that I can move on and do the other things I want to do in life."

Alexis studied her for a moment, then frowned. "In a weird, denial-ish kind of way, that makes sense. So what is it that's next on your life to-do list once this over?"

Charlotte laughed as she grabbed a tray and started setting the glasses on it. "As if you don't know," she said. "I do need to get back to the states for my niece and nephew's birthday, but figuring out how to fit my life in with Damian's is pretty high on the list."

"Sounds like a good to-do list," Alexis said.

"Having been stabbed and almost blown up in the past few days has shifted my priorities a bit."

"Smartass."

Charlotte grinned then adjusted a strap on her top. "I think I also need to have you take me shopping. You have excellent taste in clothing, and I'm not even going to ask how you guessed my size so accurately." Reaching for the tray, she gestured toward the living room.

Alexis straightened. "Having a supermodel for a mom gave me some unusual skills."

At her words, Charlotte turned and paused in the kitchen door. "And having a mom who is a cook gave *me* some unusual skills too. The team has no idea that you make this juice, do they? It's way too fresh to be anything you bought."

Surprise flashed in Alexis's eyes before she narrowed them. "They don't know nor will they ever know. Can you imagine how much of a pain in the ass Dominic and Jake would be if they thought they could get this on-demand rather than just when they are lucky enough that I bestow it on them?"

Charlotte chuckled. "Say no more. I got your back."

***

CHARLOTTE SPENT the next few hours with Mira's computer. What was emerging was less than exciting—other than the change in TL, the project had run smoothly. It had been a little delayed, but given the scale and the fact that a hurricane had happened toward the end, the delay was hardly noteworthy. And she hadn't found any evidence suggesting that the project had been considering a change in a contractor.

While she'd worked, Alexis had collected her stuff from the resort, and when she'd returned, Charlotte had taken a short break to go through it. All of her work clothes went straight back into her bag. Even some of her "leisure" clothes went back in—after a few days of Alexis's influence and her realization that she didn't have to constantly wear clothes like armor, she kept out only those that were the most comfortable. And a bathing suit. She still had her bandage on, and would for several more days, but sooner or later, she planned to be on a beach, and in the water, with Damian.

Leaning back in her chair, Charlotte gave a little shake of her head. When her mind started to conjure images of swimming and snorkeling while she was trying to figure out if Mira had information worth killing for, it was time for a break.

"I'm starving," she announced.

"Oh, thank god," Dominic said, instantly bounding to his feet. He and Damian had been going through the files of potential bombers all morning.

"No shit, Toto's everyone?" Jake said, also rising. He and Beni had been huddled over CCTV feeds from various places—some from the resort, trying to see if Freddy had made an appearance, some from the marina and surrounding areas to see if they could identify the bomber.

To Charlotte, it seemed like Jake and Beni had drawn the short straw. And judging by the way he was stretching his body and practically dancing around, Jake would probably agree.

"Toto's?" she asked, rising from her seat and joining the rest of the team in the living room. Well, the rest of the team except Alexis, who'd left to start circulating the story about the drop-off of the laptop the following morning.

"It's a beach bar about twenty minutes west of here," Beni said. "Crazy good tacos and some of the best fish on the island."

"They also have the rare distinction of serving draft beer from all three breweries on the island. Not that we'll be drinking," Jake said, pointing to the four agents, "But you shouldn't miss the opportunity. The breweries don't usually allow bars to serve competitor's beers, so Toto's is the only place you can try all three."

Charlotte knew nothing about the restaurant scene on the island, but it was hard to beat a good taco and a beer on the beach, so five minutes later, they were loaded into two cars and heading west.

She wasn't sure what she'd expected, but Toto's was not like the upscale beach bars she'd stopped at with Simon and Mira. After winding down a steep, curvy hill, Damian pulled up next to a building that looked slightly larger than a shack. No, scratch that, it looked exactly like a shack, but it did have a wraparound porch with views that were to die for of a long stretch of white sand that wrapped around a gentle bay.

Everyone placed their orders at the counter then took a seat facing the water with their drinks.

"So, did you get anything from the computer, Charlotte?" Dominic asked.

She shook her head. "Sadly, no. But I have to admit, I got a little hung up on the finances of the project just to make sure I understood them. The story I'm telling myself is that it always pays to follow the money, but honestly, I think I got lost in them because they are what's most familiar. What about you guys?"

"I think our boat-bomber is one of these three," Dominic said, sliding three images over to her.

Two were mug shots and one was an image of a military ID. She looked at each closely, but not surprising, nothing jumped out at her.

"I was thinking we could swing by the marina after lunch and talk to the harbormaster," Damian said.

She knew she needed to get back to Mira's computer, but the idea of a little break held more appeal than it should, and she nodded. "Fine with me. Maybe we can mention the computer hand over to him just in case he knows the bomber."

"That's probably a good idea," Beni said. "We don't think the harbormaster knows the guy since he probably wouldn't have mentioned him to Dominic if he did, but it can't hurt to get the word out as much as possible. And he does know we took the computer."

The waiter brought their food shortly after, and silence reigned as they all devoured their meals. As she ate, Charlotte let her mind wander from the meal to the view, then to Mira's computer. For a moment, she experienced a bit of cognitive dissonance. Palm trees lined the beach, the sand stretched for at least a mile, the turquoise water sparkled in the sun, and a light breeze caressed her skin, keeping the humidity from over-heating them. All the while, they were contemplating mayhem and attempted murder.

"I know violent crime isn't high on the island," she said, setting down one of the three sample-sized beers she'd ordered. "But what crime is prevalent in the islands? It's marketed as such a paradise, but no place is totally without violence or corruption."

Damian set his iced tea down and wiped his mouth before speaking. "That's actually the reason the task force was created. The FBI has had a small presence here for decades, but the truth is, we don't have a lot of intel on crimes in the islands."

"There are the usual, of course," Jake chimed in. "Tourists getting pickpocketed, petty thefts, that sort of thing."

"But the whispers of *more* were just that, whispers," Dominic said.

"And easy to ignore so long as they didn't impact the tourism economy," Beni said.

"So you guys are here to understand better which of those whispers bears looking into?" she asked.

"Ideally, yes," Damian said. "But we're pretty sure the politicos just want us here to make sure none of those whispers blows up and creates an incident that will impact the summit next year. They want us to *understand* the crime that affects the islands, but none of us is certain that they want us to do anything about it."

"So long as it stays swept under the rug, or only hushed about in back rooms," Dominic added. The expressions of his three teammates reflected the same frustration she heard in his voice.

"So what crimes are you finding, now that you're looking?" she asked.

"Human trafficking," Beni said.

"Drug trafficking," Jake added.

"Organized crime, if you can believe it," Dominic said.

"And those are just the top three," Damian said. "The islands are a haven for corruption and white-collar crimes too."

"And the government doesn't want you stepping into that?" Charlotte asked. She shouldn't be surprised, but she was.

"If it comes knocking, we'll take care of it," Damian said.

"But we're not supposed to rock the boat too much. A big scandal now would be a problem," Jake said.

"So, you're in CYA-mode even before the summit happens?"

All four nodded.

"Wow, that sucks," she said.

"It does," Damian confirmed. "And I'm not sure it's what any of us signed on for—"

"But we've also only been here a few months, and Director Shah has been pretty laissez-faire for the most part," Beni said.

"I hear another 'but'," Charlotte said.

"Sunita Shah isn't known for making things comfortable for other people—she has a reputation for being an excellent strategist and it's just not her style to let things go. She's the reason we all joined," Damian said. "We're being told one thing now—"

"But you don't think that's what she'll ultimately have you doing," Charlotte finished his sentence. The four agents nodded.

"We have no idea what's really going on or what her plans might be," Jake said. "But it would be just like her to lull the higher-ups into a sense of complaisance when it comes to what we're doing down here and then, once everyone has taken their attention off us, do whatever it is she has planned for us."

Charlotte smiled. "I knew I liked that woman."

"She's a little terrifying, but there's no one else we'd want to be working with down here," Beni said.

"She has clout and respect both within the agency and outside it," Dominic clarified. "If the shit hits the fan at some point, we'll all benefit from both her experience and her protection."

"That's a lot of faith to put in someone you've never worked with before," she commented.

All four looked uncomfortable for a moment, then Damian shrugged. "Like Burel said, she has a solid reputation in the agency. She's the kind of leader you want to work for if you're given the opportunity."

Charlotte thought there was more to it than that, but she opted not to push; the food had been good, the location like a postcard, and the weather ideal. She didn't want to ruin the mood. And she could always ask Damian later.

"Speaking of Director Shah, did you see that email from HQ this morning?" Beni asked, grinning. "I was in the office when it came in, and she literally told her computer, or the sender, to eat shit and die."

Dominic, Damian, and Jake all chuckled.

"It was a note about expenses," Damian said to her.

"I didn't bother reading it," Jake said. "I figure if there's something she wants us to know, she'll let us know."

"I've set up a filter where all those HQ emails go into an HQ spam folder," Dominic said. "You know the 'round-tuit' folder. When I get around to it, I'll have a look."

"And you never quite get 'round tuit' do you?" Damian said on a laugh.

"Nope, figured if there were anything I needed to know, I'd

hear it from you all or Shah," Dominic said, flashing his killer grin. Over the past few days, Charlotte had gotten used to his good looks, but now and then, it still startled her and she couldn't look away.

Beni's laugh broke the hypnotic spell of Dominic's smile, and Charlotte dragged her gaze away from him. Jesus, he was like that snake from *The Jungle Book*.

"You best stop flashing that smile around Charlotte if you don't want Rodriguez to kill you," Beni said.

Charlotte glanced at Damian, who kept his gaze on Dominic, even as he tugged Charlotte against his side. "She's made her choice, Burel. And you were never in the running," he said.

Charlotte let out a soft laugh. "He's right, but I will grant that you are pretty. Not at all my type," she said, leaning into Damian. "But you are pretty."

"Pretty," Dominic repeated. "Men aren't pretty."

"I'd have to agree with Charlotte; you are kind of pretty," Jake said.

"In a bizarre, not quite normal way," Damian added.

Beni shot Charlotte a look, and the two women laughed as the men continued to bicker. They all cleared the table as they bantered, and Dominic and Jake were still arguing when everyone climbed into their cars and started back to work.

CHAPTER TWENTY-ONE

"Guys," Damian said, drawing his teammates' attention then nodding to Charlotte, who sat alone at the table, still culling through Mira's computer. It was nine o'clock at night and most of the afternoon had been spent waiting around, but Charlotte looked exhausted.

After lunch, Damian and the team had driven to the marina where Simon O'Conner had kept his boat. There, they'd had to wait for nearly an hour for the harbormaster to return to his post from god-knows-where. Then, on their return trip home, a nice little traffic jam, caused by an overturned garbage truck, between the marina and his home, had delayed them for longer than he wanted to remember. Usually, he liked the slower pace of the island and its windy two-lane roads. Today had not been one of those days.

At least they had the identity of the bomber, though. The harbormaster had identified the photo of Nikil Balraj as the man who'd passed himself off as an officer of the law then planted a bomb on the boat. Eye witness accounts weren't as reliable as most people thought, and so he and Dominic had spent the afternoon digging up everything they could on the man and now felt pretty good about zeroing in on him.

But Charlotte was still plugging away and hadn't seemed to be making any progress—or at least none that she'd shared with them. And now she looked wiped out.

His teammates nodded then, as one, they all rose. The motion caught Charlotte's attention, and she looked up from the computer.

"You all leaving?" she said.

Jake shrugged. "I've got a few things I want to look in to, but yeah, we're wrapping up for the night."

They weren't all leaving, though. Now that their plan was in play, and the word was out about the computer handover, there was no way he, or his teammates, were leaving Charlotte unguarded. Dominic would stay outside for the next hour, then Alexis would join him for a couple more hours of watch. Beni and Jake would relieve them in the early hours of the morning. It wasn't ideal but they'd all get at least a little sleep.

But Charlotte didn't need to know because if she did, she'd want take her turn. Or at least she'd want to make sure everyone had enough bug spray, or water, or whatever to make them comfortable. And she wouldn't sleep well knowing others were out there "taking care of her." No, it wouldn't matter that this was their job.

"Find anything?" Beni asked, gesturing to the computer.

Charlotte hesitated, then shook her head. "You know, I've been consulting with the World Bank for over a decade, but I've never gotten into the weeds before. If we weren't in the position we're in, it would actually be kind of interesting."

Dominic chuckled. "If you say so, Brainiac."

Charlotte rolled her eyes at him as she rose to say goodbye. "Right, because parajumpers are so dumb."

"Don't even start with the smile," Damian said, cutting off

the grin that was beginning to make an appearance on Dominic's face at Charlotte's comment.

"You're no fun," he muttered instead.

"I'm plenty of fun, just ask—"

"Do not finish that sentence," Charlotte said, now cutting Damian off. His mouth hung open for a second, then he caught *the look* in Charlotte's eye and he snapped it shut. He supposed she did have a point; he didn't need to sexualize her in front of his teammates, not even in innuendos.

"Good choice, Rodriguez," Beni said. "So tomorrow at ten?"

That was the time they'd decided he and Charlotte would make a production of turning the computer in. She'd even made an appointment at the office just in case anyone was checking.

"Ten o'clock," Damian repeated. They had twelve hours before they forced the shit to hit the fan. He'd try to catch some sleep but he doubted he'd do more than catch one or two catnaps throughout the night.

A few minutes later, his house was quiet, and he wrapped his arms around Charlotte. "How are you doing?" he asked, dropping a kiss on the top of her head when she rested her cheek against his chest.

"Tired, which is irritating because I still have more files to go through. But also frustrated that I haven't found anything yet."

"I sent Tim and Ahmed a message about talking to them again, but I haven't heard back. If we don't hear from them by tomorrow, we'll send someone over to check," he said.

She drew back just enough to look him in the eye. "You don't think they are in danger, do you?"

He started to shake his head, then stopped. That was what made this whole situation such a shit storm; they didn't *know* very much. "I don't think so," he said. "I think if they were a target, they would have already been taken care of. I know that sounds callous, and maybe even a little haphazard, but that's what my gut tells me. They had that break-in months ago and

Mira spoke to them over a week ago. If whoever is behind this had concerns about the couple, there have already been plenty of opportunities to silence them."

"Not as reassuring as I'd hoped, but I appreciate the honesty," she said, snuggling up against him again.

He rested his cheek on her head. "You ready for bed?"

She nodded.

"You need a pain pill?"

She hesitated. "I want to say no, but I think I should say yes."

He let out a long breath. She hadn't had a pill since the morning, and it had been another long day. She'd probably needed to take one hours ago, but at least she was going to take one now.

"Why don't you go in and get ready for bed. I'll get all the lights and locks out here and bring you a glass of water."

"Then you'll come to bed too?"

"Yes, but just to sleep, Charlotte." He tried to sound resolute. And he *was* resolute. He just didn't really want to be. But after their morning and the long day they'd had, he'd be damned if he did anything that set her healing back, no matter how pleasurable it might be.

"You're no fun," she muttered, but rose onto her toes to kiss him.

"I'm a lot of fun, and you know it," he said, against her lips. "Even if you don't let me say it in public."

She smiled and dropped her hand to his waist. Dipping her fingers under the band of his jeans, she splayed her hand across the top of his ass and pulled him flush against her.

"You want me to tell Dominic just how much—and what kind of—fun I have with you?"

Again, she had a point; he really didn't want his teammates thinking about his sex life. Joking about it was one thing, but having legit details? No, he could do without that.

189

He bent his head and captured her lips in a thorough kiss, then stepped away. "Go get ready for bed. I'll be in in a minute."

"Just to sleep?"

"Those feminine wiles aren't going to work this time. Go," he said.

She snorted a soft laugh. "Fine, party pooper. But don't think I won't make you make up for it later," she said as she walked away from him and to the bedroom.

He laughed at the empty threat. "Fine, but don't think I'm not looking forward to that."

"I certainly hope so, Rodriguez. I certainly hope so."

CHAPTER TWENTY-TWO

CHARLOTTE WOKE WITH A START, her heart racing and a sheen of sweat on her brow. Not that sweating was unusual on the island —even in an air-conditioned house—but *this* kind of sweat was.

She lay still for a moment, trying to sort out just what had awakened her. A figment filtered through her mind, but she couldn't quite grasp it. In frustration, she rolled over to curl up beside Damian. Only to find his side of the bed empty.

Jerking upright, she looked at the clock. Not quite five in the morning. She cocked her head, listening for any noise, anything that would give her an idea of where in the house he might be. But she heard nothing.

Slowly, she swung her legs over the side of the bed. Her body still ached, and her stitches had started to itch, but all and all, she felt better today than she had the day before and at this point, that was all she could ask for.

The door to the bathroom was open, but a single look confirmed Damian wasn't in there, or in the closet. Her gaze landed on the closed bedroom door, and she hesitated. Was this one of those situations where she should call out to him? Or one of those situations where she should stay as quiet as possible?

She debated for a moment then opted for the latter. If something *wasn't* wrong, then she trusted Damian to recognize her form in the dark. Whereas if something *was* wrong, she didn't want to alert anyone by making her presence known.

Rising, she walked quietly across the room, cracked the door open, and slipped through. Clouds had moved in overnight and only filtered moonlight illuminated the living room. She paused in the doorway and willed her eyes to adjust. As she did, she noted just how very quiet the house was.

Her heart started pounding and tendrils of fear, real fear, started to grow and twist their way through her body. Where was Damian?

She raised a foot to step into the room when suddenly, a figure shifted on the couch in front of her. She jerked back in surprise, her hand flying to her chest, and damned if she didn't make a little "eep" sound of surprise. So much for remaining stealthy.

"Charlotte."

Relief coursed through her as air escaped her lungs in one big breath. "Damian, what are you doing out here? You scared the shit out of me."

"Sorry, didn't mean to. Just keeping watch."

Just then, the cloud cover broke for a moment and she caught a glimpse of him sitting on the sofa, a weapon in his hand.

"Did something happen?" Once again, her heart rate picked up. If her morning kept up this way, she was going to be getting a hell of a cardio workout.

He shook his head and held out his free hand out to her. She joined him on the couch, leaning against his free side.

"Beni, Jake, and I are just keeping an eye on things," he said. "We figure the closer we get to ten o'clock, the more likely it is Freddy or the bomber, or someone else, will make their move."

"Beni and Jake are here?"

With her head resting on his shoulder, she felt him nod.

"They're outside, and no, you can't go see them."

She heard a hint of humor in his voice with that last comment and she poked his side in retaliation. He let out a soft chuckle, then grabbed her hand and brought it to his lips.

"So what woke you?" he asked.

She searched her mind before answering. There *had* been something that had nagged at her, something that had woken her, but she still couldn't quite grasp it.

"I'm not sure," she said. "I had this dream. I don't remember what it was, but when I woke up, there was this urgent sense of something I needed to do or something I needed to look at. Only I can't remember now."

"You think it had something to do with this case?"

She nodded. "What else would it be? I just wish I could remember."

"Here, lie down and relax, maybe it will come to you," he said, pulling a pillow out from beside him and setting it in his lap. She wasn't sure the wisdom of this. If he needed to rise quickly, she would hinder him. But, he didn't give her any time to voice her objection as he nudged her down. When her head was resting on the pillow in his lap, he began to comb his fingers through her hair in a rhythmic, comforting way.

She sank into the relaxation, and let her mind drift, hoping it would drift to whatever it was that had awoken her. Her eyes fluttered closed and she hovered in that space between sleep and wakefulness as Damian's fingers continued to brush through her hair.

And then it came to her. "Email!" she said, jerking upright. Damian's hand flew from her head, and he tensed in response to her sudden movement.

"Sorry," she said, leaning over and kissing his cheek. "Didn't mean to startle you, but I remembered." She swung her legs off the couch as she spoke and rose.

"What did you remember?"

"May I turn a light on?" she asked. After he nodded, she answered his question. "Yesterday, Dominic mentioned setting up a filter on his system for email that comes in from HQ. I've been going through Mira's documents and emails, but I didn't think to look to see if she has any filters set up."

As she spoke, she'd flicked on a small sidelight near the dining table and located Mira's computer. "Coffee?" she asked as the screen flickered to life.

"Yes, but I'll make it," Damian said, rising from the couch.

She was on her second cup of coffee when she hit pay dirt. She looked up to tell Damian just as a streak of lightning crackled across the sky and a boom of thunder followed immediately after. The lights flickered.

"Damian?"

"Don't worry, I have a generator. I think everyone on the island does. From what I understand, at this time of year, big storms aren't common—not like during hurricane season—so hopefully, it will pass soon." He joined her at the table and leaned over to see what she was looking at.

She was pointing out what she'd found when Beni and Jake knocked on the door. In the early morning light, Charlotte could see a wall of rain headed their way and she didn't blame the two for not wanting to be out in it. They could protect her and the computer just as well from inside now that it was light and unlikely someone would be trying to sneak around.

"The storm is going to last on and off all day," Jake said, stepping into the house.

"Coffee?" Beni asked, hopefully.

"I'll get it. Charlotte was just about to tell me something she found. Why don't you tell us all as I make another pot," he said.

"I finally found the mention of the second roads contractor," she said. "It's not much, just a scanned image of a letter from RLB construction stating that, based on a prior conversation, they were following up to ask for specifics of the project to determine if a bid would be in their mutual best interest."

"Does it use that specific phrase? 'In their mutual best interest'," Jake asked, coming to stand behind her.

It did, and she pointed it out to him.

"That's weird," he mumbled. She agreed but remained silent as Beni and Jake read the entire letter, which didn't take very long as it was only three paragraphs.

"Do you know anything about RLB Construction?" Damian asked, walking into the room with coffee for Beni and Jake.

Charlotte shook her head. "I just found this two minutes ago. I haven't had a chance to look any deeper. At least now we know where Mira got the information, and we know the name of the company, so it should be easier to search for."

"Where *did* she get the information from?" Beni asked.

Charlotte repeated what she'd told Damian about looking in the filtered email. "She had a whole filtered inbox for emails that came from the new TL when he transitioned onto the project. It looks like he was just confirming with Mira that they had all the same records. The emails were all read, but rather than delete them, she kept them in the folder."

"No follow up emails or anything like that?" Damian asked as his phone rang.

Charlotte turned to Beni and Jake to answer as Damian walked away to take the call. "Like I said, I just found the letter. It was a scanned document, so unless RLB became a topic of conversation, it might be hard to search for, but we can start that right now."

"That's going to have to wait," Damian said from where he stood on the other side of the room. He held his phone by his side, dangling between his thumb and forefinger. But it was his expression that caught Charlotte's attention. For the first time since she'd known him, she caught a glimpse of what he must have looked like when he was a Ranger and on a mission. "Fierce" didn't even begin to describe it.

Beside her, she felt, more than saw, Beni and Jake come to attention.

"Damian? What happened?" she asked.

His gaze went to Beni then Jake before landing on her. "They decided not to wait for you to turn the computer in. They have Alexis, and they want us to deliver it to them."

CHAPTER TWENTY-THREE

THE ROOM DIDN'T BURST into a frenzy of noise and action as Damian had thought it might. No, instead, a deadly calm fell over it. He glanced at Beni. As a fellow Army soldier, he could see she'd gone into mission planning mode—assessing the situation of options in her mind. Jake had moved to the window and was staring out at the roiling sea and Damian didn't have a clue what he was thinking.

As for Charlotte, she remained seated, but had twisted in her chair to watch him. He didn't want to let on just how bad this situation could get, but realistically, if he wanted her prepared—and he did—he'd have to tell her everything.

"Beni, can you call Director Shah? And Jake, you need to get Dominic on the line and have him meet you and Beni at the Iguana Club in twenty minutes." Both responded without question, and as soon as the calls were finished, they placed the map they'd had out the first day on the table and gathered around.

"They want to meet us here," Damian said, pointing to a spot on the northeast side of the island. "It was a small marina and has some dry dock facilities, but it was damaged in the hurricane a few years ago and has been mostly abandoned since then."

"Who do they want to meet them?" Beni asked.

Damian's eyes flickered to Charlotte then focused on Beni. "Originally, they said just Charlotte, but I said that wasn't an option and so they accepted that it will be me and Charlotte. Unarmed, of course. And with the computer, in forty-five minutes."

"Who are they? Did you get any sense?" Jake asked.

"I think it was the bomber, Nik Balraj," Damian said. "He had a West Indian accent, so it wasn't Fredrick Althorp, but there's the possibility it was someone else local."

"What's the Iguana Club?" Charlotte asked.

"It's a bar," Beni said, pointing to a spot on the map. "It overlooks the old marina and is the best place for us to surveil the situation. We'll also be able to make our way down the mountain to the harbor relatively unseen," she added, trailing her finger down the map and voicing the plan Damian had landed on as well. The road was out of the question as his teammates would be seen, and the other side of the harbor was too treacherous.

"With this weather, I don't think we can get a drone in the air, but I'll see what I can do," Jake said, moving away from the group to make the call.

"Did they say anything else?" Charlotte asked, just as another crack of lightning lit the sky. "Alexis?" she asked.

"I heard her voice, she sounded strong, but I didn't get to talk to her," Damian answered, not wanting to spend too much time thinking of all the things that Alexis might be going through right now. The good news was that at least the two men they knew were involved appeared to be mostly into just killing their victims rather than torturing them. Or raping them. It wasn't much as far as "good news" was concerned, but at least it was something.

"What did she say?" Beni asked.

"Only my name. That's all they allowed her."

"So, tell me what we need to do?" Charlotte said as she calmly powered down the computer. She was still wearing the silk tank top and shorts she'd gone to sleep in and she looked far too pristine to be involved in any of this. Well, at least that was his completely biased opinion. He knew she could hold her own with the best of them, but he also knew that before a few days ago, it had been a long time since violence had touched her life.

He opened his mouth to say something, though he didn't know what. Maybe to say he was sorry she'd gotten involved in any of this? But he didn't have a chance because she cut him off.

"I'm fine, Damian," she said. "Well, maybe not entirely fine, but that's irrelevant. What's more relevant right now is what we're going to do to get Alexis back. They can have the computer for all I care. We have copies of everything anyway. So I just need you to tell me what to do so that we can get her back. I did promise to follow orders, and now I need you all to start giving them."

He stared at her for a moment. There was a slight tremor in her hands, but her gaze was steady, as was her voice.

"First things first," Beni cut in. "You need to change. We don't know what their plan is once you get to the marina, but if you have any lightweight pants you can wear—not jeans—and maybe a rain jacket, go put them on."

Charlotte gave a small nod then left the room, closing the bedroom door behind her.

"You going to hold it together, Rodriguez?" Beni asked.

"It's a no-go on the drone. Weather's too bad," Jake said, rejoining them at the table and giving Damian a chance to ignore Beni's question.

"The three of you and our two local agents need to get into position at the Iguana Club ASAP. It's the best way we have to get any eyes on the place before Charlotte and I head down," Damian said.

"Dominic is five minutes out," Jake said.

"And Director Shah is sending the others," Beni added.

"Good, once we have a plan, you two need to join them," he said.

"And do you have a plan?" Jake asked.

Damian stared at the map, willing it to reveal something, anything, that might be able to help them. Not surprisingly, nothing jumped out at him. Which just left him with the old stand-by.

"We go in and see how this unfolds," he said. "There's no way for us to know the set up until we have eyes on it. The best we can do is prepare for the worst."

"Weapons?" Beni asked.

"I can't carry anything obvious, but I will keep a few things tucked into my boots. I do want to be clear on one thing, though," he said.

"We know," Jake cut him off. "Charlotte's safety is the number one priority."

"If it comes to a choice between her and me, promise me you'll protect her," he said, giving each of them a hard look.

Jake nodded, but Beni rolled her eyes. "It's not going to come to that," she said. "Come on, McMullen, it's time we got on the road. Everyone have their comms units?"

Damian and Jake both nodded. They'd all checked out the tiny devices the night before so they could have them while they'd kept an eye on the house. Both Dominic and Alexis had taken theirs off when they'd finished their shifts in the early hours of the morning. It wasn't practical to leave them on while they'd been catching a quick rest, but damn, it would have been easier if they had an open communication line with Alexis.

"Damian, put yours in now," she ordered. "I assume Dominic

has his in already. We'll head out, and we'll update you as soon as we have intel."

And with that, they were gone.

Damian eyed the closed computer sitting innocently on his dining table. Did that letter from RLB Construction and Mira's innocent question start all this? And if so, was it because they didn't want it to come to light or for some other reason? All good questions but ones that would have to wait for another day.

He was sliding his earpiece in when Charlotte emerged from the bedroom wearing black leggings, grey tennis shoes, and a red windbreaker over a grey shirt. The windbreaker wouldn't keep her completely dry, but it was at least water-resistant. Then again, the rain was probably the least of their concerns.

"Will this work?" she asked, gesturing to her outfit.

He nodded, hating that they were even having this conversation. "I don't know what we might encounter, but given all the unknowns—" a boom of thunder rattled the windows, "I think it's the best you can do," he finished.

"The weather isn't really on our side today, is it?" she said more than asked.

"So long as we're not out in the open or on the water in a small craft, we should be fine," he said. "At least it stays relatively warm here, even when it rains." He offered that last bit with a wry smile.

"Always with the silver lining, Rodriguez," she said, allowing herself a small laugh. "Now, do we need to go?"

He nodded. "Give me two minutes to grab a few things. Why don't you put the computer in a bag—I might have an extra in my closet—while I wrap up, and then we'll head out in five minutes?"

She nodded and went in search of a decent computer bag while he opened a safe and pulled out a few weapons—a small but powerful handgun and two knives—all of which would fit into either the slim ankle holster he wore or his specially made boots. They weren't *quite* James Bond-ish, but they were the Army version.

"Everyone hot?" he asked, testing the tiny comms unit in his ear. Three voices answered back, Alexis's missing response was like a punch in the gut. They hadn't had too much time to plan, but it pissed him off that they hadn't considered—or prepared for—the possibility that Charlotte *wouldn't* be the target.

Charlotte emerged from the bedroom carrying an empty over-the-shoulder biker bag. Silently, he took it from her and slid the computer inside. He debated whether or not he should carry it or have Charlotte do the honors, but quickly concluded that he'd be better off if his hands were free. He walked her through his reasoning for having her maintain control of the device as he locked the house and set all the alarms. Just because he *could* be a little more lax about security here on the island than in DC, didn't mean he hadn't set up a top of the line system when he'd first moved in. In fact, he'd had a couple of buddies who worked for a private security firm fly down and do it for him because he hadn't trusted anyone on the island.

They climbed into his jeep and were heading up his driveway when the first bit of intel started coming in from Dominic.

"I hope you've had your tetanus shot, Rodriguez, those dry dock buildings are rusty as shit," he said.

"Any sign of Alexis?" he asked. Charlotte's head swiveled toward him in confusion. In response, he pointed to his ear and mouthed, "Dominic." She nodded and remained silent.

"No, but I do have a heat signature inside one of the buildings — the one furthest to the east. Hold up," he said, then paused. "Make that two heat signatures. I'm not sure where the other one came from, but it just appeared out of nowhere."

"Not possible," Damian said. "What are the options?"

Dominic didn't answer for a long moment. "Possibly from

the water," he finally said. "I'm not saying it did, but if there is a hole in the floor, there might be access to water underneath it."

"There could also be an office with a glass or Plexiglas window," Beni said, joining the conversation.

"That sounds the more likely," Jake said. "Which would mean there could be more people and we can't see them."

"All we can do is keep watch," Damian said.

"What's your ETA?" Dominic asked.

"We're fifteen minutes out," Damian said. "But we have an extra ten, maybe fifteen if we want to make them sweat it out a little bit. We'll wait at the top of the hill until you give us the go-ahead."

Beside him, Charlotte stared fixedly out the front window, but her head was cocked ever so slightly in his direction.

"Going dark on my mic for a minute," Damian said, then switched the device off. He relayed what his teammates had told him as he took her hand in his, then asked, "Do you have any questions?"

She let out a rueful chuckle. "I'm just going to follow orders, but it might be nice to know what some of those might be. Aside from knowing that Alexis is likely in some dry dock building and there is at least one other person there, I have no idea what I'm supposed to be doing once we get there. Or, perhaps more importantly, what I'm supposed to *not* do."

He grimaced. She was right. He and his teammates had each had numerous engagements like this during their careers. Maybe not exactly like this, but close enough. And they'd slid into a textbook routine for handling what was essentially a hostage situation—assess, reassess, then act. Charlotte had none of the benefits of their experience.

"There's no fixed plan. We'll take the intel we have and act appropriately." As he spoke, he swerved to miss a branch that had fallen into the road in the storm. Normally, he would have stopped to move it, but today was not a normal day.

"I want you to hold onto the computer until we see Alexis," he said. "They may threaten to kill us or some such thing, but unless there are more than two of them, they'll know they can't do that without endangering themselves."

"Meaning if they go after me, you'll retaliate?"

His blood pressure spiked at the thought. "Yes."

"Are you sure they'll know that? I mean, maybe if they know you're a former Ranger and an FBI agent, they might guess that, but do we know if they know that?"

He nodded and swerved to miss a huge pool of water that looked like it could swallow his car. "Alexis would have made sure they know."

She nodded, accepting the answer. "Okay, then what happens after we see Alexis?"

"Best outcome would be that there are only two of them and our back-up shows up right about then. Then Alexis is safe, you're safe, the computer is safe, and we have the perpetrators in custody."

"Worst case?"

"They try to kill us all or separate us. I'm not sure why they would do the latter, but the phrase 'divide and conquer' didn't come from nowhere. It's much easier to dominate, or maintain control of a situation, when a group is divided."

"Okay, so whatever we do, try to stay together once we see Alexis."

He nodded again. "Unless it looks like they really are going to kill one or the other of us then, and only then, can we agree to separate. But only from Alexis. Under no circumstances are you to leave my side unless I tell you to go."

Charlotte opened her mouth, and he could see the protest on her face. But he cut her off. "You promised you'd follow orders, Charlotte. If I tell you to run, you run. If I tell you to stay, you stay. Your safety is my top priority and you have to trust that I will do everything in my power to keep you safe."

He could feel her eyes on him even as he kept his locked on the wet road before them, the rhythmic back and forth of the windshield wipers keeping time like a metronome.

"I trust you to keep me safe, Damian. That's never been in question. But can I trust you to keep yourself safe? To do everything in your power to protect yourself, too?"

He brought her hand to his lips, then held it against his cheek for just a moment, before setting it down on his thigh and covering it with his own. "Your safety is my priority, but I have a lot to look forward to. I have no intention of letting you, me, or Alexis die today."

"I know you can't promise that no one will get hurt today, but do you promise that is your intention? That *all* our safety is your priority?"

He squeezed her hand. "Yes, I promise."

Charlotte exhaled a long breath. "Okay, so my job is to hold onto the computer, at least until we see Alexis, and do my best not to get separated from you unless you tell me to get separated from you."

Damian pulled over to the side of the road just before the turnoff to the old marina. "You sound like a pro."

She rolled her eyes. "Right, whatever. Now see if your teammates have learned anything new." She gestured to his earpiece and he dutifully turned it on.

"I'm hot," he said, letting his teammates know he was back. "Any updates?"

"Dominic and I are making our way down the hill," Beni's voice came through his earpiece. "The terrain is slowing us down, but Jake is still watching from just outside the club. We think Alexis is tied to a chair, but we'll know more once we get closer. There are now two signatures other than Alexis and we think that's it."

"Freddy and Nik?" he asked.

"Can't tell," Jake said. "Not yet anyway, but if I were a betting man, and I am, I'd say yes."

"Which means this is a two-man show," Damian said, the first good news he'd heard since the call had come in a mere thirty-five minutes ago.

"Yes, but remember one of them has a penchant for building bombs," Dominic pointed out. Which effectively meant the odds were still up in the air.

"Fuck," he muttered.

Dominic and Beni echoed his sentiment just as Jake issued a warning. "Ricci and Burel, stand down." Instantly, the sounds of the two moving through the thick tropical forest silenced.

"One of them is coming out," Jake said. As the only one with any real perspective, Damian, Beni, and Dominic were effectively blind, relying on Jake's intel to decide their next move.

"He's stepping outside. It's Balraj," Jake said. "He's moving to the building on the west side of the marina. The one closest to the parking lot."

"So, he can come up behind us?" Damian asked.

"That's my guess," Jake said.

"Then it looks like we'll be parking somewhere else. Any suggestions?"

"Drive toward the lot," Jake said. "But as soon as the road levels out, turn left and pull a U-turn so that you park perpendicular to the road you drove down on. Charlotte's door will be toward the base of the hill, which should give her some cover too."

CHARLOTTE LISTENED INTENTLY AS Damian relayed the updates from Jake about Nik Balraj. When he came to the part about their parking plan, her heart stuttered. Not since she'd left the projects had she thought about the need to take cover, and the idea made her stomach roil. Taking a deep breath, she willed it to calm the fuck down—now was not the time to get sick. They had to save Alexis and somehow capture the two men who'd caused so much damage already.

She held onto the oh-shit-handle as they bounced down the weather-beaten, little-used road, and when it leveled out, Damian did as Jake had instructed and swung the jeep around, leaving her door closest to the mountain they'd just wound down.

"Are we ready?" Damian asked, presumably to his team as his eyes were scanning the lot and the surrounding area. Other than three out-buildings, four small boats bobbing in the harbor, a multi-level boat storage building that was half collapsed, and a puddle the size of a small pond in the middle of the gravel parking area, there wasn't much to see.

"It's hard to believe that a place like this exists on the island," she said, her gaze taking in the scene. "There's so much money that flows down here. It seems like someone should have snapped this up, even with the hurricane damage."

Damian nodded. "Which makes you wonder why they haven't. I don't know the whole story about this facility since we didn't have time to dig into it, but I wonder who owns it."

"You think whoever owns this might be involved?" she asked.

Damian inclined his head in a non-committal gesture. "They may not be involved, but I wonder if maybe they run in the same circles. Regardless, we'll look into it once everyone is safe and this over," he said.

Time seemed to slow down and it was difficult for Charlotte to imagine just *when* this whole thing might really be over. But there was only one way to get from here to there. "Shall we?" she asked, reaching for the handle.

He put a hand on her arm to stop her, but cocked his head as if he were listening to something his teammates were saying.

After a minute, he spoke. "Roger that. Charlotte and I are going in."

"Everything okay?" she asked. It was a stupid question, and the second it left her mouth, she shook her head at herself. "Never mind, forget I asked. Are we ready?"

Damian nodded. "Beni and Dominic just ran into a little trouble getting through the forest, but they're back on track and should reach the area in about ten minutes, fifteen tops, which should give us time to get a better understanding of just who's here and maybe what they plan to do. You have the computer?"

She held up the bag. Once they were out of the car, she'd slip the strap over her shoulder and wear it like a courier.

"Okay, here goes," he said, then he opened his door and slid from his seat.

Charlotte took a deep breath and did the same.

"Go ahead and come around the car," Damian called to her once she'd shut her door.

She rounded the corner, and Damian held his left hand out for her. Thankful for the anchor, she quickly twined her fingers with his.

"Love you," he said.

"Love you, too," she responded.

And then, together, they walked into the lion's den.

CHAPTER TWENTY-FOUR

DAMIAN COULD FEEL Charlotte's rapid pulse in her thumb as she gripped his hand. Together, they skirted the edge of the parking lot then he pulled her to a stop as they came upon the first structure. The rain had tapered off for the moment, but dark clouds loomed in the distance. A gust of wind swirled around them, rattling the corrugated tin roof of the building by where they stood.

Not knowing what Balraj and Althorp had planned, Damian called out. "We're here. As promised and with the computer."

Silence greeted his statement and for a moment, he had a sinking feeling that maybe Balraj and Althorp had something planned that was much bigger than anything they might have anticipated. But knowing Balraj, who was in the building next to where he and Charlotte stood, could likely hear him, he refrained from raising the question with his teammates.

Though they continued to feed him intel.

"Assuming it's Althorp with Alexis, he definitely heard you. He doesn't look like he's going to come out, but he's moved closer to the door," Jake said. "And Balraj is still in the building taking his time. Assuming he doesn't have any plans to blow himself up, it might be good to try and stick close to him," he added.

Without considering it too much, Damian decided that was a sound option. Nothing in Balraj's file hinted that he was the suicidal type. Of course, Althorp didn't appear to be either, but since he'd demonstrated that he was capable of hurting people in up close and personal ways, Damian preferred to keep his distance.

"We're here!" he called out again.

Charlotte shot him a worried look but said nothing.

"The longer you wait, the more likely someone else is going to notice that Alexis Wright is missing," he said, raising his voice over the wind.

"Balraj is making a move," Jake's voice came through Damian's earpiece. Damian squeezed Charlotte's hand in warning, and not three seconds later, he appeared in the doorway to their left.

Charlotte startled, but Damian just turned his head to take in the man who'd almost killed him and Charlotte. Nik Balraj did not look a thing like any of the explosive experts Damian knew. The man was small, almost scrawny, and with his shorts hanging low on his hips, a loose-fitting tank top, and a baseball hat, he looked more like he should be hanging out on someone's porch having a beer than planting bombs.

"Where's Agent Wright?" Damian asked for show since he already knew the answer.

Balraj flashed him a toothy grin. Or it would have been if he had all of his teeth.

"Where's the computer?" he countered.

Charlotte patted the bag as Damian answered. "You won't get it until we see Agent Wright."

Balraj seemed to consider them for a moment, then he moved out of the shadows and into the light rain. "Step away from your bird, I need to search you first," Balraj said.

Damian glanced at Charlotte, who nodded. Releasing his hand, she took several steps back and away from Balraj as Damian took two toward him. Holding out his arms, Damian gestured for him to get on with it. Balraj hesitated for a moment then began to pat him down. It was over almost as fast as it had begun and Damian was pretty sure the man had learned his technique from watching TV.

Stepping back, Balraj jerked his head toward the building they already knew held Alexis. "Follow me," he said. Then in a surreal show of trust, he turned his back on them and started walking away.

Damian held out his hand, and Charlotte came forward, placing hers in his again as they followed several steps behind.

"You doing okay?" he asked. She'd been stabbed and almost drowned, and it did not escape his attention that traipsing about in a storm probably wasn't the best thing for her recovery. Thankfully, the rain had slowed to a sporadic drizzle. At least for now.

"I'm fine," she said. Of course she did. He shouldn't have wasted his breath on the question. She probably wasn't fine. Hell, *he* wasn't fine. But they had bigger things to focus on at the moment—they could sort out the emotional tangle of the situation later.

They followed Balraj into the old boathouse, pausing in the door to let their eyes adjust. Swiftly, he took in the scene.

"Interesting that they have Alexis tied to a chair in the middle of the room," he said. Charlotte cast him a questioning look. He held her gaze then lifted his shoulder ever so slightly in the direction of his ear, the one with the earpiece.

"I'm surprised they didn't use the office," she said, picking right up on the fact he was feeding intel to his colleagues.

"It's a big space for just two people to be guarding one agent," she added, almost making him smile at how quickly she jumped in.

"It's mostly empty, though, so not so hard to keep an eye on things," Damian said.

"Except for that huge pile of netting in the back, left corner," she added.

"Shut up, you two," Althorp yelled. "And come up here, closer."

They started forward, and though Damian's eyes were still sweeping the area, he was swiftly cataloging Alexis too. Her hands were bound behind her back and her ankles tied to the chair. The chair itself looked weather-beaten and for a moment, a little niggling thought slipped into his mind. But it wasn't one he could explore at the moment and so he brought his gaze up from Alexis's bound ankles to her eyes.

"You okay?" he asked. With no one around to hear her yell, they hadn't bothered to gag her.

Alexis lifted a shoulder and as she did, a cloud moved away from the sun and beam of light poured through the window illuminating her. And the red, swollen mark on her right cheek.

Charlotte sucked in a breath, but Damian squeezed her hand, willing her not to react.

"I'm fine," Alexis said, sounding not unlike Charlotte had just moments ago. He held her gaze for a moment and saw no hint of panic or doubt. He frowned, but then she gave a subtle shake of her head. He studied her for a moment and as he did, her eyes slid toward Althorp then back to his. He wasn't entirely sure what she was trying to tell him, but he had a pretty good idea.

"So, what's your plan, Althorp?" Damian said, turning to the man who held a gun in his hand. It wasn't pointed at anyone, but he was definitely ready should he need to use it.

"You know my name," he said, sounding more resigned than surprised.

Damian nodded. "I do. We know his too," he said with a jerk of his head toward Balraj. "Now, at the risk of sounding cliché, you can't possibly think you're going to get away with this."

Althorp grinned. "I disagree."

Again Damian's eyes swept the area, his mind conjuring up a hundred and one options that Althorp might be planning. "So why don't you tell me how you see this going down, then," Damian said.

Althorp chuckled then. "I'm not going to tell you shit—"

"Not even who you're working for? Because we know you didn't plan this for fun," Damian interjected.

"You're going to hand the computer over and then take a little boat ride with Nik," Althorp continued, ignoring Damian's question.

"Why would I do that?" Damian asked.

"Because if you don't, I'll kill her," he said, gesturing with his gun to Alexis. "And then her," he said, pointing to Charlotte.

"You're likely going to try to kill us all anyway. Why would we make it easy for you?" Charlotte asked.

"Because if you make it hard, I'll kill him first and you'll have to watch him die," Althorp answered.

"So, instead, you're going to send us out in a boat to die?" Charlotte pressed. She was both stalling and obtaining intel for his colleagues. He shouldn't have been surprised at her cool, but he was.

"Oh, let me guess," she said.

"No, I don't think so," Althorp cut her off. "You just need to shut up and give me the computer."

"You're going to send us out on the boat, and somewhere at some point, Nik here will bail and then the boat will blow up and it will look just like an accident. Two lovers caught out in a storm who come to a brutal end," she said, ignoring him.

"I have to admit," she continued. "It's not a bad plan. It's less suspicious than three dead people in the same boathouse. But I have to ask, to make it look real, the boat will need to be a nice boat. I mean, no one would believe that a woman like me who has the kind of money I have would be wooed out in a boat that was anything less than impeccable. You saw Ambassador O'Conner's boat. It's officially a yacht, really."

"Jesus, you talk a lot," Althorp said.

Damian just barely hid a smirk, and he caught a glimpse of Alexis's lips twitching.

Charlotte shrugged. "I'm just saying, if you're trying to deter suspicion, you have to make it look realistic and to be quite honest, I just don't see the kind of boat I'm talking about anywhere around here."

"It's in the berth behind the building," Balraj said.

"Well, hot damn," Burel said through the earpiece. Damian almost beamed with pride. Charlotte had gotten them to identify their mode of transportation and given his teammates some time to do something about it.

"Shut up," Althorp said to Balraj, who glared back at the older man.

"It better be good. I mean, if you want our death to look real," Charlotte said. "And then what about Agent Wright? It's not like you can leave her alive."

"It's past time you shut up," Althorp said, raising the gun and pointing it at Alexis's head. Charlotte's hand tightened on his, and he gave her a little squeeze. She acknowledged it with one of her own and let out a long breath.

"Fine, I'll be quiet now. Just please don't shoot Agent Wright. That Glock 22 you're carrying may be efficient, but it will be bloody and I don't do well with blood."

Charlotte's bored tone surprised a laugh out of him—one he quickly hid with a cough—and he'd admit to being impressed with her ability to identify the weapon Althorp held. Glancing over to his teammate, one of Alexis's eyebrows winged up as if to say, "what the hell?" but then he saw her lips twitch again and she averted her eyes as she fought her own smile.

"Just give me the damn computer," Althorp snapped.

Charlotte turned to Damian, and he nodded. Letting go of

his hand, she stepped away to lift the bag strap over her head. When it was free, she held it out. Althorp gestured for Balraj to take it and the man came forward, grabbing the bag on his way to stand beside Althorp.

"Look inside and make sure it's the right one," Althorp said.

Damian reached for Charlotte again and pulled her close to him as Balraj opened the bag and pulled the device out. Holding it up for Althorp to see the top—and the holographic sticker—he waited for the man to give the all-clear.

When Althorp nodded, Balraj slid it back into the bag and walked toward the office.

"It's password-protected," Charlotte said. "I couldn't get into it. Granted, I didn't try very hard since it didn't occur to me until yesterday that the computer might be important. But that's why I was taking it to the FBI. I figured maybe their people could get it unlocked and figure out if something on it was the cause of everything that's happened because I sure as hell have no idea what might be causing it."

"Do you ever shut up?" Althorp snapped, just as they heard the low rumblings of a boat engine.

Charlotte shrugged, seemingly unconcerned, but her grip on his hand was tight and she was all but glued to his side. He didn't doubt it cost her to remain so aloof and act so out of character. But she'd done an excellent job of feeding Althorp—and hopefully, whoever he was working for—the lie that she had no idea what was on the computer or why everything was happening. When they made it out of the situation, there'd be no reason to keep coming after her.

"Ready," Balraj said, strolling back into the boathouse.

"You already worked it out," Althorp said, glaring at Charlotte. "You two go with him." As he spoke, he waved them toward the door with his gun. Damian dropped his attention from the gun to Alexis, who gave him a little nod. He didn't stop the frown that formed on his lips, but she subtly jerked her head in Balraj's direction as if to tell him to get going.

Following her lead sat like a lead ball in his stomach, not because he doubted her, but because he hadn't worked enough ops with her to know if what he *thought* she was telling him was, in fact, what she was telling him. And he didn't want to be wrong about this. Not when there was a man with a gun on one side and a man with a bomb—most likely—on the other.

"Go," Alexis said. "I'll be fine."

At the flat certainty in her voice, Damian saw doubt flicker in Althorp's eyes for the first time. Another beat passed, but then he nodded and gave Charlotte's hand a little tug.

And once again, they walked hand-in-hand deeper into the lion's den.

CHAPTER TWENTY-FIVE

"OH, THAT IS A NICE BOAT," Charlotte said as she walked beside Damian toward the instrument of their death. Not that she thought they were going to die. It was a possibility, she knew, but it was one she wasn't going to contemplate.

Hopefully, her rambling commentary inside the boathouse had given Damian's team enough time to either remove whatever bomb Balraj had placed on the boat—for she knew without a doubt that was his plan—or, at the very least, put a tracker on it so if it blew up and she and Damian had to go overboard to live, they wouldn't be floating for long before they were found.

"Do you think he stole it?" she asked Damian. He shot her a look, one eyebrow raised. She shut her mouth and decided to keep her thoughts to herself. Damian and his teammates had other things to think about than the origins of the boat she and Damian were now stepping onto. Hopefully, they were discussing a plan over their communication devices because once aboard, she had nothing else to offer.

Glancing back, she saw that Althorp, and the threat of his Glock, had followed them out. Given that Balraj was, or appeared to be, unarmed, she wondered why she and Damian were following along so meekly. Especially when she knew three other agents were waiting to swoop in.

She spared one more look at the warehouse and thought she saw movement inside, but quickly looked away from the temptation to confirm. It would be nice to know if Dominic or Beni had moved inside to help Alexis, but by staring, she'd only draw Althorp's attention there.

"Tie them up," Althorp said, tossing Balraj a length of rope and gesturing her and Damian toward a bench seat that ran along the side of the back deck.

Damian gave her hand another squeeze and led her to the seating area. Within a minute, they were both tied to the little railing that sat a few inches above the edge of the boat. Charlotte hoped the speed with which Balraj tied them up meant he'd been sloppy, but there was always the chance it meant he was very proficient.

Balraj climbed up to the captain's deck and signaled to Althorp, who untied the boat and gave it a shove. The engines roared, and the smell of diesel fuel filled the air. A flicker of fear shot through Charlotte when she remembered the feel of the last explosion—the heat, the vibration of the air, and the deafening sound. Her chest tightened and she gripped the railing. Drawing on old instincts, she pulled in a breath while counting to three. Panicking now wouldn't help them

"It's okay," Damian said. He was leaning toward her, his lips practically touching her ear. They didn't have to worry about being overheard, not with the twin engines on the boat, but having him close made it both easier to hear him and gave her an anchor to focus on.

"Alexis?" she asked.

"She's fine. Althorp will have a little surprise when he re-enters the boathouse."

"Why didn't we stay? Is someone coming after us?"

"The team decided that separating Balraj and Althorp is our

best chance of taking them in alive. One or the other may still put up a fight, but now that they're both solo, our chances of each of them capitulating peacefully goes up. Not by a ton, but by enough that we had to try."

"And us?" she asked again.

"They couldn't get close enough to the boat to get a tracker on it, but Jake has the coast guard already out and waiting for us. They've been told to hang back because we don't know if this boat is rigged—"

"I think it's pretty safe to say it is," she cut in with a roll of her eyes.

Damian wagged his head. "Yeah, probably. The weather isn't helping us, but at least everyone will know where we are."

As if on cue, the boat lurched in a swell as they left the safety of the harbor and entered the open waters. The rain hadn't picked up again, but Charlotte could see a thick line moving toward them. In the distance, thunder rumbled.

"I know this boat is seaworthy—at least for now—but some of those swells look taller than the upper deck." She hadn't meant to say that. It didn't help anything to voice the obvious. But the sight of a wall of water coming toward them as the boat plummeted into a trough had her heart clambering toward her throat.

Damian wrapped his fingers around hers as best he could. "I'm not going to lie, this is going to be a rough ride, but if it makes you feel any better, there hasn't been a weather-related boat sinking in the Caribbean in decades outside of those that went down during the hurricanes. We know Balraj grew up here and has boat experience. At this point, and I know this isn't too helpful, but we need to put our faith in statistics. Chances are, if anything bad happens to us, it won't be because of the weather."

Charlotte didn't stop the wry laugh that burst from her. "No,

I supposed if we look at the statistics, we'll be fine. If only there weren't a bomb involved."

A side of Damian's lips lifted. "Yeah, if only there weren't that."

"So what's the plan?" she asked as they began to pick up speed. She knew enough about boats to know that Balraj would likely try to time his speed to ride along the tops of the swells. She'd done that once in a much smaller, nimbler craft, but she had no idea how such a big boat—and the one they were in was at least sixty feet—would manage it.

"Curl your calves under the bench and use them to hang on," Damian shouted to her over the wind. She didn't quite know what he meant, but dutifully, she tucked her feet as far under the bench as possible so that the edge of the seat cut into the back of her knees.

It didn't take long for her to find out why Damian had issued the order. Within seconds, the boat missed a swell, leaving it airborne for a split second before it dropped six feet down, landing with a jarring smack at the bottom of a trough. Charlotte's head snapped back at the impact, and she clenched her jaw to keep from biting her lip. Instinctively, she tightened the muscles in her calves and thighs to hold her in place.

She wasn't the only thing rattled by the sudden move. Everything around them seemed to protest too. The windows shook in their portals, cabinet doors jiggled against their locks, and whatever items were stored in the locked trunk on the other side of the deck, hit the top of the trunk hard enough to strain the padlock.

She jerked her gaze to Damian, but his eyes were scanning the horizon. She opened her mouth to ask him just how the boat could survive such a thing when suddenly they tipped.

"Hold on," Damian said, one of his legs shooting out to help hold her in her seat as the boat seemed to climb sideways up a swell. Charlotte chanced a look to her side only to see a wall of water not four feet away.

"Holy fuck," she muttered as she slammed her eyes shut. She didn't know if she was going to live or die today, but she sure as shit knew that watching things unfold wasn't going to give her any comfort.

Keeping her eyes closed, she leaned forward and pressed her cheek to where her hand was intertwined with Damian's.

"We are not going to fucking die today," she said. "But if we do, I love you, and I'm sorry I put us both through the last year."

In a moment of relative calm, she felt Damian's lips brush her head. "We're not going to die today. We might get a little banged up, but we're not going to die."

"You can't promise that," she muttered, not caring that she sounded petulant.

"I can, and I am," he said.

She appreciated his confidence, even if she didn't agree with him, and she held her tongue. The adrenaline coursing through her system had done its job, and a strange sense of calm fell over her. She didn't *want* to die, but if she did. She'd lived a good life, the people she loved knew she loved them, and that was really all she could ask for.

So rather than fight the fear, she embraced acceptance of whatever was to come and focused only on the feel of Damian's hand under her cheek as the boat rocked, swayed, climbed, and fell.

She didn't know how long they'd been out or how far they'd come, but slowly, she became aware that although they were still rocking with the swells, it didn't seem as violent a ride as before.

Damian's fingers brushed her cheek. "We're coming into a small harbor now. It's not fully protected, so there's still some seas to deal with, but it's much calmer than what we just came through." Again, his finger stroked her skin, now soaked with sea spray. "You can open your eyes," he added.

For a moment, she debated whether or not she wanted to— keeping the world at bay by pretending it wasn't there if she didn't see it had been working pretty well for her.

"Charlotte, I think you need to open your eyes," he said, just as the engines cut back. They didn't come to a full stop, but Balraj was throttling them back.

And then suddenly, the engines went silent, and she heard nothing but the sound of water slapping against the side of the boat.

Her head shot up, and her eyes flew open. Blinking at the sudden light, she took in their surroundings. A shallow bay, to be sure, but while one side tapered off to a low rocky point, an impressive cliff rose out of the water on the other.

"Damian?" she said in a raspy whisper.

"*Treasure Island,*" he said, explaining absolutely nothing. He must have seen the confusion on her face because he continued. "It's called Norman Island, but everyone around here says it's the island that inspired Robert Lewis Stevenson's story, *Treasure Island*. It's mostly deserted; there are a few beach bars scattered around it, but no one lives here. We've been here to dive and snorkel a few times."

"So a good place to blow up a boat since it will look like we tried to take shelter from the storm but this was the only place we could get to," she said, turning to look toward the captain's deck. She could see Balraj's back, but he was hunched over doing something, maybe on a computer, and she couldn't see anything more.

Damian nodded at her supposition. "Doing it in open water would have been the best, but assuming he's going to take the dingy to meet up with whoever is going to pick him up, this bay is a good alternative in this weather."

"Alright, we're all set," Balraj said as he jogged down the stairs to their level.

"You're oddly upbeat for someone who's about to kill two people," Charlotte said. "I assume that is the plan," she added, realizing he had never actually confirmed the theory she'd laid out in the boathouse.

Balraj bobbed his head as he eyed the knots that held her and Damian in place. "That's the plan, yeah. I don't really like killing people, but with the money I'm making from this..." He shrugged and didn't bother finishing his sentence. She should have known better than to be surprised at his nonchalance. She *did* know better; she knew men—boys—who'd killed for a baseball hat or jersey. And she had a feeling Balraj was getting paid a lot more than that. But even so, his attitude left her speechless.

"And just how much is that?" Damian asked.

Balraj grinned. "Well into the seven-figures, but if you think you're going to trick me into saying any more because you're about to die, it won't work—mostly because I don't know any more. Althorp arranged everything. He's a total douche, but whoever he's hooked up with is legit serious about getting his— or her, 'cause you know, equality and all—hands on that computer and shutting you up."

"So, what's your plan now?" Damian asked. Balraj flashed another grin but said nothing. Instead, he went to the inflatable dingy secured to the back of the boat and began untying it. She and Damian watched without a word.

When he was seated in the small boat, and the waves and tide were carrying him away, he gave them one last look. "I probably shouldn't say anything because it might make this worse, but you have about ten minutes to say your goodbyes to each other."

And with that last statement, Nik Balraj started the engine on his little getaway boat and sped toward the rocky end of the bay.

"Nice of him to let us know how much time we have to live rather than letting death come as a complete surprise," she said.

Damian switched his attention from the disappearing boat to her and flashed a grin. "Sarcasm, that's my girl," he said.

"Woman, Damian. I'm a woman."

His grin turned into a smile. "Thank god for that."

"Why are you so smiley? You have a way out of this, don't you?" she asked, her feelings of despair-driven-sarcasm morphing into something altogether more hopeful.

"I do, but we have to be quick."

"About what?"

Rather than answer, he swung his leg up and set his foot down on the bench. "Now watch your fingers, I need to bring my ankle up to my hand so I can grab the knife out of my boot. I'll be careful, but I might catch your fingers."

"Between having my fingers smashed and dying, I'm good with a couple of broken digits," she said, as he swung his leg up and wedged his toes between the edge of the boat and top rail. His boot did smash her fingers against the rail, but she bit her lip and kept her reaction to herself, not wanting to distract him.

He was carefully—and awkwardly—trying to get a grip on the knife she hadn't known he'd been carrying when the first drop of rain hit her nose. Already soaked to the bone from the sea spray, at first, she didn't even notice. But when the knife came free from its holster and Damian's leg dropped back down to the deck, relieving the pressure on her fingers, she raised her face to the sky just as the clouds opened up on them.

"It sounds weird, but this might help us," Damian said, already starting to cut through the rope that bound them both to the rail and together. "When the fibers are wet, it's easier to create friction. And yes, I know they were wet before from the ride, but I'm trying to look on the bright side."

As soon as the words left his mouth, a bolt of lightning

streaked through the sky startling her. She jerked and the knife in Damian's hand slipped, nicking her palm.

"Fuck, Charlotte, I'm sorry," he said.

It hurt like hell, but she did her best to ignore the pain. "My fault, Damian. But I hope it doesn't affect your grip." As she spoke, she twisted her hand to try and keep the blood from dripping onto the knife handle. While water was hard enough to deal with, blood was infinitely slicker.

As she twisted, the pressure of the ropes caused the blood to flow faster, but the movement also gave Damian better access to the knots.

"You okay?" he asked.

"I'll be better once we're free. I assume we're going to swim?" Thunder boomed overhead, and she ducked on instinct but managed to keep her hands steady and out of Damian's way.

"Yes, the coast guard should be here soon, but there are caves in that cliff, and I think it would be safer to swim there than to the shore, given the storm."

She'd heard about the sea caves carved into cliffs and dotted around the Virgin Islands, but hadn't been in any. Her eyes scanned the behemoth of a rock that lay about fifty meters away and it didn't take long to find what looked like an opening.

A strand of the rope gave just as another streak of lightning lit up the sky. Yes, getting out of the open water and under some cover sounded like a good plan. The shore sounded even better, but not only was it farther away, it also had no shelter from the electrical storm that looked to be gearing up for quite a show.

"Assuming Balraj was telling the truth, we have about three more minutes before our ten minutes is up. It will take me about another minute to get through this next piece, but once I do, we should be able to untangle ourselves."

"We jump right after that?" she asked, her eyes glued to the knot Damian was sawing through.

He nodded. "We jump and swim toward the cliffs. Whatever

happens, don't let go of my hand. You're a good swimmer, but I'm trained to swim in conditions like this."

"Got it," Charlotte said with a nod as the knot came loose. "Jump and swim and hold onto you like my life depends on it because it probably does. I can do that."

Damian's lips twitched at that as the rope loosened and one of her hands fell free. "I'm pretty sure you can do anything you put your mind to," he said, as both of his hands fell away.

"Except play darts. For some reason, I can't ever get the hang of it," she said, starting to believe they were going to get out of this alive. She'd like to say she never doubted they would, but that would be a lie.

Damian rose and stretched his arms. "Darts is easy. We'll play tomorrow night. You ready to make a jump?"

"As I'll ever be," she said as she rose, then promptly fell back into her seat. Only one of her hands was free. The other remained tied to the rail. "Damian?" The word squeaked out. She hadn't ever thought of herself as a squeaker, but apparently, there was a time and a place for everything.

He'd been looking at the cliff, his hand behind him, waiting for her to grab hold, but he turned at her word. It didn't take more than a split second for him to grasp the situation.

"Fuck," he said, lunging for the knife he'd left on the bench. "I'm sorry, Charlotte, but we have about a minute and a half before this boat blows and we need to get as far away as we can. This is going to hurt."

She had an inkling of what he intended to do and she braced herself for the pain. "It won't hurt as much as dying, do what you need to."

He didn't hesitate as he reached for her hand and pulled it up so the rope was taut. Flexing her hand backward, he jammed the knife between the tendons of the wrist and the rope. The tip of the knife caught the sensitive skin on the underside of her arm, but rather than focus on that pain, she zeroed in on the slide of the metal against the inside of her wrist. One, two, three slides and the rope gave way.

Relief swept through her, but it was short-lived. Without another word, Damian pulled her up and dragged her four steps to the back of the boat and then they were in the water.

The sudden change disoriented her, and it took a few seconds to realize that Damian was pulling her along, under the surface of the water and as far away from the boat as they could get in one breath. As soon as she understood what he was trying to accomplish, she started kicking her legs, propelling her forward, and using her one free arm as best she could.

They came up for air about thirty feet from the boat, but Damian quickly dragged her down again, and it was none too soon. She heard it first, the explosive boom of the boat going to its fiery death. And then she felt it, the shock waves pulsing through the water, pushing and shoving her and Damian in all sorts of directions as debris rained down on them from above.

Through it all, Damian held her close, sheltering her body as best he could as they buffeted against the onslaught. When she felt her lungs on the verge of bursting, she motioned upward. She needed air.

In two strokes, Damian broke through the surface, his body between hers and the boat, and they both gulped air. Treading water, they could see the shell of the boat still burning, surrounded by broken pieces of wood, fiberglass, and even a couple of seat cushions that had survived.

Charlotte started to smile. They weren't out of the woods yet, but they were damn close. Then suddenly, Damian shoved her behind him—not an easy task while they were both fully clothed in the water—and any relief she might have felt dissolved at the tension she felt radiating from him.

It took her a few seconds to understand his actions, but then she heard it too, the distinct sound of a boat coming toward them. She hoped it was the Coast Guard, but as Damian seemed to believe, it was better to be cautious.

"Be ready to dive deep if we need to, but don't let go," he said as the silhouette of the boat came into view. The rain prevented them from seeing much until it was almost upon them.

"Agent Rodriguez, this is Captain Marquez of the US Coast Guard. We have you on our radar and will be throwing out buoys," a voice announced.

"Can you hear me?" Damian shouted back.

A beat passed. "Yes, are you in need of medical attention? We have a medic onboard."

"Leave the buoys and go after Balraj," Damian shouted.

"Negative, Agent Rodriguez," came the reply.

"He took a dingy around the bend. He'll be heading back to one of the US islands. Go after him. We'll take the buoys and swim to the caves. Send a local boat to pick us up. We're fine, and we don't want Balraj to get away if we can help it."

Silence followed his orders, but then the sound of a buoy hitting the water echoed against the walls of the cliff.

"There's a boat from the Marine Research Center fifteen minutes away. They've answered the call and will be here as soon as they unmoor. Take the floatation device and take shelter. We won't leave until we see you have the rings."

She and Damian didn't hesitate, and they both swam forward and grabbed the bright orange circles.

"Go," Damian shouted over the rain. "He only has a twelve-minute lead and he would have had to switch boats from the dingy to something else."

Charlotte half expected the Coast Guard to change their mind and insist on picking them up before going in pursuit, but maybe they received orders from somewhere else because without another word, the engines came to life again, and the boat disappeared into the blanket of rain.

She and Damian treaded water for a moment, floating up

and down in the boat's wake, then he turned to her. "Ready for a little swim? The cave has a little beach inside, so once we're in, we can get out of the water if we need to."

"I don't mind the water," she said, "In fact, I find there is very little I mind right now. We survived, we're here. Anything else is just gravy."

CHAPTER TWENTY-SIX

DAMIAN GUIDED Charlotte into the shelter of the cave just as the heart of the storm moved overhead. He'd been trained for this kind of stuff, but damn she put him to shame. Sure, she'd had a moment on the boat where she'd struggled to keep it together, but though he'd always admired her strength, she'd taken his breath away today.

The cave started out deep, but as it curved along the inside of the cliff, it led to a small beach where they could rest. As soon as his feet could touch the sand, he hauled her into his arms and kissed her. Then when that wasn't enough, he pulled her tight against his body and just held her—assuring himself she was there, worshipping her for being the woman she was, and just being as grateful for her as he'd ever been in his life.

When the adrenaline in his system slowed to a low thrum, he led them to the beach, where they both sank to the sand. Charlotte climbed into his lap, and again, he simply held on. Whatever he'd done in life to deserve her, he didn't know, but he sure as hell wasn't ever going to let go. Which meant he had one more secret left to tell her.

"March thirteenth and November twenty-second," he said.

Charlotte tried to pull back, but he didn't let her. He needed to tell her.

"I was married once. Long before I met you and before you ask, no, I didn't love her. It was tragic, really, all of it. But she was a woman I'd met and yes, I had a brief thing with her but she was into a lot of the guys from the base and I'm pretty sure she wasn't seeing me exclusively. In retrospect, I should have seen the signs. I should have seen that she was hopping from man to man as a way to take her pain away. But at twenty-four, I didn't have that much insight.

"She came to me one night. It was three days before Halloween and I was getting ready to go out with some of the guys from my team. She was crying and told me she was pregnant."

"Oh, Damian," Charlotte said, but he couldn't think about the tenderness in her voice. Not yet.

"I honestly don't know if it was mine or not, but at least I was able to see she needed help. She had no one, no family, nothing. And so I offered to marry her until she got her feet on the ground. That way, she'd at least have a stable place to live, benefits, healthcare, that kind of thing. I know I didn't need to marry her to give her a place to live, but there weren't benefits for domestic partners at the time and so marriage was the only way to get both her and the baby healthcare since I couldn't afford to pay for it out of pocket.

"We agreed it would be short term and two days later we were married at City Hall. Less than three weeks later, she lost the baby," he said.

"November twenty-second," Charlotte said.

He nodded, his cheek resting on the top of her head. "She was a wreck. And again, in retrospect, I understand why. Not only where hormones involved, and not only did she genuinely love the baby, but I think to her, the baby offered her a way, or a perceived way, to make right everything that had gone wrong in her life. I think she saw the baby as her redemption in some ways."

"And you?"

He took a deep breath and let it out slowly before speaking. "Me? It was sad, I felt bad for her, but beyond that, I didn't *feel* much of anything. I didn't feel like my life had changed, I didn't feel like the loss really impacted me at all. I wasn't the one who'd been experiencing any of the pregnancy symptoms. I wasn't the one who felt any attachment to it." He paused as those words sunk in.

"Listen to me. I just called the baby an 'it' and as callous as that sounds, that's how I felt. I didn't hate her or begrudge her or the baby or anything like that. But I had *no* emotional attachment to it. I would have cared for him or her whether it had been mine or not and I like to think I would have fallen in love with the kid if I'd ever had the chance to meet it, but as it was, I'd barely gotten used to the idea of a baby being part of my life when suddenly it was gone."

"You're not alone in being ambivalent about a pregnancy," Charlotte said. "It's not talked about often, but believe me, I have enough friends who have kids to know that not everyone is thrilled from day one about a baby, even if it is planned."

"Yes, well, Linda—that was her name—wasn't so understanding. She couldn't understand why I wasn't as devastated as she was. She couldn't understand why my world hadn't fallen apart like hers had.

"I did my best. Or at least I like to think I did the best my twenty-four year-old-self could do. I gave her space, I gave her a home, she even used the healthcare to get some counseling which I think was probably the best thing she could have done."

Charlotte squeezed him and snuggled closer. "But it wasn't enough, was it. Not for her?"

Damian took another shuddering breath. "No, it wasn't. On March thirteenth, we had a big fight. Or I guess that's what she would have called it. She yelled at me for hours about how cold I was, how insensitive I was, how I was little more than a monster because I didn't feel the same things she felt about the loss of the baby. I let her yell. At that point, I engaged with her as little as possible because nothing I did or said was ever enough." He paused, remembering that awful night. Then forcing himself, he continued. "I finally got tired of her yelling at me and suggested that maybe she should move out. You should have seen her face, Char. It was like I'd struck her or something. She just froze, mid-tirade, then started crying. A few seconds later, she grabbed the car keys and left the apartment.

"Four hours later, the police knocked on my door to tell me she'd been in an accident. She'd driven into a tree. They said it was possible she'd fallen asleep at the wheel but I," he hesitated. "I don't think she did. I don't think it was an accident. I sent a woman to her death because I didn't care enough, Char."

"Damian—"

"I know what you're going to say," he said, cutting her off. "I know it wasn't my fault, I know I couldn't force myself to feel what she wanted me to feel. And most of all, I know her issues were much deeper than just what she saw, or didn't see, in me. But still, those memories, the words she hurled at me, they stuck with me, and over the years, I couldn't help but wonder if she was right. I *know* she wasn't," he said, tightening his arms around Charlotte. With Charlotte in his life, he knew for a fact that he could—did—feel honest, pure, and real emotions. And more to the point, he realized that he'd always had the capacity for them—he might show them differently or handle them differently than others, but he most definitely *had* them.

"But sometimes logic doesn't always trump the doubts we feel about ourselves," Charlotte said, finishing his thought.

He nodded. "And those two days are hard for me because I can still hear her voice calling me nothing more than an automaton, calling me heartless. And then I hear the police telling me she was dead."

"I'm so sorry," Charlotte said as she leaned into him. Just those three simple words. Those three words—and her presence —did more for his heart than anything else. She saw him—all of him—and not only did she see him, but she leaned *into* him. She didn't tell him he was wrong or try to make it right, and in the space that she created for him, he found an anchor he didn't know he needed.

"You know I love you, right?" he said, burying his face in her hair, before resting his lips against the warmth of her neck.

"I do. And I hope you know the same," she said, tilting her head back to meet his eyes.

He pulled back just enough to look into the dark brown pools. "I do," he said. "I really do."

A hint of a smile teased her lips, but before it could go any further, he dipped his head and brushed his lips against hers. It was a sweet kiss, both a promise and a vow. When he drew away, she smiled at him. It was his favorite kind of smile from her—wide, honest, and open.

She ran her fingers through his hair, and he closed his eyes in bliss.

"As much as I'm glad we've had the chance to work through everything that kept us apart, maybe next time we have an argument we don't have to be so dramatic about it? You know, maybe we could just talk about it, like adults, and not need to get blown up and stabbed and things like that?"

A bark of laughter burst from him. God he loved her. "That sounds like a solid plan. Pinky promise?" he said.

She rose and brushed her lips against his again. "Pinky promise," she said.

"Good," he said, gazing down at her. "I'm glad we have that resolved because I think our ride is here."

CHAPTER TWENTY-SEVEN

DAMIAN'S TEAMMATES were waiting for them when they reached the dock. Traveling in the large, well equipped marine research vessel had made for a much smoother ride back than the one on the way out. Of course, it also helped that the storm had abated and that they hadn't been tied up and subjected to wind, rain, and sea spray. That Dr. Nia Lewis and Captain John Peters had given them each some dry clothes to wear had been icing on the cake.

"Thank you, Dr. Lewis," Charlotte said, hugging the woman before stepping onto the dock.

"Call me Nia, please," the doctor replied, following her. "And when the weather gets better, let me know if you want to go out with us someday. That offer stands," she added.

Charlotte assured Nia that she'd reach out when she'd had a chance to catch her breath. The two women had hit it off on the blessedly brief trip. At the age of thirty-three, Nia Lewis held a joint Ph.D. in marine biology and oceanography and was director of the research center on the island—the most prominent center in the Caribbean. Like Charlotte, she was an impressive woman, and it didn't surprise Damian in the least that they'd clicked almost instantly.

Damian quickly introduced Nia and John to his teammates, then pulled Alexis aside as Jake, Dominic, and Beni thanked the rescuers.

"Are you okay?" he asked.

Alexis nodded. "I'm fine. Dominic and Beni were in the building by the time Althorp got back from helping Balraj. He's not talking, but he's in custody," she said.

"And Balraj?"

Alexis lifted a shoulder. "He disappeared into the wind. The Coast Guard boat wasn't far behind, and they are still looking, but he ditched the dingy just around the bay from where he left you and Charlotte, and hasn't been seen since."

"And the island's being searched?" he asked.

Alexis frowned. "Director Shah is working on getting permission to do that. She had permission for the Coast Guard to go into British territory to pursue the boat you and Charlotte were on, but getting authorization to conduct a foot search of the island is another beast."

"And he'll be gone by the time she gets that," he muttered. The FBI always had to contend with issues of jurisdiction, but it was especially challenging in the Caribbean with so many different territories in such close proximity to each other. Although knowing that Balraj likely knew very little about the broader operation took some of the sting out of losing him.

He glanced over his shoulder to see his teammates and Charlotte still in conversation with Nia and John. Adrenaline had gotten them far, but it wouldn't last much longer and Charlotte was starting to look a little fatigued.

Turning back to Alexis, his gaze roamed over her swollen cheek and the small cut just below her right eye.

"You gave yourself up on purpose, didn't you?" he asked. It was the thought that had niggled at him when he and Charlotte had first walked into the boathouse. Alexis wasn't the type to lose her cool—no one on the team was—but even so, she'd seem oddly self-assured when they'd finally found her.

She turned and focused on the group standing less than fifteen feet away. When she didn't answer, he filled in the blanks.

"You put it out that *you* were going to be meeting with Charlotte to receive the computer, didn't you? And maybe even suggested that she was handing it over to you because you were her friend—someone she would care about if you were taken hostage." As the words tumbled out, the surer he was that Alexis had orchestrated her own capture. And worse, he had a pretty good idea why.

"You did it so that we—I—could control the situation, didn't you? You did it so that Charlotte and I wouldn't have to sit around and wonder when Althorp might make his move against us. And so that when we did make the exchange, I would have the rest of the team at my back."

For a long time, Alexis remained silent. Then, without taking her eyes from the group, she spoke. "Sometimes, the anxiety that comes from the waiting, especially when you're waiting for the unknown, is harder than anything else. Director Shah knew about and supported my plan, but I knew you and the team might think differently." She paused then turned to meet his gaze. "I know it's not good to keep secrets like Director Shah and I did, but honestly, I'd do it again if I had to. Charlotte may be tough, she may have more life experience than most women in her position, but being taken by surprise—and probably quite literally *taken*, since there was no way Althorp was going to let her live—is something else altogether. The fear and the helplessness can be paralyzing. I didn't want that for her and I knew the best way to prevent it would be to make sure that you and the team had control over the situation. Maybe not complete control, but more control than you would have had otherwise, and at least you'd know when and where you would be meeting Althorp and Balraj."

Damian stared at Alexis, his eyes searching hers. She spoke of the fear and the helplessness with a familiarity that chilled him. It also raised a lot of questions he instinctively knew he'd not get answers to, not yet anyway. He still didn't like that she'd made the decisions she had without consulting the team, but that she'd done it so that Charlotte wouldn't ever have that same bleak look in her eyes that had flashed in Alexis's, tempered his frustration.

"I appreciate you looking out for Charlotte, I really do," he said. "But you need to remember we're a team now. No one person's life is more important than anyone else's, and it doesn't do anyone any good in the long run if we all go around playing god and making decisions on our own that affect us all."

Her pale blue eyes held his, then after a moment, she nodded. He wanted more assurance from her than that, but the team started moving toward them. "We'll talk more later," he said as Charlotte reached his side and slid her hand into his.

Alexis muttered some response that he missed as Charlotte reached out and pulled her into a one-arm hug. The two women talked as they all made their way to their cars—Beni's SUV and Jake's Jeep now pulled alongside Damian's.

"Director Shah wants a debrief with everyone in two hours," Beni said, falling into step beside him. "She said at the office, but if you want to meet at your place, I'm sure she wouldn't mind." She nodded toward Charlotte as she spoke. The thought of Director Shah in his house was a little disconcerting, but he agreed with Beni—there was no way he was going to drag Charlotte back out of the house to his office for a debrief.

"Would you mind arranging that?" he asked.

Beni nodded. "You get the sense this isn't over?" she asked.

His hand tightened around Charlotte's, and she glanced over. He smiled at her and though her brow furrowed in question, he turned his attention back to Beni. "I think the danger to Charlotte is probably over. It's well known that not only is she talking to the FBI but that we have the computer and Althorp now, too. There'd be no reason for anyone to go after her if they believe that what they *thought* she might know has either been shared with the FBI and/or is on the computer. But do I think this is over altogether?" He shook his head. "If this is about the rogue letter from RLB Construction, someone went to a lot of trouble to keep it from coming to light. I could see someone wanting to do that if there was actual misconduct, but just the hint of it?" he shook his head again. "It doesn't make sense. I think what we stumbled into this week is just a whisper of something bigger."

Beni nodded. "I agree. Will be interesting to see what Director Shah says."

They stopped beside his car, and Charlotte let go of his hand to make her way to the passenger seat, still in conversation with Alexis and Dominic.

Damian crossed his arms over his chest and let his gaze drift over the boathouse. He truly did believe the danger to Charlotte was over, but as to the rest, unease settled in his stomach. Maybe he and Beni were paranoid. Maybe their years in the Army had made them jumpy. But he didn't think so.

"I guess there's only one way to find out," he said, opening his car door. "See you in two hours?"

Beni nodded. "I'll call Director Shah and let you know if there're any issues. If not, we'll see you in two hours. And Charlotte," she said, leaning around him to speak to Charlotte, who was now seated in the passenger seat. "Take care of your wound. When you get home, be sure to clean it off and get some antibiotic ointment on it. Let me know if it looks red or swollen or anything like that?"

Charlotte nodded, then Beni looked at him for his assurance and he nodded too.

"Great, see you both in two hours," she said, then turned and walked away.

He slid into his seat and leaned over to brush a kiss across Charlotte's lips. She obliged, bringing her hand up to rest on his neck.

"I don't know what's happening in two hours," she said. "But it sounds like something that includes more than just you and me, so why don't you hurry up and get us home and we can make the most of the time we have."

Slowly, a grin spread across his face. "Anyone ever tell you, you're bossy?" he said, pulling back and started the engine.

Charlotte chuckled. "All the time, and you know you like it."

He laughed and grabbed her hand. "I definitely don't mind. Not at all."

CHAPTER TWENTY-EIGHT

DAMIAN STEPPED out of his bedroom, closing the door behind him. He'd left Charlotte lying in bed, sort of reading, sort of napping. There was no question it had been a helluva day, but his teammates, and Director Shah, were coming to talk business, and as much as he trusted her, there were just some things that needed to remain within the Bureau. As a woman with significant security clearance herself, Charlotte hadn't minded being left out, but that didn't mean *he* didn't feel a little put out at the interruption. He knew he and the team needed the debrief, but still, he wouldn't have minded if they could have done it the next morning.

"Hey, Rodriguez," Jake said, walking through the front door Damian held open. "For later," he said, holding up a six-pack of a local ale as he continued into the kitchen.

One by one, the rest of his team filed in, followed by Director Shah. She paused at the threshold as her gaze swept the room, then she stepped inside and made her way to the table. Within minutes, they were all seated.

"I won't take too much of your time," Shah stated, flashing a look at Jake, who grinned at her. "You do all deserve to relax a bit tonight, but as I'm sure you've all surmised, what we stumbled into these last few days is likely bigger than we originally thought."

"Beni and Alexis have debriefed me on the events of today, so we don't need to go through that, but Damian, we need to know what, if anything, Nik Balraj said to you while you were out on the water."

Damian knew the question was coming and was able to answer succinctly—the gist of it being that Balraj had told them very little.

When he finished, Shah nodded. "That aligns with our current theory that he was little more than a hired hand. We'll be transferring Althorp to the FBI detention center in Florida, where he'll be questioned more thoroughly, but for now, I want to share with you what I learned this morning.

"First, the Team Leader that took over the project just before it was completed is named Duncan Calloway. He's generally known as an international businessman, but of the sort that no one can say what he actually does. By our records, what he actually does is very little—mostly just introducing people to other people. Some of those people having more integrity than others," she said.

"So a sketchy TL takes over the project. But based on our initial review of the files, it didn't look like anything sketchy actually went down," Dominic said.

Shah inclined her head. "The only irregularity we found was the mention of RLB Construction as a potential replacement for the roads work."

"We didn't have a chance to look into them, but it sounds like you did?" Beni asked.

"I did," Shah said. "RLB is owned by Roberta Barret and her husband, Lawrence."

"Are they above board?" Jake asked.

"By all appearances, yes," Shah answered.

"But Roberta Barret was married to Vice President Matthews," Beni said.

Damian frowned. "Okay, that's a weird connection, but Calvin Matthews wasn't even in office yet when RLB sent the letter to the Bank. And it's not like it's his current wife or anything. Not that he has one," he added. The fact that the young, good looking Vice President wasn't married was a topic of conversation in just about every political circle. The fact that he, a Democrat, had run on a ticket with a female Republican, and together the pair had made a historic sweep in the election two years earlier, was often a distant second to his marital status when it came to the level of interest in him.

"She is his ex," Beni said. "But they're still close. Roberta and her husband even campaigned for him during the election. Turns out, Matthews is also the one who introduced them."

"But even if that's the case, Damian's right, Matthews hadn't won the election when RLB wrote the letter," Alexis said.

"He hadn't, but he and Ann-Marie Cunningham were so far ahead in the polls, that they'd all *but* been elected," Shah said.

"And why do I get the sense, there's more?" Damian asked.

"Because there's a reason I picked you for this task force, your instincts, and everyone else's on this team are uncanny," Shah said. "So yes, you're right, there's more. Duncan Calloway was a fraternity brother of Calvin Matthews while at Harvard and, even though residents of Tildas Island and the other US Virgin Islands can't vote in federal elections, Matthews still made a trip down here after the hurricane hit that summer and before the election. There's no doubt he cares about the island— once he was elected, he followed through on every one of the promises he made during his visit—but he's also smart enough to know that everyone living here probably has family on the mainland who *can* vote."

"So we have a vice presidential candidate make a campaign stop here on the island. Then shortly after that one of his buddies is appointed TL of a World Bank project without any obvious prior experience. And *then* his ex-wife's business is being considered as a supplier," Alexis summarized.

"Given his focus on fighting for the people," Jake said, highlighting Matthews' primary campaign focus, "using his power to benefit his ex-wife and a friend probably isn't something you'd want to get around."

Damian didn't have a hard time imagining the scenario Jake painted. He'd seen people do crazier things for and with political power. But even so, it didn't sit right, not as it applied to Matthews.

"But that wasn't just how Matthews stumped for his campaign. If you look at his career and what he's done since he's been in office, there isn't anything to suggest he's in it for his own gain," he said.

No, Matthews and his running mate, President Cunningham, were a rare set of politicians and from what Damian knew of them, he just couldn't wrap his mind around what Shah was suggesting. Politically, the two belonged to different parties, but both had long histories of fighting for the people who elected them, Cunningham through her fiscal responsibility and government accountability measures, and Matthews through his focus on social progress, including healthcare, education, and eradication of poverty. When Cunningham won the nomination of the party, she'd not only shocked her own cohorts when she'd announced Calvin Matthews as her running mate, she'd shocked the entire country. It had taken the pair a tremendous amount of marketing to convince the voters of their commitment, but once they had, their popularity had skyrocketed. The country was starving for leaders who put the people first, and in Cunningham and Matthews, they seemed to have found it. And while the pair had their detractors, as all administrations did, for the most part, their approval ratings hovered around the highest of any administration.

"I agree," Shah said, surprising him. "However, we've all been around enough to know that what we see is very rarely the truth. It's too early to say if he's involved or not, but the coincidences can't be overlooked or minimized."

"So what now, then?" Beni asked.

"Now, we keep digging into Duncan Calloway and RLB and keep an eye on Vice President Matthews," she said. "If we can get Althorp talking, that may help, but I'll be honest, I don't think he's a talker and I'm not counting on getting anything useful out of him. At least not anytime soon."

Shah rose from her seat, and everyone followed suit. She paused and let her eyes drift over them before she met Damian's gaze. "We might be opening a Pandora's Box and we all need to be ready for what that might entail. But for tonight, relax and enjoy yourselves, you deserve it, you earned it. And tomorrow, we'll make a plan."

Everyone murmured their assent, and Damian followed her to the door. "How's Charlotte?" Shah asked, pausing on the porch.

"Tired, but good."

Shah smiled. "She's a good one, Rodriguez. For selfish reasons, I'd love to have her around more as we prepare for the summit, but more importantly, I hope to see more of her for your sake."

He smiled. "I don't think there will be any doubt about that. We haven't sorted out the details, but she'll be around."

Shah smiled back. "Good, I'm glad to hear that. Now, go on with your celebration and I'll see you tomorrow."

He gave her a little salute before closing the door and turning back to his teammates. Only to see all four of them eyeing him.

"What?" he asked.

Jake cleared his throat. "So, um, are we kickin' it tonight?

Should I grab the beer? Or are, you know, you and Charlotte wanting *alone* time?"

The bedroom door opened and Charlotte stepped out. "We had *alone* time before you got here, and we'll have *alone* time after you're gone," she said as she walked toward Damian and slipped under his arm. He pulled her tight and dropped a kiss on the top of her head.

"I don't know about you all," she said. "But I could use a beer right about now."

THE END

Did you enjoy Damian's and Charlotte's story?
Are you curious about book number 2 featuring Alexis' story?
Get your copy of NIGHT DECEPTION or read on to find an extract on the following pages!

Did you know that we first meet Damian & Charlotte in my award-winning **Windsor Series**? They make their first appearance in book 2, THESE SORROWS WE SEE.
The complete Windsor Series is available with Kindle Unlimited.

EXTRACT OF
NIGHT DECEPTION

#2 Tildas Island

PROLOGUE

Isiah Clarke stood behind the bar drying glasses as Marty, his second in command, mixed up a batch of Painkillers for the group of tourists sitting at table eleven. He slid a clean rag into a glass, wiping away the condensation left over from the dishwasher, as his gaze swept the room. As it always did, pride teased the corners of his mind when he took in the scene.

After more than a decade as a Navy SEAL, he'd needed something to do with his time—and his life—so he'd bought a piece of land perched high on a bluff on Tildas Island and started building a bar. Slowly, he'd transformed his little bit of paradise into a place everyone, but more particularly locals, felt comfortable.

His gaze slid over the patrons then to the long screened-in veranda. Now that night had settled over the Caribbean, he couldn't see the collection of islands that lay beyond the shores of Tildas. Nor could he see the deep, vibrant ravines that ran down the sides of the mountain to the shore, or the swirling blues of the Caribbean Sea. But they were there, and just knowing that soothed his soul a little bit.

As he set the glass down in one of the tidy rows that lined

the shelf, the hairs on his arms stood up and a prickle of energy whispered across the back of his neck. He looked up to see the source of his unease just as *she* stepped into the bar.

He hadn't seen her in months, not since the end of December and it was now the end of February, but she wasn't a woman he'd easily forget. She paused in the door and, as always, everything about her—from the cut of her clothes, to the simple gold chain that hung from her neck, to the perfect hair and nails—screamed *expensive*. But it was more than all that that drew his attention; it was the way she carried herself. Even when she'd walked into his bar that first time there hadn't been a lick of self-consciousness about her. No, she'd walked in like she fucking owned the place. And while he generally avoided tourists as much as possible, and she wasn't his type, he had to admire her confidence.

Out of the corner of his eye, he watched as she approached. Her deep blue dress crossed over her breasts then fell in waves to the floor. Her long dark hair was pulled into a high ponytail that fell straight between her shoulder blades, and as she stepped, he caught glimpses of her pale toenail polish. With her smooth skin, pale blue eyes, high cheekbones, and full lips, she was a stunning woman.

Even if she wasn't his type.

"Double Laphroaig," she said when Marty turned toward her. The same drink she'd ordered in each of her previous five visits.

Marty grinned. "Good to see you again. No Painkiller or Mojito today?" he asked. The same question he'd asked in each of her past visits.

"Get the woman her drink, Marty," Isiah said on an exhale. "If she'd wanted a Painkiller or Mojito, she would have ordered one," he added. As he spoke, she turned her head toward him, and the air left his lungs. Very carefully, he set down the glass he'd been holding.

"What happened?" he asked with a nod toward her cheek. Growing up, he'd seen the same kind of mark on his mother's face enough times to know what it meant. And though he had no right to ask, he wasn't going to ignore it.

"Walked into a door," she said with a shrug. His eyes lingered as she returned her attention to Marty who was adding a small piece of ice to her drink, the way she liked it. She didn't appear to be self-conscious about the bruising or cut that marred her right cheek, not like he would have expected if she'd been a victim of domestic violence, but still...

"Let me know if you need any help fixing that door." Somehow he managed to sound casual though his stomach churned with acid at the thought of some man hitting her.

She flicked a small smile in his direction, then took her drink from Marty and placed twenty-five dollars onto the counter. "I took care of it myself," she said, then she slid off the barstool and headed to the veranda.

Isiah picked up another glass and began drying it as he watched her walk away.

"What do you think her story is?" Marty asked, grabbing a lime wedge from the container and adding it to a gin and tonic. She'd taken her preferred seat in the corner with her back to the wall of the bar, and sat staring out into the darkness, as if she could actually see the view through the thick of night. She quietly sipped her drink, not once looking around her or pulling out her phone.

"I've got no clue," Isiah answered honestly. He'd been around the block enough to get a good read on most people and it wasn't often that people stumped him. But that woman most definitely stumped him.

Or she would have if he gave her much thought.

Which he didn't.

Because she wasn't his type.

Alexis rolled the tumbler between her fingers and let her head fall back against the wall. It had been a hell of a day—overall, a good one, but still, getting kidnapped, tied up, and yes, even hit a couple of times, earned her a drink. Or two.

Even if it was—more or less—part of her job.

As an FBI agent, and part of a special task force based on Tildas Island, not once had she doubted that her teammates had had her back. But even so, the memory of the rope cutting into her wrists, and the forced immobility that came with being tied to a chair, had driven her to visit The Shack and to the distraction that was Isiah Clarke.

Yes, she knew his name. She knew a lot about Isiah Clarke, thanks to her family's security team. She knew the kind of things that should be shared between friends, or lovers, as a relationship develops, and as trust grows. But that wasn't how her family rolled. Not anymore.

And so she knew all about Isiah Clarke. Product of a broken home and an abusive father, he'd enlisted in the Navy at eighteen and worked his way to becoming a distinguished SEAL. He'd sent home all of his paychecks so that his younger sister could go to college and his mother could get her own coffee shop and inn up and running (once she'd kicked her now ex-husband to the curb for the last time). After retiring eight years ago, he'd bought the land for The Shack and from what her security had told her, Isiah was a good man, running a solid business and keeping his nose clean.

Awareness shimmered across her skin, and Alexis knew Isiah was looking over at her. From his position behind the bar, most of her face was hidden from his view. But that didn't stop him from looking. Or her from noticing.

Which was exactly why she'd come tonight. Isiah was a man her friends would definitely refer to as eye candy. He had eyes so dark they were almost black, sharp features, and thick hair that he wore in a clean, short cut. He hadn't let his build slip from his SEAL days—at least not enough to notice—and his six foot two frame all but begged to be touched. That she'd noticed him the first time she'd set foot in The Shack wasn't a surprise. But tonight, it wasn't his looks that pulled her back to the bar.

No, tonight, the uncomfortable awareness she felt around him was just what she needed to take her mind off the events of the day. So, sitting in her corner, sipping her drink, she welcomed the way her pulse accelerated in his presence. She lingered over the question of whether or not he was watching her. And yes, she even craved the way every nerve in her body came painfully alive when she looked at him.

It was the distraction she needed, even if she never acted on it. Not that she hadn't thought about it, because she had. Frequently. But as they say, it takes two to tango and every indication Isiah had given her told her he wasn't up for the dance.

She took a sip of her drink and thought back to the night he'd had made it very clear that while she might not mind the prickling awareness between them, he wasn't comfortable with it. From the moment she'd arrived, he'd avoided looking at her or speaking to her—not even sharing any of the standard island pleasantries. But it was when Isiah had called Marty over to take her drink order when she'd been standing across the bar from him that she'd grasped just how strongly he felt about putting distance between them. And being an adult, Alexis acknowledged that since it was his bar, and he couldn't leave, it was up to her to withdraw. Which she had. Until tonight.

But tonight, she needed his nearness to take her mind from the ropes and the guns and violence. Maybe it was selfish of her, but if it was, so be it. After all, it was just one night and Isiah Clarke struck her as a big boy, able to handle whatever he thought of her.

Closing her eyes for a moment, she savored the peace that

the whiskey, and the comforts—and discomforts—The Shack brought. In her mind's eye, she conjured the view of distant islands dotting the seascape, rising up from the bright blue of the Caribbean. She saw the lush, green mountains interrupted by brilliant orange and red Flamboyant trees. And she felt the sweet sting of the sun touching her skin as its heat cut through the humid air.

"Need another?"

Alexis's eyes jerked open to find Isiah standing in front of her. Not once in her prior visits had he ever come to check on her. The Shack didn't have tableside service. It was one of the things she liked about it.

Her gaze held his, then dropped to her glass. Her empty glass. She didn't remember finishing it, but the proof was before her. She debated for a moment—she'd had a beer with her teammates before coming here, and then the double Laphroaig. She didn't need another drink, but then again, she wasn't even close to tipsy and she was walking home, anyway.

"A single this time, please."

Isiah nodded and reached for her glass. Their fingers brushed when she handed it to him and a jolt of energy flooded her nerves. She fought the urge to jerk her hand back from the simple touch that was somehow so intimate. It was only her years of training that made it possible for her to pretend there was nothing out of the ordinary. She released the glass into his keeping and murmured a quiet thank you.

Yes, this distraction was exactly what she needed to take her mind off the day she'd had.

And all the memories it had dredged up.

Made in the USA
Columbia, SC
18 April 2023

15443371R00162